THE BRIDE WILL KEEP HER NAME

ALSO BY JAN GOLDSTEIN

The Prince of Nantucket
All That Matters

JAN
GOLDSTEIN

the

BRIDE

will keep

her

NAME

A NOVEL

THREE RIVERS PRESS
NEW YORK

Copyright © 2009 by Jan Goldstein

All rights reserved.
Published in the United States by Three Rivers Press, an imprint of the
Crown Publishing Group, a division of Random House, Inc., New York.
www.crownpublishing.com

THREE RIVERS PRESS and the Tugboat design are registered trademarks of
Random House, Inc.

Originally published in hardcover in the United States by Shaye Areheart Books,
an imprint of the Crown Publishing Group, a division of
Random House, Inc., New York, in 2009.

Cataloging-in-Publication Data is available on request from the Library of Congress.

ISBN   978-0-307-34593-6

Printed in the United States of America

Design by Lynne Amft

10 9 8 7 6 5 4 3 2 1

First Paperback Edition

For my children

THE BRIDE WILL KEEP HER NAME

1

*B*e careful what you wish for.

These six little seeds of warning were long ago generously planted and watered in my unconscious by the inimitable Melanie Mandelbaum, a fifty-eight-year-old executive buyer for Bergdorf's, affectionately known to my father and to me, her daughter, as the *buzzkiller of Long Island.*

My friend Katrina once described my mother as *Oprah in a size 4, only white . . . and Jewish.* She pretty much nailed her. The woman is a nonstopping, ever-talking, advice-giving force of nature who has always insisted on having a hand in everything.

According to Dr. Seymour Unterman, Madison Avenue proctologist to the rich and irregular, her chronic state of constipation is a result of a life lived over the speed limit. As with my friends' mothers, I had discovered that, along with all of the considerable good it has certainly accomplished, this "need for speed" is apparently one of the side effects of the women's lib movement.

These women of my mother's generation had worked to have it all, do it all, accomplish it all, which, we daughters have come to discover, means moms who played at paying attention while distracted with more pressing concerns like jobs, arranging childless evenings in the city, and noting who was getting appointed to what prestigious committee. They were the ones who went back to their careers as soon as they'd pushed out their babies, running like lab rats on cocaine—mothers who spilled the contents of takeout onto paper plates and offered it up as a home-cooked meal.

These guilt-riddled women were forced to navigate their nonstop, strive-for-everything, *yes, damn it, I can have it all because Gloria Steinem told me so* lives by tossing back wee fistfuls of Xanax and almost single-handedly turning therapy in America into a boom profession as a consequence of not, in fact, having actually gotten it *all.*

This was my mother.

As a kid I remember her bathroom being equipped with a Rolodex, a three-line phone, and a large bottle of Maalox. To my mother, you couldn't waste time simply *doing your business;* you had to actually *do* business. She'd swoop in for dinner or pop into my room at homework time only to disappear seconds later on a phone call or to race off to a meeting in the city, leaving my dad to see to the more mundane childhood endeavors, such as building a dud-free volcano for the fifth-grade science fair or composing a haiku about baby spiders.

Would she ever simply sit and watch me do whatever it was daughters do, maybe even *kvell,* as Bubbe would say? *Fuggedabouddit.* Not even with an act of Congress, four Ambien, and a liter of scotch.

On the day of my bat mitzvah, she was constantly up and busy—checking on the food, retouching her makeup, conferring with the rabbi about some VIP who'd just arrived and would be requiring recognition. He and my dad, the superhumanly patient Morty Mandelbaum, had to all but hold her down during my actual solo.

Don't get me wrong. She always loved me. I knew this because she'd say those exact words after inevitably doing things her way. Like the time she'd signed me up for the Mommy and Me classes, only sending me with our nanny so, you know, it was really Nanny and Me, which, of course, my mom spun proudly by pointing out that she loved me and, unlike the other girls, I was picking up some Spanish.

And this senior Bergdorf buyer who'd failed to receive the bump to management she felt she'd long deserved, whose wildly successful money-raising, temple sisterhood events had for years been the envy of religious institutions all over Long Island, this Energizer bunny with the newly tightened ass, could always be counted on to drop her awesome little minimantra—*Be Careful What You Wish For*—at the most inopportune moments.

Like the time you'd fallen during the tap-dance recital, splitting your costume before God and the collective families of the Little Princess Dance Academy of West Hempstead.

"You wanted this, remember?" she'd lovingly observed, tearing off what was left of your tights. "Be careful what you wish for, Madison, and you'll never be embarrassed or disappointed."

Or when you were eleven, trying to become the "teacher's pet" by actually taking care of the teacher's pet, a six-foot python you had volunteered to house during winter vacation that was last seen slinking down your parents' toilet bowl from where it presumably ended up swimming with the fishes somewhere out in Long Island Sound.

"You wanted to be the teacher's pet? Welcome to the doghouse. Don't I always say . . ."

And there it was, good old *Be Careful What You Wish For.* Like hot sun on a child's ice-cream cone.

But then the world changed in ways my mother was unprepared for.

Like when we got a lesson in sex education from the president and his intern that suddenly made politics *really* interesting. Or when Britney kissed Madonna live on television. Or the horror of watching the twin towers fall, Bubbe rushing to wrap me in her protective embrace while my mother sat, arms around herself, staring at the screen, alone. From IMs to iPods to iMacs—which my mother refused to learn to navigate— to her shock and awe when her champion Hillary lost to Barack, the world for her was becoming increasingly incomprehensible.

And then came my sin of managing to graduate Wellesley magna cum laude without her having to pull any strings, receiving a master's in art history that she was fond of pointing out was of dubious worth in today's information-driven economy, a marketplace that required targeting a specialty, not generalizing and thinking it would get you somewhere.

Indeed, through the years of my life, her warnings of the perils of dreaming too big or reaching too far have been as constant as a daughter's desire to please. But somehow, with two best friends working on my confidence file, with breasts too small and baby fat on my hips that refused diets and the gym, I have come to the conclusion that being *careful* about what you wish for makes about as much sense as enrolling your daughter in Girl Scouts to get a deal on the cookies. (Have you met my mother?)

And now at the *lived a little but just you wait* age of twenty-eight, I am taking this moment to officially declare my candidacy for independence and here announce that I have forever deleted the glass-half-empty sentiment of *Be Careful What You Wish For* from my hard drive.

I am here to shout to the world, amid church bells and the sound of a thousand shofars, that wishes *do* come true.

My proof? Simply that in one week from tonight I, Madison Leah Mandelbaum, am set to marry the awesomely sweet, astoundingly smart, phenomenally hot *Colin Wordsworth Darcy,* he of the dazzling dark eyes and perfectly Episcopalian chiseled chin, the son of Diana Steinberg Darcy of Fifth Avenue-opposite-the-Met (a totally secular Jew but a Jew nevertheless, rendering Colin kosher in the eyes of the Talmud and JDate) and Sir Hugh Aubrey Darcy of London (heralded British barrister, *not of the tribe,* whose distant cousinhood to the Queen nevertheless has conferred on him what Bubbe likes to call a certain *royal yichus*).

Now, one week before the event, alone in my Village apartment, working diligently on my vows, trading e-mails with my mother who was maddeningly tweaking the seating chart for the umpteenth time, those six little words of hers have been noodling my brain, trying to get an invitation to the big event.

Be Careful What You Wish For.

Get lost, I order, banishing them from my enchanted world.

Never for a second entertaining the possibility that in less than twenty-four hours . . . they would be back to stay.

2

To get a bead on Colin Darcy and me, you had to start with Hugh, and I don't mean his father who goes by that name. I refer to that other Brit with the last name of Grant, with whom I'd fallen in love at thirteen, having seen his film *Four Weddings and a Funeral* once for every year of my life.

I had driven my parents into submission, insisting the actor had to be invited to my bat mitzvah or my life would be over. After much breath holding and threats of boycotting my own affair, they finally agreed. Soon after, an RSVP arrived claiming Hugh Grant was "regrettably busy shooting a film in London" on the particular weekend in question and lamentably had to decline the invitation. At the bottom of the neatly handwritten note was a postscript in which the actor expressed his certainty that I would be "particularly dazzling" on the occasion.

From the beaming face of my dad, the irrepressible teddy bear and supersuccessful CPA Morty Mandelbaum, I slowly deduced that Hugh had received some help with his response.

Shoot fifteen years into the future to April 15 of last year—fourteen months ago. I was with my two best friends on the steps of the Metropolitan Museum. ("Best friends" doesn't cover it. They're the sisters I never had.)

Abs (short for Abby—but also due to the fact that since her teens she'd been almost ludicrously possessed of this impressive little six-pack) was a Toobin of the Broadway *Toobins*. Her father and uncle produced last year's best musical and, when we were sixteen, got us into the opening of *Rent* when you couldn't touch tickets for less than the cost of her mother's facelift. We'd been inseparable since age three. We'd met Kat in third grade and almost immediately became a trio of BFFs. Kat, the magnificently practical Katrina Fitzsimmons, daughter to the Park Avenue disaster of Jeffrey and Tabby Fitzsimmons, had developed her shoot-from-the-lip style organically. It had been her particular "blessing" to spend her childhood and teen years in alternating side-by-side tenth-floor penthouses in an arrangement deemed altogether progressive by her globe-trotting, peripatetic parents who shared a rich mutual loathing for each other that was always generously in evidence whenever Kat and her friends were around.

We were brown-bagging it as we often did on Wednesdays when I looked up and *bam,* there he was, seriously hot. He was smiling at me with this kind of unworldly confidence that wasn't shot through with the transparent come-on you detected in guys about to make their move.

"Good afternoon, ladies," he said, greeting us with a voice bright and bold like a David Hockney canvas. "I don't mean to disturb your lunch but I wondered how three works of art managed to escape the museum?"

OK, it was a line, but, trust me, coming from that face and with that accent, he sold it. He had Hugh's to-die-for British pedigree that had always made me weak in the pit of my stomach. We had barely exchanged names when the fact-finding Katrina asked Colin what it was he did for a living. He smiled, and his gaze locked on mine in a way that sent little lightning bolts through me.

"I'm an investigative reporter for NBC. What I do is try to uncover the truth, if that doesn't sound too grandiose," he said with a laugh.

And then leaning in, his incredibly blue eyes on mine, he said the most remarkable thing.

"Really, you have to forgive me 'cause I absolutely never do this, but I have the strangest feeling that you are going to be part of my life. Isn't that wild?"

I knew Katrina, not one to give people the benefit of the doubt, had bought it as a line he must have used before. Abby was smitten. But all I wondered was whether there was any possible response that wouldn't make me sound as if I'd dumped my brains in the East River and replaced them with Jell-O. It was a mad and outrageous thing to say and I was rendered mute. His eyes were on me exclusively. He didn't even look at Katrina, who was tall, with short, ginger hair and a Cameron Diaz figure, or at Abby, who was Natalie Portman–like beautiful and possessed of a pair of awesome breasts, which she'd had since she was twelve.

Seven and a half hours later we were on a first date. He took me to Babbo in the Village where, contrary to my normal dating procedure of pick and nibble, Colin encouraged me to actually eat the parmigiana I'd ordered. He said he hated women who always talked about their weight when, as far as he was concerned, a good meal was part of the joy of being alive. Not partaking was, he said, and I was struck by the words he used, denying the person you were with *the pleasure of your pleasure.*

I immediately inhaled the meatball he offered me and nearly passed out.

It blew me away that he seemed so interested in my love of art, enchanted that I'd envisioned fairies dancing on lily pads on Monet's *Giverny* paintings when visiting the Met with my family at ten or how, at twelve, I'd been drawn to the passionate drippings of Jackson Pollock in a visit to MoMA. He seemed to understand that kind of love at first sight. For an Oxford man who'd come to the States and graduated from Columbia's School of Journalism, Colin was amazingly open to the dreams of someone other than himself. Men don't come at you like that, confident enough to let you talk, not having to fill up the conversation with noise about what they've accomplished to prove they are worthy of a hookup.

It was later that night, after his lips gently brushed across mine outside my Village walk-up, that I remembered words my bubbe had once shared with me. I'd been in the ninth grade and she'd surprised me by coming to the high school to pick me up. We strolled the park, having one of our *woman-to-woman* chats she'd started after my bat mitzvah.

"How did you know Zayde was the right man for you?" I'd asked her between licks of the chocolate-chocolate-chip ice cream cones we both favored.

She paused, smiled this glowing smile, and said, "Your heart tells your head, sweetheart, and your head, if it's smart, it follows."

As I watched Colin disappear into the growing mist that night fourteen months ago, I realized that was exactly what was happening—my head was following my heart.

Never once since that magical, perfect evening did I think it even remotely possible that the roles would get reversed.

3

The Peter Hoyt Gallery
Sunday—June 10—5:26 P.m.
6 days, 2 hours, 34 minutes to the wedding

I stood in the smaller of the two rooms in the SoHo gallery I have managed for the past two years, studying a newly delivered painting. The owners and I had recently agreed to show the work of a transplanted Croatian artist, and his first offering had just arrived that afternoon. My assistant, Sasha, a blond NYU brainiac, *very* Gwyneth Paltrow, had helped me hang the work and I had minutes to view it before racing out to a very special dinner with—wait for it—my fiancé.

The spectacular nude female figure on the canvas before me was bathed in bronze and dancing with wild abandon along a sandy shoreline. Azure waters lapped at her feet and her arms swayed above her as she tilted her face upward toward a celebratory sun.

But something subtle was going on here. Was that the look of ecstasy on her face or its opposite? Was this stunning woman laughing or crying? Was the sun warming or burning her? It seemed to me it could be viewed both ways.

I checked my notes. The piece was titled *The Dance of Life*.

And I noticed now that the shoreline stretched on into the distance. The artist's technique of spatial arrangement gave the viewer a feeling that there was no finality to the dance. It went on endlessly, a dance of tears or joy, depending on your mood or perspective.

The word "perspective," as every good art grad knew, came from the

Latin *perspicere,* meaning "to see through." In my study of art I had always been struck by the fact that an artist creates perspective through what are, essentially, *lies*. Artists employ tricks through shading, foreshortened lines, objects painted smaller as their distance from the observer increases—all to tell a story that isn't real. In actuality, what they do is to create the feeling of depth that doesn't exist. It is an illusion. And yet, we the viewer, the art aficionado, stand and stare and are lured into that world by the sheer magic of the deception. It has never failed to thrill me.

And then and there, filled with the excitement of my impending wedding to the man I adored, I began dancing, mirroring the nude in the painting. I swayed here and there, back and forth with abandon.

"Excuse me." A voice sounded behind me.

I swung around, embarrassed.

"My mother left a package here the other day. The name is Hobbs. Katherine. They said they'd hold it in the office?"

"Oh," I said with a self-conscious smile. "No problem. Let me check."

I skipped back, searched, and returned a minute later.

"Sorry, I didn't find anything. You sure it was here?"

"I probably got the galleries mixed up." He shrugged sheepishly. "Thanks anyway."

There was a funny little expression on his face as he turned and exited. He'd probably thought I was weird to be dancing around the gallery, but I didn't care. I busted a move and screamed.

"Madison is rocking the house tonight," called out Sasha, six years and countless party nights my junior, as she entered with coffee she'd picked up for us.

"You better believe it," I shouted.

I resumed my dance, skipping and leaping between the Jasper Johns and a triptych of aging faces by a Connecticut artist in her nineties.

"Colin and I are going to our favorite little spot in the Village. Home of the magical first date." I smiled. "Sharing our vows for the first time. It's giving me goose bumps. Look at me," I said, holding out my arms.

"Oh, please, please, let me hear them?" Sasha begged. "I can seriously give you feedback before you lay them on him."

I shook my head adamantly. And gazing at her, it struck me once more that she was stunningly beautiful and blonder than most of Fire Island and could easily have been making tons of money modeling but preferred our little gallery and, who knew, maybe my humble company.

Still, *no deal.*

"The first one has got to be Colin," I explained with a grin.

I abruptly burst into a shriek of excitement and anticipation. I felt like I was back in ninth grade when, in a move I later found out had been brokered by Abby (I could only guess what she had bartered), eleventh-grade hottie Billy Mason had just asked me to the Spring JamFest. Only this was way better.

Checking my watch, I headed into the small office off the back of the larger gallery space. Retrieving my purse from the drawer in my desk, I threw on my handwoven green cape Colin had purchased for me the previous month. Tossing it over my shoulder, I turned to my computer to log out.

There was a single new e-mail blinking its presence in the corner of the screen, the sender identified simply as >A FRIEND<.

I'd been getting more and more congratulatory little communiqués from friends and acquaintances as the big day drew closer. The perks of being a bride, Colin had noted. They all wanted a piece of the fairy tale. Who wouldn't?

I smiled and opened the e-mail, read the brief message quickly, and then paused.

I didn't get it and read it again.

Was this some kind of joke? I stared at the words.

DO YOU REALLY KNOW THE MAN YOU ARE ABOUT TO MARRY?

The next line was even more stark and outrageous.

COLIN DARCY IS NOT WHO HE APPEARS TO BE.

I slammed the laptop shut and raced out of the gallery.

Hurrying down the street, the crazy message clung to me. Someone we knew was obviously playing games, probably one of his co-workers, or maybe it was his dearest friend, Benjamin Sachs. *Big Ben,* Colin called the guy who towered over us at at six feet seven. More to the point, he was a Wall Street lawyer and slightly demented.

Looking up at the signpost, I was reminded I was walking on a street named Prince. How perfect was that? And mine was waiting for me at Babbo.

Turning the corner onto MacDougal, I had already shaken off the e-mail and was experiencing tiny electric goose bumps as I anticipated hearing my groom's vows. And filled with that transcendent thought, I danced my way up to Greenwich Village.

4

Colin was standing in front of the restaurant, wearing a dark jacket and pants and an open white shirt, with a boyish grin on his handsome face as I rushed into his arms.

"Here's the future Mrs. Darcy." He grinned as I ran to him and gave me a full-lipped kiss. "Vow time?"

"Let's *do* it," I said with a playful shake of my head.

He put his arm around me and we walked into our favorite little two-story hot spot with the best Italian this side of Mulberry Street. You could wait a month to get into this place, but somehow, whenever we wanted it, Colin pulled some strings and, like that, we were in.

We headed upstairs to the cozier loft, its yellow walls glowing with reflections of the candlelight. Perfect. I sat down and the excitement of what we were doing caught up with me.

As he removed his jacket and hung it over the back of the chair, I gazed across the small, white-clothed table at Colin. He was grinning back at me, and I thought I saw a hint of nervousness in his eyes. My dad, after meeting Colin the first time, remarked that his eyes were so amazingly blue they reminded him of the first time he'd seen Paul Newman on-screen. I teased him for being "one of the girls," and I think he was embarrassed the next time Colin looked his way.

As Colin ordered, I drank in the rest of the face I loved: his strong jaw, the dimple in his chin; his wavy, Patrick Dempsey–like dark locks in which my fingers adored getting lost. As Abs and Kat agreed—the man had it going on. Best part, he was my man.

Colin reached for a paper in his pocket and I got a shiver up my arms. Wow. We were doing this. Vow time.

You've heard them at a thousand weddings. Brides and grooms pledging their undying love amid tears and jokes often bordering on the inane but which many of us, closeted as well as wear-it-on-your-sleeve romantics, eat up with a big spoon. Vows like:

G R O O M : *I, William, choose you, Loren, to be my wife. Before friends and family I promise to love and cherish you through good times and bad. I promise to try to remember to put down the toilet seat and replace the toilet roll when it finishes. I promise to remember this day with maple syrup and roses. I will love you always.*

B R I D E : *I, Loren, choose you, William, to be my husband. Before friends and family, I promise to love and cherish you through every obstacle that may come into our path. I promise to become proficient at programming the TiVo and refilling the windshield wash when it runs out. I will comfort you when your team loses and drink beer with you when they win. I will love you always.*

And there's the little touch that Brad Pitt and Jennifer Aniston promised each other: *I vow to split the difference on the thermostat,* which I'd long ago ruled out appropriating, since we all know how that one ended.

The waiter poured out two glasses of Chianti. We didn't need the menus. Colin knew what I wanted, and, unlike my mother, who always insisted on ordering for herself with meticulous detail, I left it to my guy. And when he'd finished and turned back to me, reaching across the table for my hand as he'd done that first night fourteen months ago, I melted.

"Ready?" He grinned.

I nodded, excited.

He reached into his jacket and drew a folded yellow-lined paper out of his pocket and slowly opened it.

I raised my eyebrows, gritting my teeth.

"You first," I begged nervously.

"Chicken?" he teased. "OK," he said as he nodded. "I'll bite the bullet. Now, it's not exact just yet, so if there's something you don't like, you tell me, all right?"

"You got it." I smiled, touched by his vulnerability.

This was a man who, on a daily basis, reported before millions on television. And sitting there across from me, his fingers gripping his modest piece of paper, he was like a schoolboy. I loved it.

Taking a deep breath, Colin began.

"I, Colin Darcy, take you, Madison Mandelbaum, to be my wife."

I froze at the words. I couldn't breathe. This wasn't a little girl's daydream; this was really, truly happening.

"I promise you love and laughter and sweet kisses on your nose in the middle of the night."

God, my heart was pounding. It was like we were there under the canopy already. He was gazing into my eyes across the prosciutto and fresh-baked Italian bread and I was spellbound, eleven years old and twenty-eight all at once.

"I vow to deliver to you the fullness of my heart and to entrust you with my dreams even as I cherish yours." His eyes held mine with intensity. "I promise you truth and honesty and to be as constant as your love, which is beyond reproach. And one thing more . . ."

He seemed to tremble, and his voice caught in his throat and he had to clear it and begin again.

"The boy in me holds out his hand to the girl in you. I will ever be her playmate."

Oh my.

"The man in me holds out his love to the woman in you. And there it will remain for as long as we two are blessed with life."

Wow.

Could any woman want more than this—truth and honesty and a promise of constant love? We both smiled and as a tear rolled down my cheek, we clasped hands.

"Excuse me."

Jolted from our reverie, we looked up to find two older women standing there, beaming and breathless like aging rock groupies.

"Yes?" I said.

The taller of the two, her silver hair pulled back in a bun, gazed at me.

"We were just finishing our meal over there," she said, pointing to a nearby table, "and we couldn't help but overhear this gentleman's words to you. We don't mean to pry but"—she giggled—"are you two about to be married?"

"In six days her name goes from Mandelbaum to Darcy." Colin beamed and glanced back at me with a big fat grin.

I have to admit, I liked the sound of that. *Mandelbaum* was my family name and all, but, sorry, Dad, it's always been one matzo ball of a heavy moniker. Colin and Madison *Darcy* had a lightness I was looking forward to.

"Those were the most beautiful words we've ever heard a man express," said the other elderly woman, bundled in a long dark green sweater, her soft green eyes brimming like a young girl's.

"He's a prince," I said, looking over at him.

"That must make you some kind of princess," chimed in the smaller woman in the sweater. "Good for you, darling. Every woman should feel like that at least once in her life."

"What a lovely thought," I said, moved. "And is that how you felt with your husband?"

"My husband?"

The women burst into laughter.

"My gracious, no. Henry was a boor."

She turned and put her arm around the taller lady.

"But then I found Grace here." She winked happily. "Now we're both princesses every day. Best of luck to you."

And giggling like schoolgirls, they beamed at us, waved, and walked off, arm in arm.

Colin and I shared a look of surprise and then tumbled into laughter.

"Forgive me. Are you Madison Mandelbaum?"

I glanced up at the dark-haired hostess.

"I am," I answered, mildly startled.

"There's a call for you at the front desk."

"Here?" I responded, confused. "Who would phone the restaurant?" I checked the cell in my bag, but there were no missed calls.

"You're extremely popular," teased Colin as I shrugged and rose to follow the hostess. "I want vows when you get back," he called after me, clearly pleased with himself.

A moment later I was handed a phone by the hostess table downstairs.

"This is Madison."

"You received my e-mail?" asked a metallic-sounding male voice.

I froze.

"Who is this?" I asked, slightly freaked out.

There was no answer.

"Look, if you're one of Colin's friends, this isn't funny and if you're one of mine, you're dead," I said, only half-jokingly.

"I'm neither," the person replied enigmatically. "Let's just say I am looking out for you."

"Uh, I'm pretty sure I'm not the one here who needs help," I taunted, suspiciously. "Ben, is that you?"

"I beg to differ," the caller insisted evenly. "I want to keep you from making the mistake of your life."

"Are you mentally disturbed?" I blurted.

"Two words for you, Madison," the caller said.

Cut him off, my brain shouted.

"Rebecca Farris."

"You are seriously disturbed, my friend," I spat back.

But he was gone.

I don't know how long I stared at the phone before handing it back to the hostess. She gave me a rather curious look as I did and I quickly turned from her gaze.

How could he have known I was in this particular location? My eyes darted among the customers. Was he here? A shudder went down my spine. I suddenly had the creepy notion I was being followed.

Unsettled, I found myself silently repeating the name the caller had mentioned.

Rebecca Farris.

It meant nothing.

Annoyed at having our special time interrupted, I took a stab at placing the voice but could come up with nothing. Cursing the caller, whoever he was, I climbed the steps back to Colin.

5

"I was beginning to wonder if I'd been dumped," Colin joked as he rose and motioned to the waiter to return with the food he'd had him keep warm in the kitchen.

He slipped back into his seat as the dinners were placed back before us.

I glanced up to find a quizzical look on Colin's face.

"You look a little weird, Maddie," he said, lightly concerned. "Everything all right?"

"Mmm." I nodded, taking a quick gulp of wine.

I wanted to tell him about the e-mail, and the totally bizarre call. But why disturb him? Besides, I was already upset enough for both of us. No, I told myself, I needed to protect him. This was our wedding week. Why should I ruin this special time for Colin? I was certain he would do absolutely the same for me. I forced a smile and did my best to shake it off.

"Your turn then?"

"Hmmm?" I said, digging into my macadamia-dusted tortellini.

"Your vows?"

"Oh, right," I answered, furrowing my brow.

I smiled as I held up my hand while chewing my food and stalling. I wanted to force myself to read them, to see the look on his face at the words I'd mulled over, the vows that kept me awake wondering if they were good enough, smart enough, meaningful enough for him. But the mood felt different. The call, outlandish and ludicrous as it was, had, despite my efforts, gotten to me. I was agitated, and the vows were too special to share like this. I needed it to be just right.

"Yours were so beautiful," I said, forming my excuse. "I need just a *scootch* more time to get them just right. Rain check until tomorrow?" I asked as sweetly as possible.

He eyed me in mock exasperation. We'd made a date. It was supposed to be tonight. He'd come through and here I was wimping out.

"I don't know," he said, mulling it over. "I'm going to need some serious enticement."

"I think I can arrange that," I said with a nod.

"All right," he agreed, letting me off the hook. "But those vows better be pretty damn spectacular."

As we rode the taxi back to his place the name *Rebecca Farris* floated into my consciousness. *Forget it. The caller was a crackpot.* I was angry with myself for not letting it go. *Didn't you hear those amazing vows?* I reminded myself, glancing over at Colin as we pulled up in front of his West End Avenue apartment building. *You are one lucky bride-to-be, Madison Mandelbaum,* I insisted.

Exiting the taxi, before Colin could hand the driver the fare, I lunged for him, knocking him back against the cab.

He broke away, shaking his head with laughter.

"Hold that thought," he said, turning and handing the fare through the driver's window.

Then, turning back to me, Colin grinned and opened his arms. With a joyous scream, I leaped up, smothering him with kisses as he carried me through the door of the building, up the elevator, and into his totally delicious bed.

6

I lay there in the middle of the night, having made love as only Colin and I could . . . wild, combustible, parched on the inside and drinking each other's love. I thought back to our first time. I'd been afraid to respond like that. I was overwhelmed. Colin was so gorgeous and I remember thinking, was my body good enough for him? What would he think about the baby fat that had stuck to my hips like a sticky bun ever since puberty? My breasts, as far as I was concerned, had always been too small. ("Just right," Bubbe had called them when I'd confided in her after Jason Stein tried to cop a feel in eighth grade and let it be known that Maddie Mandelbaum was *flatter than a pancake*.)

Back in junior high, I couldn't help but stare at Abby's breasts when we'd try on bras at Bloomingdale's. I would wonder what God was thinking to take all that extra boob material and stick it on her when it would have been a lot fairer to distribute it more evenly. But Colin had told me I was beautiful and, for the first time in my life, I believed it. I never even knew it could be like that before him. The way he touched me, his lips and hands exploring my flesh as if discovering uncharted territory. I recalled the tiny, exquisite orgasmic shocks that detonated in recesses of my body I hadn't known were there.

I lifted myself up on one arm and gazed at Colin lying there, all gorgeous and peaceful. He had this great habit of rolling up behind me after our lovemaking and lifting his knees up so he fit right up there in the crook of my legs. *Spooning,* Bubbe called it. She told me that she and my grandfather used to sleep like that every night of their lives until his arthritis got too bad. I imagined them younger and hot for each other, and, even though they were poor for years, she told me they were rich with love.

The best kind of rich, she'd said.

I hoped we would always be like that. Colin had one leg out on top of the sheet and I studied his nakedness, the taut lines of his physique, the muscles along his arms, the firmness of his broad magnificent back, his killer ass. It bummed me to think that, years from now, when gravity would have its way with our body parts, it would be *his* butt that would no doubt weather time better than mine.

Still, mine was a pretty good one. A little fleshy but Colin seemed to love it and that was all that mattered. At least my mom gave me that much. Even approaching sixty she looked pretty good. Oh yeah, a tuck here, a tighten-up there, but it was mostly the original work. My dad still loved looking at her, I could tell. I wondered if she felt the same way? Even with his teddy bear paunch around the middle, Morty Mandelbaum had a sweet smile and kind eyes, and I loved the way he stared adoringly at the women of his life. I would count myself lucky to get that look from Colin when we're their age.

I got up to pee and, on returning, found myself at the large window to the right of the bed, staring out at Colin's view of the Hudson. It was such a great apartment. Even though I hadn't officially moved in, I'd been here more than my place for months. The plan was to stay here another year and then, who knew—a loft in SoHo, maybe out to the coast, wherever Colin's career took us. Art was everywhere, as long as we were together. And we would be. *Always.*

Remembering my vows, I headed into the small living room to retrieve his laptop. Plopping myself on his striped red-and-black sofa that I knew I'd replace, I logged on to my e-mail. I'd sent the vows to myself and figured now was a good time to review. As the screen opened on my webmail, I paused, remembering. Clicking on the last e-mail, I forced myself to reread its disgusting words.

DO YOU REALLY KNOW THE MAN YOU ARE ABOUT TO MARRY?
COLIN DARCY IS NOT WHO HE APPEARS TO BE.

My body tensed with rebellion. I could hear that voice on the phone at Babbo's, the twisted individual who'd sent the e-mail, the sick jerk who had the chutzpah to suggest he was looking out for me.

But, like a stone in your shoe, the name the mystery man had linked to Colin nagged at me, refusing to shake free.

Googling, I typed the name REBECCA FARRIS into the search engine. In less than a second the screen filled with results.

I scrolled down to a *New York Post* article dated July 5 of last year. Curiously, I clicked on it and began to read:

> Rebecca Farris, a twenty-five-year-old aspiring artist, was found dead in her Queens apartment yesterday. Her nude body was discovered in the bathtub along with a curling iron and hair dryer, indicating that she died from electrocution. A suicide note was found nearby.
>
> Neighbors reported that the attractive woman seemed happy, though they were unaware of her ties to the company known as Elite Escorts, a premier online escort service said to cater to a high-powered clientele. Acquaintances interviewed refused to believe the young woman would take her own life and told police they were certain of foul play.

Tragic story, I thought to myself, *but what did any of this have to do with Colin?*

I scrolled to another story. It was also about the death of Rebecca Farris. This one was on a blog titled NY CrimeSeen. There was a color photo of a lovely young woman in a red halter dress, a gold pendant hanging from her neck. Her long blond hair framed olive skin and her green eyes. She had a smile like Julia Roberts, big and ready to burst into laughter.

What would make a person like that give up on the world? It made about as much sense as the bizarre suggestion that Colin was connected to an escort who had decided to bathe with her electrical appliances.

Still, the e-mail, the caller, the dead girl, they wouldn't leave me. So I did the only thing I could. Knocking over a pile of books on the nightstand, I woke him up.

Startled, Colin sat up in bed.

"Madison," he said, squinting in the small light of the bedside lamp I'd switched on to see his face. "What is it?"

"Well, it's crazy, really. But what do you know about Rebecca Farris?"

"Rebecca Farris?" he repeated.

I watched him and it seemed obvious I'd hit a nerve.

"What? Why the hell are you asking me this in the middle of the night?"

But there was no mistaking the wince at the corner of his eyes. His face grew grim. My heart sank. Could he have known her? I sucked in some air.

"Someone I think who knows you is playing some kind of game. I got this anonymous e-mail . . ."

"About Farris? Why, what did they say?" he demanded uncharacteristically.

"Whoa, newsboy. Why are you getting so worked up?" I said, taken aback by his strong reaction. "I just figured it was all a mistake."

"Yeah. A *big* one," he said.

I felt my heart stop. I'd never even heard the woman's name before that night.

"Colin?"

He groaned as if it were something he didn't want to have to answer.

"Please?"

He fixed me with a pained look that froze me to my spot at the end of the bed.

And then, his jaw muscles clenching, Colin launched into the most disturbing story I'd ever heard.

7

"I had just arrived at the station that day last April," Colin began, "and this young woman stumbled in. She looked deranged, drunk, or both. They couldn't tell. One of the secretaries helped her over to a couch and when she inquired whether she could get anything for her, the woman, astoundingly, asked for me. She had seen my report the previous night on the sex scandal that had erupted between a personal escort and state senator Ted Mason. She had mascara running down her cheeks and a slight cut over her eye. I told her she looked like she needed medical attention, if she'd just wait right there I would get someone, but she grabbed me by the shirt. There was a wild intensity about her, her eyes pleading. It was something she needed to do. She insisted I listen to her. And then she offered me something any reporter or journalist would trade their mother for . . ."

Colin's face constricted, as if the pain of the memory even now was difficult for him.

" 'I have someone even higher up for you,' she said. And then she offered up *Jamison Walker.*"

I was stunned. The state's attorney general was a familiar figure on TV and in the press. He'd served as district attorney in New York City before having been elected to statewide office five years earlier. He'd easily won reelection last year. Once while home from college I'd found my mother staring at then DA Walker holding a televised press conference and remarking at how handsome he was. For once, I had had to agree with her taste.

"Let me get this again," I said, shaking my head. "Farris was accusing Jamison Walker of a *sex* scandal?!"

Colin nodded.

"She told me Walker had been meeting her for six months at the Red Lion Inn in the Berkshires. He would register the room under another name and always pay in cash. They had met through an online escort service where she was known as Monet, she said, because of her love of art. He had begun asking for her exclusively and he offered to make a private arrangement and cut out the escort service, paying her directly.

"She told me he'd made promises to introduce her to people in the art world who could help her career. When she reminded him of this fact, insisting he use his contacts as he'd sworn he would, he got angry. She told me she was tired of being used by men, especially a guy like this who she'd come to believe really cared about her. So she pushed back. She told him she was going to tell his wife and go to the press if he didn't keep his word."

I had sat through every major on-air report Colin had filed in his three years with the network. Never once had he spoken of Farris and Walker. *That* one I would have remembered.

Colin avoided my eyes. He actually appeared to be ashamed, maybe even guilty. My stomach quivered.

"Bob Hopkins who, you know, hired me is a personal friend of Walker's. He heard about the story and came to me. I told him we had a potential blockbuster exclusive. You know what the guy does?"

Colin flashed me a look that was a mix of anger and hurt.

"Shut me down. He swore he'd been tipped off that someone was out to get Walker and insisted he'd done some research and had reports that showed Farris had been under psychiatric care. He told me Farris had to have manufactured the account she'd given me. He insisted he had solid sources for his assertions of Walker's innocence and pointed to the fact that I had no proof other than Farris's assertions to discount his version."

"What did you do?"

Colin's face was dark, his jaw muscles working.

"I told him to give me a week. There was something about Farris that told me she was telling the truth. He was like another person. The son of a bitch threatened to end my career. Said if I insisted on pursuing the story he'd make sure I didn't get hired anywhere. Told me I needed to be smart and that the lure of journalistic glory had been the siren song that had crashed many a promising career."

He paused, biting down on his lip.

"Rebecca Farris died on July 4. Independence Day. You believe that?"

"And you never saw her again before her death?"

"No," he answered solemnly.

"And that's it?" I asked, waiting for more.

Colin turned to me.

"That *was* it."

Was it? I tensed for what was coming.

"Three weeks ago I was putting papers in my safe deposit box, getting ready for the wedding."

"Papers?"

"Yeah. Good old Big Ben, being a best buddy *and* a lawyer, suggested, with the marriage and all, that I revise my will."

I was surprised.

"You have a will?"

I'd never even thought about the subject.

Colin shrugged. "It's a British thing, I suppose—everything in its place. Anyway, I was getting it out and there it was, the Farris file that I'd put away for safekeeping after Hopkins had shut down the story. Couldn't get rid of it, I don't know why. I took it back to the office and had just slipped it out of my briefcase when I turned to find Hopkins eyeing me suspiciously. I wasn't sure if he'd seen it, but since then he's been asking daily for updates on every story I've been pursuing. I got this hot tip," he said as he brightened. "May turn into something big, we'll know in a day or two."

And then his face grew dark once more.

"What is it, Colin?"

"I backed off the story Farris brought me and she ended up killing herself. Because I let her down."

"It wasn't your fault," I offered, pained at seeing what was clearly an ongoing anguish he'd kept hidden.

"She came to me, Madison. *Me*. I let Hopkins scare me off." He glanced back with a fierce determination. "I won't let that happen again."

I was moved and saddened and strangely proud he cared this much about helping someone who sounded like she'd needed it. I could have killed the caller. He'd pressed me just enough to bring this whole subject up and now look at what it was doing to the man I loved.

"An anonymous e-mail?"

"What, babe?" I responded, lost in my self-recriminations.

Colin turned back.

"Why would someone e-mail you about Rebecca Farris?"

"Who knows?" I shrugged, trying to play it down. "Maybe some colleague you scooped and he wants to get back and stir up trouble. It's New York."

I smiled and snuggled up in his arms.

"In five days I get to be Mrs. Colin Darcy. That's all that matters, right?"

He raised his head and slowly began to nod. I could feel him let go of the tension he was carrying.

"Yeah," he said, turning to me, trying for a smile. "That's what matters."

Moments later, as I stood in the shower, the hot water cascading over my skin, healing me, I finally let go of the anger caused by the crazed caller. He was not going to get to me again. Instead, I did what I always did in quiet moments like this one. I closed my eyes and envisioned our being pronounced husband and wife. I wanted that kiss to last forever, but I'd settle for the start of hors d'oeuvres. As a little girl I'd dreamed of that moment, when everyone I cared about would be there and the man of my dreams would gather me in his arms and the magic and love would be more real than the fear that kept people like my mother from being truly happy.

I stood in the shower, my arms wrapped around myself, and then I felt the delicious surprise of Colin's arms enveloping me as he stepped into the shower. He stood behind me, pressing his nakedness into my body, bending his lips to my neck that arched back, responding to him with a need and hunger that, as always, never left me feeling anything less than utterly alive.

Afterward, Colin seemed himself again as he dressed, kissed me good-bye, and headed out for an early morning run. My hair and body wrapped in towels, I was putting water into the coffeemaker when my cell rang in the other room. By the tone I knew it was a text. I glanced up at the clock. It wasn't even six in the morning.

Retrieving the phone, I checked the text. Immediately I was sorry I had. It was from him. The caller. The terse few words of his message said simply: "Do you believe me now?" with a photo attached.

Bracing myself, I opened it. I was stunned to find a photo of Colin and a woman I now knew was Rebecca Farris. They were smiling, and she was clinging to his arm in a way that suggested more than a professional relationship. My mouth went dry and there was a pounding at my temples.

I went to the laptop and bluetoothed it onto the bigger screen. As the sun began to rise outside the window, I stared at my fiancé and the woman he'd just insisted he'd seen only once.

And then I noticed it. The *New York Times* rolled up in his arm. Maybe I had just watched too many *CSI* shows or maybe my mother's cynicism had now, in the week of my greatest joy, decided to emerge or maybe the mystery caller had somehow managed to screw with my head just enough, but I was compelled to check it out.

I clicked on the photo; isolated the newspaper, and like some crime scene detective, hit the zoom button. I could hear my heart reprimanding me, saying that someone who knew her fiancé inside and out like I did would let suspicions fall off her shoulders. *The man of your dreams, Madison, he already explained everything. He hadn't seen her since April of a year ago, right?* I knew that was right. The words had come from his lips, lips I worshipped.

I zoomed in tighter. The newspaper remained blurry and unreadable. Tighter still and the top of the *Times* came into view. I highlighted the date and zoomed in further, blowing it up. As it crystallized before me, I stared at the date and bit my lip so hard I drew blood.

July 1, it read. Last year.

Two months *after* Colin said he had last seen Farris!

I cross-checked the date with the article. Yes, she had died on the fourth. The photo had been taken only three days earlier.

A wave of nausea welled up and I gripped the edge of the sofa. I looked back at the date. *July 1?!* Colin and I had been together three months by that time. We were already madly in love.

I was unable to breathe. Pulling myself to my feet, I staggered back into the bedroom. This wasn't happening. It felt like I was having an out-of-body experience and I couldn't find my way back into my own skin.

As I collapsed onto the bed my mind raced with panic. Instinctively, I reached for the phone.

As I did, one thought formed in my brain. I *needed* the truth. I loved Colin Darcy to the stars and back, but before we stepped under the canopy in five days, I vowed to myself I would find it.

8

Monday, 7:15 a.m.

5 days, 12 hours, 45 minutes to the wedding

"First thing we need is a command post," Kat called out as she blew through the door of Abby's Chelsea apartment, still wearing her aquamarine workout leotard and gold headband.

She'd been in a sunrise yoga class when I'd put in the SOS call and had come straight from downward dog.

"OK, we're not the NYPD. Easy girl," Abs responded over the whir of the beans she was grinding in her tiny hiccup of a kitchen.

As for me, I couldn't stop pacing the narrow lane between the sofa and the modern glass coffee table shoehorned into the modest-size living room that had become even more crowded by Abby's newly acquired twin soft-leather chairs.

Kat tossed down her sports bag and immediately plopped herself unceremoniously down into one of the brown guardians.

"Are you sweating, Katrina?" Abby immediately protested. "Because there's a no-sweat rule when sitting on the new leather."

"Trust me, it dried in the cab over," Katrina shot back, feeling her forehead and wiping it on her leotard. "All right, Maddie. Spill it. How long have you suspected?"

"What are you talking about?"

"You know, the whole 'Colin's a liar' thing."

"He's not a liar!" I insisted, banging my knee on the glass table. "Shit!"

"All men are liars," Kat corrected, popping some nuts from a jar on the end table. "They can't help it. It's in their DNA along with the cheating gene and the not-asking-for-directions gene and that whole rearranging-the-equipment thing they've got going on down there."

"We're not saying Colin's a liar," Abby chimed in supportively as she hurried in with a mug for each of us. "You're talking about her very-soon-to-be-husband. You remember that, Katrina, *don't you?*" she scolded, giving her a cold look that didn't escape me.

"Oh, really," Kat responded, cradling her mug. "Then may I ask what the hell are we doing here? I heard emergency and I split right before shavasana," she complained, removing her fuchsia leggings. "Now, there's no point going to yoga if you don't get the shavasana."

"Isn't that the part at the end when you just lie there and do nothing?"

"Damn straight," Kat retorted. "That's the reward I get for the hell of going through the rest of it."

"*That's* your reward?" Abs remarked with that arched eyebrow thing she's done ever since we met in kindergarten when she'd flashed it at Mrs. Ingersoll, who'd passed by and let out a giant fart that had nearly knocked us over.

"I got an idea for you, Kat," Abs said, grabbing coasters for both our mugs. "Why don't you just skip the yoga, stay in bed, do shavasana for another hour in the comfort of your own apartment? You'd save yourself the cost of the class, not to mention the horror of three dozen asses staring you in the face before you've even had your morning coffee."

"Ladies, could we concentrate on the problem?" I blurted impatiently.

"Sorry, Maddie," Abby said reassuringly. "I think we're just, you know, nervous for you. You get this strange call. You find out things you didn't know, it's got to be upsetting. But there's most probably nothing to it and an explanation we'll all laugh about someday."

Abby took her place next to me on the couch and immediately began rubbing the back of my neck.

"It's just ridiculous I know," I insisted with a worried laugh. "I mean, Colin's the greatest, right?"

"Amazing," Abs concurred, pressing a little harder.

"He's perfect. Tall, handsome, rich, successful, *British*. Women would do anything to be where I am."

"Sell their firstborn."

"Give up whole careers . . ."

"Hell, yeah."

"Not me," Kat interjected from the depths of the deep leather seat in which she'd been steadily sinking. "I wouldn't trade my job in the DA's office for any man *or* woman. Too hard to get where I am to give that up for something as transitory as love."

I looked up, hurt, and caught Abby glaring at Katrina.

"What?" Kat responded. "You know the statistics."

"You're not being helpful here," Abby said pointedly. "This is the week of our best friend's wedding. Get over yourself."

"Hey," Kat said with a shrug. "Just trying to provide a little perspective."

"Drink your java," Abs ordered, then turned back to me. "Maybe it's nothing, Maddie. You and Colin, you're just the yin and yang. He's so into you. You ask me, someone's messing with your head."

Kat started humming "Ironic" by Alanis Morrisette.

"And Colin doesn't have some hidden woman. He loves you to death, Madison. We've all seen it," Abby assured me before turning on Kat again. "Why the hell are you being so difficult?"

"They've all got secrets. I say check him out. The man needs to be vetted."

"He's not running for office, he's going to be her husband."

"All the more reason," Kat declared. "Think about it. You won't let someone into the Oval Office without knowing when was the last time they picked their nose, but a guy is going to move into your heart and home and you don't so much as run his driving record. *Hello?*"

"I Googled him," I offered weakly.

"*And* let me remind you that when she met him, all three of us MySpaced and Facebooked him," Abby defended.

"Oooh," Katrina said as she waved her hands in the air, "we went the whole Homeland Security route. Wake up. Terrorists have a freakin' Facebook page. They're cool. No worries."

"You've been in the DA's office too long."

"Two years?"

"Then two years too long," Abby observed. "You've devolved into a flaming cynic. How do you ever expect to find a man with an attitude like that?"

"Eyes open, Abs," Kat countered, sipping her coffee. "You got a bagel or something?"

She jumped up and headed for the kitchen.

"Full disclosure. The men I meet know right from the get-go I'm no-nonsense. They screw me over, I'm outta there."

"Well," Abby deadpanned, "that explains why you haven't been laid in six months."

"No," Kat corrected, lifting an eyebrow. "That's because I've decided to try the big C."

That got our attention.

"You what?" Abby and I exclaimed in unison.

"That's right, ladies. *Celibacy.* It's the ecstasy of a new generation."

"What happened to *bringing sexy back*?"

"Came and went," Kat quipped. "Besides, you forget who my parents are," she noted soberly as she munched away. "Mr. and Mrs. Never-Leave-One-Another-Unscorched?"

"Katrina . . ."

"No, no. Fifteen years they're divorced and they still can't let it be. Why opt for ten words of why you despise each other when *twenty* are just as easily available?"

"Are you done?" Abs demanded. "We're here because of Madison. *She's* the one in trouble. She's hurting, Katrina. Can't you see that? Can't you get past all that shit and see what our girl here is going through? This is her *wedding* week, damn it."

I looked up at Abs gratefully. Then over at Kat who gazed at me now, her bravado gone, her face clearly pained.

"I know." She nodded with a groan. "I'm sorry, Maddie. You've always been my vault. I could always go to you with my secrets, and I knew they were safe. I guess the whole marital thing has me spooked for lots of reasons, some selfish, I guess."

"It's OK, Kat," I said. "I get that."

"Last night my mother threatened that if my dad was going to your wedding, she wouldn't attend. We had a major blowout. It reminded me of all the crappy feelings I have about marriage."

She put down her coffee and came to the sofa, kneeling down beside me.

"But that has nothing to do with you, Madison. Abby's right. Irritatingly, sometimes," Kat admitted, giving my defender a begrudging little smile. "I'm here to help. Hey, the three of us are more 'family' than family. We go deeper than blood."

"Thanks," I said, taking both of their hands in mine. "It's just that I'm scared, you guys. Why would this caller want to warn me? Who is he and why would he try to ruin everything?"

"People are troublemakers. They can't stand when someone else finds happiness," Abs explained. "I mean, look at Kat."

"Nice," Katrina shot back.

"And there's this rather obvious lie I don't know what to do with."

"Look, Madison," Abby cautioned. "Who knows you better than *we* do? We understand you need to be certain that you are marrying the guy you think you are. So, what's your heart saying?"

I looked back at them with a sad smile.

"My heart's in love," I said, then shrugged and shook my head. "But my head, it's totally confused. None of this makes sense. I have to know the truth or I'll never be able to walk down that aisle and look at Colin the way I'm meant to."

We held hands in silence for a minute or two before Abby jumped in with a plan.

"Katrina, they must have a file on Rebecca Farris's suicide down at your office, right?"

"I suppose," Kat answered.

"Couldn't you maybe dig that up, see what it tells us?"

"What's that going to prove?" I asked. "The police declared it a suicide."

"Right and the whole damn government told us there were WMDs in Iraq," Abby insisted. "You have to check the evidence for yourself."

"OK, OK, I like your thinking." Kat jumped up, mind spinning. "You told me the article you Googled said her friends suspected foul play. Now maybe Colin knew about that and for some reason had to sit on the story."

A ray of hope went off in me.

"He *did* say that Rebecca confessed to having had an ongoing sexual relationship with Jamison Walker . . ."

"Whoa," Kat cried out, getting up and holding her head like a bomb had just gone off in it. "The attorney goddamn general?!"

"Colin said that his boss at the station quashed his investigation and promised to end his career if he didn't leave it alone."

"There you go," Kat declared. "Conspiracy. Very Washington. Love it."

"But why would he lie about the last time he'd seen Rebecca? Was he . . . ?"

"Madison?" Abs asked, her hand on mine.

"Was he *doing* her while he was doing me, because I seriously couldn't take that . . ."

"OK, let's not get ahead of ourselves," she cautioned. "Kat will check the file, see what she can find. I'm sure there's an explanation. It's going to be all right, Maddie. You'll see." She brightened. "Colin's a good guy. We're going to prove it. And, by the way, don't forget, we have a two thirty appointment."

"We do?" I answered, my mind still on what Katrina might discover.

"Your wedding dress?" she reminded me. "Your final fitting?"

"Oh, right." I nodded, jolted.

"Your mom says she'll be there, so put your game face on. It's *your* dress, Madison. Remember, it doesn't require her approval."

The dream of a dress I'd selected had not exactly warmed the haute couture eye of the veteran clothing doyenne Melanie Mandelbaum.

"It would be nice, though," I heard myself say wistfully without meaning to.

Kat showered quickly as Abs changed into the business smart suit of a publishing house assistant editor. I put the mugs in the sink and changed into the gallery clothes I'd brought. We were ready to leave for our respective jobs when my cell beeped. I froze. Abby took my cell and checked it out.

It was from Colin.

COUNTING THE MINUTES UNTIL SATURDAY NIGHT.
I LOVE YOU MORE THAN YOU KNOW, MADISON.

"Hey, what did I tell you?" Abby screamed.

I allowed myself a relieved smile.

"I'm telling you. Nothing to worry about," Abby assured me. "He loves you big time, girlfriend."

Even Katrina grinned.

And then, as we had a thousand times before, we wrapped arms around one another.

"Thanks, ladies. I really need you this week," I told them, shaking a little.

"You got us," Kat said.

"Like always," Abby added, squeezing my hand.

"What are we waiting for?" Kat abruptly announced, breaking away and grabbing her briefcase with bravado.

"We're smart, resourceful, and capable of kicking serious ass. Let's go solve this thing so our girl here can have her fairy tale."

9

I brooded all morning while shepherding customers who ebbed in and out of the gallery. I paced, drank coffee, and fielded text messages from Abs, Kat, and my mother, confirming our 2:30 appointment for the final fitting of THE DRESS.

I also sent Colin two sweet little reminders. We had kept this ritual of exchanged love notes every day since our engagement ten months earlier. I was not going to let that change with all that had occurred. *Especially* with all that had occurred. It was as much for me as for him. I needed to keep my vision of who we were alive, even as parts of the dream I'd inhabited for so long threatened to come undone.

"Madison? Did you hear me?"

I was staring at the woman dancing in the nude again, lost in my thoughts, when I glanced up to find the owner, Peter Hoyt, gazing at me, a funny expression on his tanned, forty-eight-year-old, half-the-year-in-California face.

"Hi," I said, surprised.

"Is everything all right?" he asked, deeply concerned.

Could he read my thoughts?

"I've been trying to get your attention. It's like you're not even in the room."

"Of course, she's not in the room, you idiot," said Brigitte, his Scandinavian-born wife, ten years his junior, with a laugh.

She had just entered the gallery, a take-out tray of Starbucks in her hand.

"The young woman is to be married at the end of the week, silly."
She smiled at me, shaking her head at her clueless husband.

"Men, Madison. They have no head for the important matters. Coffee?"

"Thanks," I answered, not sure I needed the added caffeine on top of the emotional jag I already had going on, but I took a cup anyway.

Brigitte handed another cup to Peter and then paused to gaze at the painting.

"Look, Peter, she has my breasts."

Peter turned red and glanced at me uncomfortably.

Like Madonna or cable TV, Brigitte never censored anything. Maybe it was the cultural difference. I owed my job managing the gallery to her. Well, her and, as she would never let me forget, to my mother.

The two had met at Bergdorf's four years earlier when I was working at MoMA after my master's work at Columbia. Brigitte was slamming a rather nasty saleswoman for refusing to acknowledge that the dress the woman had insisted she try on was unflatteringly matronly for the hot body Brigitte possessed. My mother passed by, was appalled at the way this wild customer was acting, and interceded. Within a minute, she conceded Brigitte's point, impressed at her sense of fashion, and the two ended up having lunch.

Then, the story goes, there was talk of a daughter, the art maven, which led to the stunning coincidence of the job opening at the gallery that Brigitte and her husband were about to open in SoHo. To my surprise, they had proven to be amazingly hands-off, spending half the year on the West Coast and allowing me complete autonomy when it came to acquisitions.

"The reason Peter is lingering about uncomfortably, Madison, is because he has something he needs to discuss with you," Brigitte said before reclining on the antique chaise longue as she continued to study the nude in the painting.

I turned to Peter.

He seemed genuinely unsure of how to proceed. His gentle, fine features were suddenly drawn taut. *Great,* I thought to myself, *more bad news.*

"It's about your after-hours. Specifically when you close up, Madison," he began hesitantly.

"Yes?" I hadn't the slightest clue as to what he could possibly be intending to say.

"Look." He shifted on his feet. "We found these," he said.

And, with major discomfort, he pulled a pair of thong panties out of his jacket pocket. "It was under the Rauschenberg this morning."

"My God." I all but laughed, staring at the sheer bit of material in his hand.

"*Sexy* underwear," cooed Brigitte appreciatively and gave me a wink.

"Yes, well," Peter said as he swallowed, completely embarrassed, "the point is, we don't mind what you do on your own time."

"No," I blurted, realizing now what he was thinking.

"I mean . . ."

"You don't understand. They're not my . . ."

"Hey, I wouldn't object," offered Brigitte, sipping her coffee and trying to be helpful. "Art is a big turn-on for me, too."

My phone beeped.

"It's just that we prefer . . ."

"You're not hearing me," I countered, taken aback at the suggestion I would do something like that in the gallery.

But the beeping cell was making a play for my attention. My eyes darted from him to the cell. It was a text from Kat. I held up a hand.

"If you'll just . . ."

"I know for women of your generation, the spirit can move a person at moments that are not exactly convenient," Peter said, making a stab at his take on the sexual appetites of twenty-eight-year-old females.

"Peter, you sound like that fellow in the suspenders. You know, Larry King?" Brigitte laughed. "And what do you mean 'of her generation'?"

"Brigitte, please," Peter stammered. "I'm just trying to," he said, turning to me in obvious pain. "Madison, what I'm trying to say is, in the future, if you could refrain from actually having . . ."

"Peter," I protested, exasperated, as he stood red-faced before me, not getting it.

He stared at me, confused, as I averted my eyes quickly to the cell message.

A & M.

THE ARCH @ NOON.

IMPT!

K

My heart sank. Katrina hadn't indicated if it was good or bad, just important.

"It's nothing to be ashamed of, Madison," Brigitte offered proudly. "Peter and I have done it in all kinds of places."

"Brigitte!" Peter objected, and he looked as if he might pass out.

"Barneys. Top-floor dressing room."

"Honey, please," Peter again begged, growing more flustered as he clung to the thong underwear.

"Once in a church in Taos, New Mexico. Those pews were very uncomfortable . . ."

"Brigitte, stop!" Peter snapped.

I was still staring at my cell message. Then I checked the clock. It was a quarter to twelve.

"Madison," Peter demanded, nearly apoplectic. "Are you listening to me?"

The sight of those slender panties in his outstretched hands snapped me back to the moment.

"These," I insisted, taking them from Peter's hand, "are not mine. Do you understand? If they belong to Sasha, I'll make your wishes and concerns, not to mention my own, expressly clear. I am not," I declared, growing loud for emphasis, "repeat, NOT having sex in this gallery."

There was a slight gasp that came from the doorway, not fifteen feet away.

Peter, Brigitte, and I looked up to find an older, well-dressed, white-haired couple, regular customers I recognized, standing there in some state of shock, unable to move.

"I think we'll come back another time," said the gentleman uneasily.

The two turned and headed for the door.

"Mr. and Mrs. Hanson!" I called out. "You don't understand. I didn't mean . . ."

But they were already halfway down the block.

I turned back to Peter, who looked stricken with horror at what had just transpired. Brigitte, on the other hand, was in hysterics.

Flustered, Peter strode from the smaller gallery into the next room. Brigitte rose and came over, placing her arm around my shoulder, conspiratorially.

"Peter's installed a new high-tech security camera in the gallery. It's the size of a fingernail. They actually *hide* them in the frames of the paintings. Thinks he's James Bond. Downloads it daily. Ridiculous expense. He insists it's to trip up would-be thieves who can jam the old system but, between you and me," she said with a wink, "I think he's checking out the after-hours action."

She broke into laughter and headed back to the office.

My cell rang. I remembered Kat and immediately picked up.

"Katrina?"

"No, the father of the bride," came my dad's playful baritone. "How's my favorite daughter?"

"Fine. It's all fine," I mumbled, distracted by Kat's text. "What's up, Dad?"

"Does anything have to be up for me to check in on my little girl during the most important week of her life?"

"Of course not," I told him, trying not to sound worried. "It's all good."

"I just was thinking that you have to be going a little crazy with all the plans, the dress, the who knows what all. I only wanted to remind you to enjoy everything. It goes by so fast."

"Yeah," I said, closing my eyes. "Thanks."

"I remember the week leading up to your mother's and my wedding," he said, and I could hear the emotion in his voice. "I was nervous as all hell and your mother of course was like a queen bee running the rest of the drones around the hive. I think she was as nervous as I was, but we dealt with that differently. You know her."

"Dad . . ."

"I know, I know. I'm getting sentimental. OK, give me a minute. Thing of it was, in the middle of her checking and triple-checking the guest list I forced her to come with me outside. There was this full, giant golden moon and I just wanted us to appreciate the moment 'cause"—his voice faltered—"like I said," he continued as he cleared his throat, "it goes by so fast."

I glanced away from Kat's text message.

"OK, Dad. I hear you . . ."

"Good. Lecture's over."

I mouthed to Brigitte that I had to go, jotting a note that Sasha would be in by one. She nodded and I headed out, switching to the earpiece as I went.

"You share what I said with Colin," my father urged. "He's probably a bunch of nerves over there at the station. I caught his piece on the governor's income taxes. Smart. Good reporting. You two are going to make a helluva couple."

"I've got to run, Dad," I said, heading out of the gallery and starting down Prince Street. "See you tomorrow. We're having dinner with Sir Hugh, remember?"

"Ooh, right," Dad said. "The *other* father."

"He's getting in from London in the afternoon so he'll probably be tired. Maybe give him a break on the history trivia. I'm a little nervous. I haven't spent that much time with him."

"Keep your cool. I'm sure he's a nice guy. Look at his son."

I turned north at MacDougal. My father's sweet attempts to reach out to me threatened to unleash all the emotions I was fighting to contain.

"Dad?"

"Yeah, Blue Eyes," he answered, using the childhood name he'd given me as a baby.

I stopped and took a breath.

"Thanks. For the call," I said, my voice breaking.

"Madison. You OK, honey?" he asked, filled with sudden concern.

"Yeah. Yeah, sure," I lied. "I just really appreciate you taking the time . . ."

"Go. Enjoy yourself. I got to eat my salad," he said scornfully. "Six weeks like this. Your mother thinks I'll never make it into that tux. Day after your wedding I'm headed to Katz's for pastrami. Ciao."

"Bye, Dad."

I crossed Bleeker and made my way up to Washington Square. Kat would be waiting there. She'd found something. Whatever it was, I prayed it wouldn't make things worse.

Isn't there a rule somewhere that every bride gets her wish the week of her wedding?

Take it from me, there *should* be.

10

When we were teens, the Washington Square Arch was the meeting spot for the three of us every weekend. Standing at the bottom of Fifth Avenue, it was modeled on the Arc de Triomphe in Paris. It marked the symbolic entrance to Washington Square and the village beyond. As teens, Kat, Abs, and I would wander the shops, grabbing lunch, checking out the music, the boys, the scene. As far as I could remember, we had never met for anything as serious as this.

Nearing the fountain, I could see Abby getting out of a cab at the northern edge of the square. Kat was already there by the arch, waiting. Seeing me forty yards off, Abs waved enthusiastically. Kat did not. She simply turned toward me, her face solemn, her lips pressed tightly together. My stomach lurched. I knew the look. It couldn't be good.

The thought of turning around, of walking away, pinged inside my head. Whatever it was Kat had to tell me, I didn't want to know it, did I? It had all been near perfection less than twenty-four hours earlier. What if I just chose to ignore this, whatever it was, and forget about the inconsistencies in Colin's story he'd shared that morning—the wrong dates, Rebecca Farris—erase it all. Couldn't I do that?

Turn around, Madison, I told myself. *Run.*

Abby was looking back at me as if she knew exactly what I was thinking. She motioned to me.

OK. I would just go over and thank Kat and Abs for their help and very calmly explain that I would no longer need it. I was all set to marry Colin Darcy and I loved everything about him. If he had some history that could possibly be construed as slightly problematic, well then so what, who didn't? He was still the same man I'd fallen in love with. Wasn't he? *Come on, Madison,* wasn't *he? Listen to your heart, girl, and tell your head to shove it.*

A strong breeze blew through the square. I drew a deep breath. Colin Darcy was going to be my husband, I told myself. I wouldn't enter marriage by hiding.

I pressed forward, dodging several musicians setting up for a noon-time session.

Whatever it was, I could handle it. I needed to know *everything*.

11

It was a June day, but I was aware of the cool gust of wind that seemed out of place, which is exactly how I felt right then as Kat took a tan, nondescript folder from her briefcase and pulled us over to a nearby bench.

"This case is not open," she instructed, and the tone of her voice was strained and uncharacteristically worried. "I shouldn't be showing this to you. I could seriously lose my job. I have to get this right back."

"OK." Abby hurried her along. "We get it. Big problem. You—out on a limb. Let's hear it."

Kat pursed her lips, studied us, and then pushed on.

"This was a back-burner, outside-the-normal-channels homicide investigation that stretched out several months before, for some strange reason, it was suddenly sealed. The order must have come from pretty high up the chain, because no one just above me knew anything about it or had the authorization to get it for me."

"What do you mean?" I asked. "How did you? . . ."

"Turns out, I'd fixed up the DA's personal secretary with this guy I used to date. Actually I was doing it to get back at him because this woman is so into herself she's practically a Hilton. Who knew it would work? Apparently they're madly in love and according to her she owes me big time so"—she held up the file—"favor paid."

Kat looked at me, hesitating. I realized she didn't want to tell me what she'd found in the file and, at the same time, knew she had to.

"There was a diary found in the apartment where Rebecca Farris died. The pages the investigation zeros in on are those from the last three months of her life," she said, opening the band on the file. "Several of the entries are noted."

She flipped through the file to the photocopied excerpts and drew them out, handing them to me.

Abby pulled closer on the bench, and together we read the high-lighted section from April 12.

> **When he touches me I feel clean. Not like I'm some high-class whore the way it is with the others. He asks a lot about the other men. Tonight he got mad. I think he's jealous. I think I like it.**

Abs looked at me, then back at Kat who knelt in front of us, scruti-nizing our response.

"What's this got to do with . . . ?"

"Keep reading," Kat instructed, biting her lower lip in that strange, exaggerated way she did just before she was completely freaked out.

I'd first noticed that quirk back in high school, just before Kat told Abby and me her dad was dating our tenth-grade English teacher. A few years later she flashed it again just before letting spill that her mom had detected a lump. Seeing it now was *not* a good sign.

Abby flipped the page to a new excerpt from the diary dated a month after the last one.

> **He was rough with me during sex for the first time tonight. I didn't understand and when I begged him to tell me what was wrong he finally confessed he needed to end it. Us. There's an-other woman. Some hotshot with an art degree from Columbia.**

I gasped.

Abby put her hand on mine and squeezed hard.

I looked up at Kat, who was still biting her bottom lip and studying my reaction. I took a quick breath and turned back to the diary entry.

Probably some rich bitch who thinks she's entitled to other
women's men. It's terrible to say, I guess, but I wish she were dead.
I made the mistake of saying that out loud and he got so angry
with me I thought I was the one who was going to die. There were
bruises on my body after we had sex and I cried until he kissed me
over and over and told me he loved me.

I sat there, staring at the diary page.

"You aren't the only one who graduated with a degree in art from
Columbia," Abby pointed out unconvincingly.

"Yeah," Kat said bitterly. "Though maybe fewer are connected to a
man with the same name as her fiancé."

"What are you talking about?" I protested. "Colin's not mentioned
in any of this."

Kat just gazed at me without saying word.

I shook my head, but she just smiled at me sadly and waited.

I looked at Abby and she swallowed hard, then turned to the next
diary entry.

And there it was.

Only a few lines, but they would fuel my worst fears and alter
everything.

I told him I couldn't go on like this. He warned me not to make
any trouble. There would be consequences. Why do men make
you feel loved and important and then always, always break your
heart? He can't get away with this. I'm not something you use up
and throw away. I'll tell if I have to. I'll make him pay.

Colin, Colin, how could you do this to me?

I couldn't breathe. My head was on fire.

Kat and Abby were frantically calling my name, but their voices
seemed distant. I turned and looked out at the square. Everything seemed

confused, splattered, tangled. People, instruments, nannies pushing babies in strollers—all were melting into lacerating reds and blacks and yellows. It was like standing inside a Jackson Pollock canvas, frenzied lashings of color whipping me from all angles.

Abby had a bottle of water at my lips, insisting I take a drink. I tried but my lips wouldn't work and the liquid poured down my top, soaking me to the bra.

I shot forward.

"This isn't happening," I cried out.

Abby reached for me, trying to console me as I railed at Katrina.

"Why did you bring me this?!" I pleaded, marching on her. "Why, Kat?" I cried. "Why?"

Kat gazed at me, sad but determined.

"You asked me to help you," she said simply. "Isn't it better to know the truth now before it's too late?"

I looked at her, angry and wild. And then I broke away and headed out of the square.

"Where are you going?" Abby shouted, racing to catch up.

I turned back. I was cornered and desperate and didn't know what to do with any of it. People were staring at me, but all of it meant nothing.

"I'm going to find him," I shouted suddenly. "I'm going to confront him with this!"

"No," Kat called out, coming to me.

I gazed into her resolute face and all at once broke into jagged gasps and tears.

"Madison, listen to me," she said, putting her arms around me and trying to steady me. "You aren't going to show this to Colin because, if this is true, and that has not been established, your confronting him could have all kinds of consequences."

I pulled back and stared at her.

"What does *that* mean?" I probed, alarmed. "Are you suggesting that Colin would, that he could ever *hurt* me? Because if you think that, you just don't know him."

"No, Madison," she countered. "The point is, maybe it's you who doesn't know *him*."

"Kat, don't," Abby warned.

"We have to," Kat shot over at her. "If we don't, who will?"

I stared at her, stunned, not wanting to hear what she had to say.

"Madison. You've already established that he lied to you. There are these disturbing calls someone is making, someone who knows more than the police. On top of it, I have here suppressed evidence that suggests there might be more to Colin Darcy than any of us realize."

"We're supposed to be married in five days!" I pleaded.

"Yes," Kat acknowledged. "That means there's still time."

I didn't understand. "Time for what?" I asked.

"To find out, Madison," she said, her eyes searching mine. "If you should or not."

The question had been floating through some part of my consciousness, and I had not wanted to give it air. But Katrina had done it for me, and her words rose up and roared: *deal with me*.

"Colin's father is coming in, guests are arriving," Abby worried aloud to Kat. "How can she go through with everything she has to do this week? Maybe she could postpone . . ."

"Are you nuts?" Kat shot back. "She postpones and everyone will want answers. No, we have to do this behind the scenes. We have to know if Colin has secrets that could hurt our girl."

"There's got to be some kind of logical explanation," I offered, bargaining. "Maybe he was helping her and she confused it with something else."

I searched my friends' faces for support.

"Maybe," Kat said firmly. "And maybe, like the weirdo caller said, he isn't the man you think he is. Look, Madison. We're going to find out everything we can. We have five days before you have to cross that bridge. OK?"

And Kat took me into her arms and I felt Abby embrace us both from behind and all I wanted was to wake up and see my prince waiting there. He would take me into his arms and let me know it was all just some horrible dream and that he was everything I'd come to know and love and look forward to being with for the rest of my life.

As I gazed with tears in my eyes over the shoulders of my best friends, it was the words of a dead girl that kept playing out in my head.

Colin, Colin, how could you do this to me?

12

I phoned the gallery. Sasha had arrived and the Hoyts had gone to lunch.

"I'll need you to hold down the fort this afternoon," I said. "I, um, have my dress fitting and . . ."

"Oh. My. God," she cried, sounding freaked. "*The Dress.* I am so stoked for you. Are you, like, totally psyched or what?"

That would not be the word I would use to describe my current state of mind, I was certain.

"Yeah." I humored her. "It's a rush."

"A rush? It's HUGE. It's bank. It's bangin'."

Even in my current state, I couldn't help but laugh. "OK, Sasha, who *are* you? Because you sound like some airhead from the mall in New Jersey."

"You got me there," Sasha answered in the usual East Coast elite tone I was used to hearing from the summa cum laude. "I was approached to audition for a one-line role as a sort of Lindsey/Britney knockoff in the new Woody Allen movie, so I'm practicing. It's really exhausting talking like a ditz, you know? How do they keep it up?"

"Talking about keeping things up, Peter and Brigitte found a pair of thong underwear this morning."

"Damn. I was looking for those."

"Yeah, well, you might want to find another venue for entertaining posthours. Give me a break here, will you?"

"Are they going to fire me? Jeez, Madison, I'm sorry. My boyfriend and I got carried away. The whole art thing."

"Yeah, I know. It's a big turn-on."

"Right. You get it too. It's the whole creative vibe. Orgasmic colors, all that."

"TMI. Gotta go now."

Katrina headed back to the office to see if she could dig up anything that might show that Rebecca Farris was unstable and might have possibly imagined a relationship with other men, including Colin. For all we knew, Katrina pointed out, the woman had seen Colin on television and developed a crush. I could certainly buy that. Only we all knew that it would hardly explain the photograph or why he had lied as to the last time he'd seen her.

Abby and I wandered up Fifth Avenue arm in arm, she literally holding me up.

"Why would he lie?" I asked, unable to wrap my brain around it. "He loves me, Abs. I know he does."

She nodded silently. Her eyes seemed to be pleading with me not to have to go there.

"He made me believe him."

Abby pulled her arm around me tighter.

"Maddie," she started, then paused.

"Go on, say it," I told her.

"Liars can make you believe them if they're good enough. They can even make themselves believe it."

"Abby." I pulled away.

"No, Madison," she said, coming toward me. "I'm not saying he was lying, only that when we love someone, naturally we want to see them in the best light. Believe what they tell us is true. I saw the same file you did. I don't know what to think, but I promise, Madison. You are my best friend and I am going to help you find the truth. I won't leave you. Kat won't leave you. We're in this together."

I looked at her, too blown away by events to be grateful. I shook my head in disbelief and gazed down.

My eyes focused on the colorful chalk drawing beneath us. It was a stunning rendition of the Raphael cherub, Cupid, as painted in the Renaissance. The arrow in his bow was at the ready and he was aiming it directly at the observer.

The caption above his head asked: GOT LOVE?

Perfect question. I thought I had. I was desperate now to believe it had not all been an illusion.

I stared at the cherub beneath my feet. I must have seen Cupid and his bow depicted hundreds of times and never once given thought to the natural implications of being struck by an arrow.

You are wounded.

13

Bernini's Bridal on Fortieth off Broadway was one of the temples to wedding haute couture to which most brides could only hope to aspire.

I wasn't one of them. I was happy with a simple gown. I didn't need a cutting-edge creation by Vera Wang or Stella McCartney. But my mother, of course, would never hear of it. She'd insisted on the best, meaning the highest profile, if for no other reason than her business associates and friends would hear about it and set in motion the buzz. And Melanie Mandelbaum, if you must know, and you must, was all about *the buzz.*

It was her drug of choice.

As Abby and I raced up to the third-floor home of the celebrated Bernini Bridal salon, I knew she would be sitting in judgment, never knowing, as was often the case, what I was going through.

Would I dare to tell my mom about the heartache that was confronting me? The mystery man's maddening calls, catching my fiancé in a terrible lie, confronting a possible crime in which the man of my dreams may have had a hand—all five days before my wedding?

Are you kidding me? *Be careful what you wish for,* remember?

For all of her success—the loving husband, a daughter who had received more than decent scores on her SATs and never once been in on a drug buy, a wonderful and nurturing mother who was bubbe to the world, the bang-up reputation she'd created in her chosen field, and the fact that the ladies of the sisterhood of Temple Israel of West Hempstead believed she walked on water—yes, despite all the praise, the reveling in buzz, the spotlight and attention, my mom was the *unhappiest* woman I knew.

Because she didn't get that it wasn't all about *her*. That her mantra of being careful what you wished for was a form of control that ended up pushing others away. That anything she did or accomplished had the shelf life of a gnat, always killing herself to impress the world when, in fact, she was her own harshest critic.

But mostly I saw her as the unhappiest woman I knew for one simple reason—she didn't get that, despite a lifetime of convincing herself to the contrary, she really *did* have it all.

14

Abby and I walked through the door into the plush outer waiting room of Bernini's. Several large, framed photographs of gorgeous, size 2 women modeling spectacular wedding gowns hung on the wall. Two cushy love seats faced each other, between them a dark wood table upon which sat two compilations of even more photographs, these of actual brides wearing their dazzling wedding day dresses.

"We beat her here," Abby noted as she sat down and flipped through one of the display books.

"She doesn't like to wait, remember?" I said, trying to prepare myself. "She always shows a few minutes late to avoid it."

"Madison . . ."

"I swear, Abs"—I tensed—"if you ask me if I'm OK one more time, I'm going to freak."

"Right." She nodded and went back to the photographs.

Suddenly, the inner door flew open and "Bernini" himself appeared.

"Do my ears deceive, or did I hear the bride of the year has arrived?" He laughed, clapping his hands together and wiggling his outstretched fingers in my direction. "Kiss-kiss, lovey. Come to mama."

And shooting a glance at a startled and bemused Abby, I reluctantly obeyed.

As I had discovered in two previous visits, Bernini was, in actuality, a forty-four-year-old gay Asian-Brit with the fabulous name of Quentin Woo ("Q" to insiders).

"Greetings. I have arrived." I heard a familiar voice behind me.

I turned around to find my mother bursting through the door, her arms filled with assorted bags.

Quentin immediately went to her.

"The queen of couture arrives," he cooed.

"Q, you are our god," she sang as the two double faux-kissed on each cheek.

"And look who got here first, my daughter, the bride, and her BBW, Abby."

"I think you mean BFF," Abby corrected, giggling at the faux pas.

But my mom had moved on, hugging both of us as the Bergdorf bags she was holding bounced off our bodies.

"What have you got there, Mom?" I asked.

"Oh, you know me. Just a few accessories I thought we might try out."

"What kind of accessories would I wear with a wedding gown?" I asked.

"Well, they're mostly things I might need," she said brightly, "but you never know. Now, Quentin. I've already put the word out that she will be wearing an original Bernini, and the women are dying to get a glimpse. But not before Saturday night," she teased.

"Mom, I've got a lot to do today so if we could just . . ."

Her ubiquitous phone rang and, deftly retrieving her earpiece, she popped it on, holding up her finger like a baton.

"Melanie here, yes? Ah, Richard. That would be perfect. Let me know when the others have arrived. And don't let the fall line get mixed with the summer. We had a mess last year. Ciao."

She threw down her bags, tossed off her cape, and whirled around to face the three of us. "All right. I'm ready," she declared. "Let's get this show on the road. Quentin?"

"Mom."

"Let's see the finished product, shall we?"

"Mom?"

"Come, Madison. I'm due back at Bergdorf's and meeting a client for drinks at Pierre's and your father for a quick bite and something at Lincoln Center after that. An opera or jazz concert, anyway, something with music, so, tick-tock, come along."

She took Quentin's arm and started for the inner sanctum of Bernini's.

"Mother," I insisted again.

"Yes, Madison, what is it?" she said, looking me over with alarm.

I glanced back at Abby, who was nodding encouragement at me, and then pulled my mother aside.

"I'm not on your timetable, all right? This is my wedding and I want to get it right."

"So do I, Madison," she insisted, hurt I might suggest otherwise. "The mother of the bride is the one who looks out for her little girl. Think of me as your champion." She smiled. "This is a big day. A *big* deal. You never know when something could go wrong, and I'm here to make sure it doesn't."

Her words detonated like tiny concussion bombs.

Something *was* wrong, I wanted to scream. Couldn't she tell? Just look in my eyes, Mom. For once, take the time to *see* me.

But she was too revved up, ready to do her thing, one foot out the door. I could never confide in her. Not even if she begged me to forgive her for missing my piano recital in third grade because she needed to attend a fashion show with Christie Brinkley and four hundred of her nearest and dearest friends.

But mostly I couldn't say anything because she was the one person who had raised objections to Colin from the start.

"His eyes," she'd commented when, at her suggestion, I'd brought him over for Sunday brunch to meet the family.

"Yeah," I'd agreed, not following and thinking she found them as sexy as Dad and I did.

"They're probing eyes," she'd clarified. "Like they're looking for something in you, something private that he has no business knowing."

Was she certifiable?

"Where the hell do you get *that* from?" I'd demanded.

"Maybe it's the fact he uncovers dirt for a living."

"He's an investigative reporter!" I'd objected, really hating her for raining on my choice. "And the station's talking about a bump to week-end anchor sometime soon. Then who knows? They say the networks are noticing. And don't count out CNN."

"What," she had answered with that little tone of cynicism in her voice, "so you're saying he's the next Anderson Cooper? Be careful what you wish for, dear. Men taste success, they leave you behind."

I was stunned and hurt. She didn't get that Colin saw *me* as his suc-cess. She would have to accept him, I'd decided. He was *my* choice.

And now, here we were.

So, pulling myself together, I flashed my mother a fleeting mask of a smile and stepped forward.

"Let's do it," I said.

15

At Quentin's insistence, my mother and Abs remained on the other side of the royal blue curtain as his two assistants, a pins-in-her-mouth little Vietnamese woman, and a tall, black, and muscular gentleman, bent over, making slight adjustments on the gown. As was Quentin's custom, the mirror in front of me was covered so as to allow me the full effect when all was ready.

Quentin smiled at me knowingly. I'd almost forgotten our secret. My mother had no idea that following the initial sketch that she'd approved months earlier, I'd asked for several modifications. It would be too late for her to make changes now.

"There are only a few exceptionally elegant women," Quentin declared loud enough so Abs and my mother could hear him. "Goddesses of style and fashion. Women like Grace Kelly and Jackie O, both of whom wielded enormous influence on fashion."

He eyed me up and down while scratching the top of his head lightly with the little finger of his right hand.

"It was Jackie who told me as I attended to Caroline's nuptials while working for Carolina Herrera that of all the dresses I would create, I would find the wedding dress the greatest thrill and challenge. And, cupcake, she was right."

He paused, stroking his chin as he looked me over from head to toe and then, with a small grin, he gestured to his assistants who, with a flourish, removed the cloth in front of the mirror.

I stared straight ahead at the incongruous sight in front of me and, in that moment, everything that had been gnawing at me—the maddening mystery caller, the diary, Farris—all seemed to slip away.

The dress was breathtaking ivory bliss, all layered and luscious like an overflowing glass of champagne. And, though I'd thought about something simple, casually elegant, there I was, beyond any wishful thinking and fanciful wannabe imaginings, looking—dare I say it—*beautiful*?

"Dior, Ricci, Balenciaga," Quentin trumpeted as he turned me around, "bite your collective tongues. I have achieved nirvana."

He drew the curtain, and I looked down into the stunned and awed expression on Abby's face. It seemed as if she'd just been hit by a really spectacular dawn. Our eyes locked and I thought we both might cry as she mouthed the word "wow" over and over.

And then I found my mother. She was gazing at me in this strange, weird way that I couldn't recall ever seeing before. She appeared seized with some long-lost emotion that had taken her by surprise, her lips slightly open, and, for once—was it possible?—she appeared at a loss for words.

My mother rose from her chair as her eyes wandered over me from head to toe.

"The poetry of the wedding dress is all," Quentin cooed as he came over to make one little adjustment to the waist. "It flatters the bride's body. She feels on that day she has dreamed of all her life as if she knows herself inside and out. That she is facing a spectacular future with the man of her dreams and, *comme ça,* all is right with the world."

My mother continued to stare. I couldn't remember her ever taking this much time to look at me. Was she seeing me or was it herself she was viewing, years ago when she was young?

There was a sudden burst of music and we all jumped.

Suddenly the little Vietnamese woman and the tall man of muscles had exploded into a wild dance, moving to the rhythm coming from the baby grand piano in the corner. I looked up and saw Quentin, who had just erupted in song, banging the ivories and regaling us with his salonified version of Elton John's "Crocodile Rock."

"Come on, Madison," he called out over the music. "Let's take her out for a test drive, shall we?"

Dance? Here, now?

My mother was already on her cell. I guess our moment had passed.

My eyes locked on Abby. She alone knew the roller coaster I was riding.

She shrugged her shoulders, as if to say, with all that was going on, why *not* dance? With a little smile, she stood, and, ever so slightly, began moving her shoulders to the beat.

"Are you kidding me?" I said, grinning for the first time since daylight.

The woman, pins still protruding from between her lips, took my hand and began shaking her hips, beckoning me with her smile.

So, right there in Bernini Bridal, with Quentin and his Rockettes rocking out, wearing the fabulous dress that had, however briefly, stopped my mother cold, with my heart on hold and my life in the air, I, Madison Mandelbaum, broke down and *busted out a move.*

"You go, girl," Abs called out.

The tiny lady stepped forward and twirled me around before I was intercepted by the tall, dark, ripped assistant who whirled us in a sweeping ballroom-like circle before pausing and gyrating his package in my direction.

"Whoa," roared Abby, coming in for some of the action.

Amid the wild scene I heard the faint sounds of my cell going off. Still moving, I danced over to where it was. Catching the private CID, I shimmied to the far side of the room, glancing back to find Abby cutting loose as the little Vietnamese woman attempted to pull my cell-tethered mother into the action.

"Yeah?" I answered, Quentin's Elton ringing in my ears.

"I told you about Colin Darcy."

I froze, then quickly glanced back to find Abby bumping hips with Mr. Biceps and my mother being twirled by the little Vietnamese woman as she continued her conversation on the phone. The music faded into the background as I turned my back on the room and faced the window overlooking Fortieth Street.

"OK, look. I've had enough of these calls. Who are you?" I demanded.

"That's not important, Madison," said the voice on the other end. "*Who* exactly is Colin Darcy? That would seem the more pertinent question."

"You are ruining the biggest week of my life! What did Colin ever do to you?"

"I told you, I want to keep you from making a monumental mistake."

"You don't even know Colin," I spat.

"No, darling," the man answered assuredly. "It's you who doesn't know him. Rebecca Farris was no suicide."

I held my breath.

"By the way, you *do* look rather amazing in that dress."

My head shot up and I stared out the window, eyes darting along the street.

"Where are you, you son of a bitch?"

And then I spied a figure across the street. He was in a tan raincoat, staring up at the window, an old-fashioned fedora hat on his head.

"Don't move!" I spat, racing for the door.

"Madison, what is it?" Abby shouted with alarm.

The music died instantly.

"Madison, what in God's name do you think you're doing?" my mother cried out.

"You cannot go out of here in that Bernini. I forbid it!" shouted a frenzied Quentin.

Frantically, I unzipped the gown. It fell to the ground in a heap. I heard Quentin scream out as if I'd murdered his offspring. But I had no time for that.

In bridal slip and heels, I threw open the door and bolted down to the street.

16

I raced into the traffic on Fortieth, cars screeching all around me. A truck driver busted out the expletives as I dashed in front of him, but I had a mission.

I got to the other side of the street where I had seen the man from the window, only to find he'd already vanished. I pivoted around on the sidewalk, looking up the street and down.

"Lady, you got some problem?" a man selling hot dogs asked from his nearby cart.

I glared back at him and then out over the traffic, down toward Sixth.

"Forgive my observation," he called out, "but I think maybe, you forgot something? Like, maybe your dress?"

"Hey, is this one of those reality TV shows?" his customer barked excitedly. "Come on, where are the cameras?"

And then I saw him a hundred feet off. The figure in the tan rain-coat and fedora was hustling around the corner onto Fifth.

"Madison!" Abby called out as she burst from the building across the street.

"Madison Mandelbaum, you return here this instant!" my mother cried shrilly.

Sorry, no time. I was already racing down Fortieth. In a flash, I charged around the corner onto Fifth.

My eyes were lasered onto that hat bobbing up and down out of the crowd ahead of me. I was only vaguely aware of the looks, shrieks, and roars of approval I was getting from the pedestrians and drivers as I raced half-naked up the sidewalk.

There was only one thought in my mind at that moment, to confront the bastard who was ruining my life. But I was falling farther behind as I zigged and zagged, trying to make up the distance.

"Need a lift?"

I looked over without breaking my stride.

A helmeted, middle-aged woman on a scooter had slowed along the curb as she headed uptown.

Without a word, I ran into the street, pulled up my slip, and straddled the small seat. Throwing my arms around the stranger, I pointed up ahead at the man in the hat.

"Follow that fedora!" I roared.

We exploded forward into traffic, my eyes fixed on the moving hat and tan raincoat making their way up past the New York Public Library.

And then, out of nowhere, the figure suddenly diverted to a taxi at the curb. He glanced back in my direction and then opened the door and got in. The Good Samaritan shepherding me understood instinctively.

"I watch *Law and Order*," she yelled over her shoulder. "I got this."

We sped forward, hot on the bumper of the yellow cab. And then, after the next block, we caught a break. The light was changing. *Yes!* The taxi would be forced to stop.

A dozen cars back, my scooter lady threaded her way through traffic and slowly maneuvered us up amid scattered whistles and catcalls pouring from vehicles all around us.

In seconds, we would be alongside the yellow cab and I would finally get a look at this guy.

But what would I do? I suddenly wondered as we eased forward. Threaten to report him? What would be the charge, interfering with a wedding? Implicating my fiancé in a crime no one knew about? Who was I going to tell? My mind raced. The publicity would destroy Colin's reputation. Even the suggestion could lose him his job. And I'd be the one responsible.

I could see the tabloid headlines: BRIDE RUINS GROOM'S LIFE ON THEIR WAY TO EVER AFTER!

I panicked. But as we approached the cab, I was determined to see this mysterious caller for myself. To confront him, face-to-face.

Then, finally, we were there.

As we pulled alongside the cab, I turned to my right to peer into the window. I could see the side of the man's face. He was clean-shaven and smaller than I expected. His hat and hand obscured a closer view. I reached out and knocked on his window.

"Roll down the window, you coward!" I shouted.

And then the light changed and, in a flash, the taxi shot forward. The woman stepped on the gas, trying to keep up, but it was too late. In seconds the cab had disappeared into a sea of yellow taxis.

The lady pulled over by FAO Schwarz. A contingent of men and women dressed in the colorful regalia of the British Royal Guard were in formation outside. They stood at attention, forming a corridor for a beautiful young woman and her chivalrous escort as they made their way into the store.

"There goes every little girl's vision," I said to the woman.

She turned back to me and removed her helmet. A bounty of silver-flecked dark locks tumbled out. She was maybe my mother's age. The woman gazed at me, her demeanor sweet but determined.

"I don't know who that man was to you," she said plainly. "I only know that if he's running, he's not worth it, hon. You find a man who will stick it out with you through the good and bad. That's the one worth holding on to."

Her words hit home. I nodded.

"You're right. Of course, you're right."

"I admire your pluck, girl."

"I have pluck?" I said, shaking my head. "Thanks."

"Just one thing. The next time you decide to chase after someone, you might want to rethink your outfit."

I looked down at my slip and then up into the eyes of a family visiting New York, the man aiming his video camera at me as his wife swatted him.

"Can I drop you somewhere?"

"Definitely. Thanks."

I clung to the woman as she scootered over and down Sixth, then back to Fortieth. Abby was pacing the sidewalk as we pulled up.

My mother was on the phone, and Quentin and his dancing assistants were huddled by the door.

"Madison," Abby called out, running to me.

"There you are," my mother snapped. "Do you know how embarrassing this is for me?" I turned and thanked the woman.

She smiled, glanced up at my mother, shook her head, and drove off.

"Well," my mother demanded, backed up by the Bernini trio. "Have you gone completely insane?"

"It happens," Quentin observed. "Brides sometimes get this brain meltdown. It's quite insidious. Thank God, we rescued *Le Dress.*"

"Leave her alone!" Abby yelled, silencing everyone en masse. "She's having a very tough day. Give her a break, can't you?"

I turned to her, eyes filled with gratitude. Abby was my hero.

As she helped me back into my clothes in the middle of the sidewalk, I glanced over at my mother, who was busy making little jokes with Quentin and his sidekicks, no doubt about her slightly whacked daughter, smoothing things over in her inimitable fashion.

As Abby helped me into my blouse I avoided the curious eyes of passersby. I was sick at what I was becoming. I was determined to follow the advice of the woman on the scooter. "You find a man who will stick it out with you through the good and bad. That's the one worth holding on to."

She was right.

Whatever Colin may have done or not have done, he was that guy.

If it was true yesterday, how could anything or anyone change that today?

I slipped out of my heels and handed them to Abby.

"Come on," I said with renewed determination. "I've got some marriage vows to polish."

17

I was back at the gallery in time for a five thirty appointment with a couple purchasing a Madaket sunset I had found for them by a Nantucket artist. The three calls I'd already received from my mother demanding an explanation for that afternoon's outrageous behavior had gone unreturned. And I was relieved to have never heard from Katrina. I refused to deal with any more of it. My new strategy for this wreck of a day was to meet Colin back at his apartment and jump his bones. That was my plan and I was sticking to it.

I let Sasha go early. She'd covered my ass all afternoon and, besides, it guaranteed Peter would find zero panties beneath any of the art the next morning.

The couple purchased the painting in all of five minutes. They were newlyweds and this was their first art acquisition as a married couple. I felt I'd finally done something right that day.

I had often daydreamed about the art that Colin and I would have in our home one day. Classic, modern, abstract? What artists would we collect? I didn't know what we could afford, but that didn't stop me from dreaming big. I wanted a mix of contemporary artists with those who had died and left something behind that continued to touch the eye and imagination. That was the artist's immortality.

And just as quickly as the good feelings had come, they disappeared. The news clipping of Rebecca Farris's death I'd read that morning said she had been an aspiring artist. I found myself wondering what sort of art she had liked. What work might she have created had she lived? I was

angry with myself for thinking about her. It brought up disturbing images of her and Colin when I was trying to get back to my image of him
and me.

As if hearing my thoughts, a text message came in for me. It was
from Colin, and it contained only two words.

TOP / NOW!

My adrenaline started pumping. I knew what it meant immediately.

The way it worked was this. On the days he was on the news broadcast, Colin would appear somewhere around the ten- to twelve-minute
mark with a local story. Should he ever track down an exclusive, something significant in the world of political news, his report would come at
the *top* of the program. This had happened only once before when he'd
broken a story about a secret slush fund being held by a local congress-
man who was tied to the mob. Colin had been the toast of the station for
the next month. That had been the story that had raised his profile. He'd
even received a personal note from Brian Williams.

Now, astoundingly, five days before our wedding, he'd apparently
done it again. I raced to my laptop and clicked on the live simulcast of
the six o'clock news.

As the show uploaded, my mind flashed back to the first time I'd seen
Colin on TV. It was right after we'd met. Kat, Abby, and I had decided we
needed to check him out and see if he was for real. He was doing a live interview from Albany, reporting on Spitzer's first day in office. He was a
natural, interviewing aides to the new governor and even provoking one
newly elected assemblywoman to giggle as she stared into his baby blues
and melted on camera. I was floored. This hunk was pursuing *me*?

I'd once believed I was consigned to the Joey Kagens of the world.
He was the horndog with braces who had volunteered to help me lose my
virginity in the ninth grade. I declined his tempting offer, but he was the
first in a long line of losers. I never got the hot ones. Until Colin.

The broadcast began and I leaned into my laptop. The anchor, Ron Calhoun, announced *breaking news*. They were going to go live to Colin Darcy at City Hall.

My heart was pumping.

And then, there he was. Standing on the street just in front of the historic white building only minutes south of me.

"Good evening, Ron," Colin said solemnly into the camera, his hair catching a breeze.

He looked amazing.

"I'm coming to you live from City Hall here in lower Manhattan where explosive information has come to light implicating Mayor Gerald Pittman in a kickback scheme involving money for patronage that, if borne out, could bring down his administration, forcing him from office."

"Holy shit," I whispered.

"Reliable sources have provided this reporter with credible evidence that seems to confirm that at least two independently owned companies hired by the city to handle, in one case, borough waste management and, in the other, replacement of City Hall's outdated communications system, have both been channeling funds to the mayor in return for his favorable role in steering the award of those contracts to their organizations. Sources further suggest that the kickbacks do not end there but may in fact point to a widespread pattern of secret payments involving up to a dozen private companies who have enriched the mayor by channeling funds through clandestine overseas accounts."

"Shocking news, Colin," the anchor responded. "Has the mayor's office issued a response to these accusations?"

"When we contacted them earlier today, there was no official comment," Colin replied. "Just before we went on the air, city and state authorities assured me that our report is certain to trigger an immediate and open investigation that, as we have said, almost certainly would bring about a change in administration and, as one federal official suggested, a 'sweeping set of reforms.' A related item, Ron. With Senator Corwin's recent selection as the next secretary of commerce, Governor Williams has been preparing to make an interim appointment as New York's junior senator. The leading candidate was widely rumored to be Mayor Gerald Pittman. Revelations today would now seem to favor Attorney General Jamison Walker, whose office has said it will have no comment. We will, of course, bring you an update as further details become available. This is Colin Darcy reporting from City Hall. Back to you, Ron."

"Holy mother," I shouted, bursting out of my chair.

Colin had broken a major story all right. *Ginormous.* The mother lode. His name would be everywhere. There'd be no living with him. I started to shake, unable to dial my BlackBerry fast enough.

"Good. You're here."

I whirled around to find Katrina in the doorway.

"Did you hear?" I said, totally off the charts with excitement. "Colin just broke this *major* story involving the mayor. I've got to reach him. He is going to be so up, he'll never come down." I laughed, grabbing the phone. "The sex is going to be seriously amazing."

As I fumbled with the digits I glanced up, unable to hide my enormous grin.

Katrina had this seriously grave look about her. No reaction to the big news. Nothing. What was her *problem*?

And then I saw the white envelope in her hand. She glanced down at it solemnly as if afraid to hand it over.

I took a step back.

"Not now, Kat." I shook my head. "This is a big night, a really big night for Colin and me. Whatever you have there I don't want to see it."

"Madison . . ."

"Katrina, now listen to me," I said, as if bargaining for a reprieve. "I just want to shut this whole thing down. I'm getting married in five days and this is going to a be a very big week, a *very* big week for Colin and me, so if you've got something to show me that's going to make me want to scream or jump off the Brooklyn Bridge, I'd rather you not. OK?"

I was half laughing, half terrified. My eyes darted once more to the envelope in her hand and then glanced away.

Kat slowly walked up to me until we were facing each other.

"I'm your friend, Maddie," she said softly. "I love you. You know that. I would never ever want to do anything to hurt you. But I couldn't live with myself if I didn't pass this along. Look at it or don't, that's up to you. But they say the truth shall set you free, right?"

"Yeah, well," I answered with a nervous laugh. "Maybe this week not so much."

"OK, but let me ask you this one question. Knowing Colin like you do, think of the way he's committed to getting at the truth no matter where it leads. What would he do if the situation were reversed? Would he want to know everything or just part of the story?"

I stared back at her without an answer.

"If you decide to look at this, whatever you choose to do with it—I will stand by you. I'm here to hell and back. But you asked for my help. I feel an obligation to share everything I know. That's the only kind of friend I know how to be. I love you, kiddo."

She kissed me on the forehead and turned to leave.

"Oh," she said, pivoting back. "Congratulate Colin on the scoop. Way to go."

And placing the white legal-size envelope on my desk, she left the office.

I glared at the envelope as if it might incinerate if I just stared hard enough.

Colin had just delivered the biggest story of his career. He was my guy and, damn, I was going to celebrate his big day and to hell with the rest of it.

I went to the envelope. Whatever was in there, I couldn't leave it around the office. Cursing it, I picked it up and stuffed it in my bag.

Then, hitting the lights, I headed out to party with my man.

18

Colin was dancing on the bed toasting the world, himself, us, even the Yankees while, drunk on my fourth mojito, I lay in open blouse and panties, gazing up at him from the floor of his apartment.

"It was like channeling lightning, Madison!" he roared, downing more mojito from the large glass pitcher of drinks we'd made. "The story was right there in my palm, and I knew the minute we went live it was going to blow a hole in the political ozone layer."

Some of the drink in his pitcher made it down his throat, but an equal amount splashed down his neck onto his naked chest as he stood in his boxers and socks totally tripping to the fortune of this very enormous, career-boosting "get."

"Here's to you, Mr. Darcy," I said, raising my glass, the drink buzzing in my head. "NBC is going to kiss your hot little ass."

"You know," Colin said, laughing, "they just might." He drank again. "Oh and Maddie, I forgot to tell you," he added, the alcohol buzzing through him. "They want me on *Today* in the morning. And *AM America* and the, whaddaya call it"—he snapped his fingers, trying to remember—"you know, the show with what's her name, blond, married to that director, Mike Nichols?"

"Good Morning America."

"That's not her name." He laughed through the alcohol. "But whatever, they want me. And get this"—he poured more drink down himself—"Larry King's people called."

"Larry King?" I repeated, slightly slurred.

"You got that, babe," Colin crowed. *"Larry fucking King."*

I loved seeing Colin so happy. It reminded me of the wild night when he'd spontaneously asked me to marry him on the heels of rather tragic events in the streets of Verona.

It was at a performance of *Romeo and Juliet* in Central Park at the end of last summer. The Delacorte was filled like always. It was a humid late August night and, even in the theater's totally open outdoor setting, we were dying. You could smell the audience sweating. I had suggested to Colin at the intermission that maybe we ought to just escape and head back to his place or mine for a cool shower and some AC. But he seemed really taken with the production and insisted we couldn't miss the powerful second half. When it was finally, mercifully over, I was ready to strip down right there, buy a bag of ice, and roll in it.

But as the actors took their bows to a roaring ovation, I noticed Colin was gone. I looked up the aisle toward the exit. I figured he must have really had to pee. And then, above the din of applause and cheering, I heard a familiar voice ring out.

"Madison Mandelbaum!"

Stunned, I turned around and stared up at the stage.

Colin was standing there among the disconcerted actors who didn't seem to have any more of a clue as to what was going on than the rest of us. Shouts arose. I honestly thought the actor playing Romeo was going to run him through. But Colin begged the indulgence of the acting company and audience.

"I know this is completely outrageous and the performance was astounding, truly." He bowed gallantly to the actors who seemed rather placated by his gesture, even touched and bemused. "But, kind ladies and gentleman, it occurs to me that sometimes we must say *enough* to tragedy."

What on earth was he *talking* about?

"Tragedy sometimes seems the default setting of our daily lives," Colin continued as the audience listened in rapt silence. "Backstabbing in the workplace and in our government . . ."

A murmur of agreement rippled through the crowd.

"Unkind critics . . ."

The actors nodded and laughed.

"Even, as in tonight's play, tragic love."

I held my breath. Apparently so did the rest gathered in the stifling theater, because I was aware at that moment that everyone around me was completely and utterly silent.

"Given all that, I say to you, we must grab for happiness wherever and whenever we can find it. I think the man from Stratford, were he alive today, would completely agree. And so"—he cleared his throat—"I would like to make a proposal . . ."

And only then did I realize what was about to happen, and my heart stopped.

"Sitting over here to the left and some fourteen rows back is *my* Juliet."

He pointed in my direction. A stagehand grabbed hold of a spotlight and, in a flash, I could feel every eye on me.

Colin dropped theatrically to one knee as electric excitement rippled through the crowd.

"With your indulgence, ladies and gentlemen, I make my proposal."

I held my breath.

"Madison Mandelbaum, will you agree to star in the role I hope you'll play for our lifetime? Will you do me the honor of becoming my wife?"

And with all eyes and the spotlight upon me, as stunned and over-whelmed as I was, I somehow found my voice and, with a force that shocked even me as the words left my lips, I shouted for all to hear.

"Yes, Colin Darcy," I called out excitedly from where I stood. "I would love to become your wife!"

A deafening roar went up from the audience and both Capulets and Montagues cheered from the stage as I moved through my row, raced up the aisle, and was lifted up onto the stage and into Colin's arms.

We barely noticed as the drops of rain began to fall and quickly picked up velocity. It was a curtain call like no other. Actors took prop crowns and placed them on our heads and we felt, for all the world, like New York royalty, drenched to the bone and ecstatic beyond dreaming.

Now, mojito covered, I rose to where he was on the bed. We reached for each other. Colin was filled with unbridled hunger, floating on the surging empowerment of love mixed with accomplishment. I felt his heat and returned it as we made love with abandon.

And yet, through the mojito buzz and the bliss, a nagging ache rose up within me, threatening to ruin the delicious high of our moment. Doubt that I hadn't gone looking for had insinuated itself into my life. Some—OK, just my mother and Kat—thought that I had been crazy to get engaged to a man I'd only been dating for four months, but it had all felt so right. But now, I could feel myself being jolted by the disquieting notion that for all my passion, I was making love to a man who possibly could have betrayed me.

I fought the invader, pushing back against it even as I pulled tighter toward Colin, wrapping myself around him as if to protect both of us. And then, sticky with the spilled alcohol and our lovemaking, we fell back onto the pillows, totally blissed out.

We drifted off in each other's arms and it was several hours before I woke as Colin groaned to life, disentangling our bodies as he quickly got up, showered, dressed, kissed me good-bye, and headed off into the darkness for his early call at the studio.

I got up to pee, threw some water on my face, and pulled back my hair, gazing at my reflection in the mirror. I was flushed with the afterglow of sex. I went to my handbag to retrieve my vows. I would meet him after the *Today* appearance and finally read him the vows I'd written. It would be perfect.

Reaching into the bag, I saw the envelope Kat had brought to my office and paused at the memory of her words. I swallowed hard as I stared at it before picking up the bag and flinging it into the living room.

I trust him, I told myself. *I don't want to know anymore.* I shut my eyes tightly as if it might make everything else go away. As I did, something Kat had said earlier about vetting the man you were going to marry popped into my head. It had sounded so ridiculous. You either knew about a person or you didn't, my heart asserted. But my head argued for Kat. She made sense, it reasoned. We investigate every corner of a politician but not the people we let into our hearts?

The argument led me to Colin's laptop. I felt like a spy inside what was practically my own home, but I humored the nagging voice in my mind. OK, I'd show it who was boss.

Was he really the son of Sir Hugh and Diana? I laughed at myself as I Googled Sir Hugh Aubrey. Up came a series of newspaper references to cases he'd argued in the London courts. I found a bio on the Royal Justice site and clicked on it. His education, titles, assorted judicial appointments, his connection to the Queen and, there it was at the bottom, formerly married to Lady Diana Darcy (*Lady?* I'd have hardly used that word to describe her), *father of one son, Colin Wordsworth.* Take that, Katrina.

Next I checked out Columbia where he'd received his master's. In no time I'd located a photo of him with his graduating class in the website archives. Date. Degree. This was fun.

What else? Oh, yeah. Before moving here after college he'd attended Oxford. Even rowed for their boat team, he'd told me. *Skulling* or whatever it was. As I called up the Oxford site and searched the archives there, I giggled to myself. I'd never seen a shot of him in college. Why hadn't I done this before?

I searched through the year he would have graduated and for some reason was unable to find him listed. I broadened my search a few years. Maybe he'd graduated early or he could have taken an extra year? Again, nothing. That was strange. It could have easily been an oversight, some clerical mistake, I assured myself. I tried connecting *Oxford* to Colin's name but, once again, came up blank.

I got what was becoming a familiar quiver in the pit of my stomach.

I checked the clock and did a quick calculation. It would be nine thirty in the morning in England. This was stupid I knew, but I suddenly couldn't let go of it. Where was any mention of him at Oxford? I went to the website and retrieved the phone number. Grabbing my BlackBerry, I entered the overseas and country codes and the university's number. In seconds I reached someone who connected me with the alumni office. I explained that I was looking to find photos for an honor being bestowed on one of their alumni whom, I pointed out, really selling it, had made quite a name for himself as a reporter in America.

"Brilliant," the woman exclaimed, sounding impressed.

She explained that they now had all of their photos and records digitalized so it would take but a moment.

"Colin Darcy, is it?" she repeated a minute later.

"Colin *Wordsworth* Darcy," I clarified.

"What year did he graduate?"

"1999," I said.

"Yes," she acknowledged, sounding disappointed. "I have a *Charles Patrick Darcy* and a *Louise* with that surname. But I'm afraid I'm not turning up any record for a *Colin Darcy* having graduated Oxford in the past, well, thirty years."

I felt the air leave my body.

"Are you positive?" I pressed.

"Yes," she insisted. "Quite certain. Sorry. Perhaps you meant to phone Cambridge? Please don't take offense, but Americans often seem to confuse us." She laughed warmly.

"No, um, thanks," I said, and hung up.

Devastated, I stared at the wall, trying to fathom what I'd found.

Why would Colin possibly say he had graduated from Oxford if he hadn't?

And then my brain coughed up the only question that could follow.

What *else* didn't I know?

Immediately I rushed into the living room and grabbed my bag. Heart racing, I sunk to the floor. Reaching in, I drew out the envelope I knew I didn't want to see.

With a shallow breath, I tore it open.

19

I was looking at a set of fingerprints mounted in tiny squares on a rectangular spreadsheet.

What was this supposed to mean?

Next, there was a photograph in a smaller envelope. The handwriting on the front identified it as "The apartment of Rebecca Farris."

I took out the photo. It was of a bathtub. I recoiled.

A hand—limp, lifeless—hung over the side of the tub.

Hers.

I turned the photo over and discovered a block-letter description.

DECEASED, REBECCA FARRIS, 25,

DEATH BY ELECTROCUTION

(HAIR DRYER/CURLING IRON CONNECTED TO LIVE CURRENT,

FOUND IN WATER BESIDE THE BODY)

I had known all this from what Katrina had shown us earlier. Still, I cringed at seeing it. A chill raced from the base of my spine, up my back, and into the rest of me. It was awful. Tragic. Horrific.

I turned back to the rectangular spreadsheet and again examined the fingerprints. I was puzzled. I was no expert, but, as I looked closely, the prints seemed to be no more than smudges. Partial prints at best. I could make out what looked like the top of a thumb, maybe half a palm, nothing like you see in the movies or on television.

And what was the point of all this? Searching in the envelope I couldn't see anything else that explained what it was I was supposed to be seeing or what any of this had to do with Colin.

Why had Kat given this to me?

And then, peering into the envelope out of frustration, I saw one last item in the packet. It was a small, folded note. I opened it and immediately recognized Kat's handwriting.

If you've decided to look and have come this far, call me.

I leaned back against the tub. Why would she . . . ?

And then, like a friend's hand, it came to me. The contents would be enigmatic to anyone else into whose lap this might mistakenly fall. The note was meant for my eyes only.

I knew at once it was Kat's way of protecting me, of not allowing anyone to connect the dots of this information, even as I had failed to do.

I checked the time. Four forty-five. Did I dare call this early? Then again, could I bear waiting? The answer to that was an emphatic no, rendering the first question moot.

I felt the sting of sneaking around behind Colin's back, but I could see no alternative. I'd been drawn into this and had pulled my girlfriends into it as well. I had to know what Katrina was trying to tell me.

I stepped out onto the apartment balcony to get some air to clear my head. The early morning noise of the city rushed up to greet me. Cars roaring up the street, an occasional horn, the distant wail of a siren, the thud of a machine pounding at some nearby construction site, all reminded me the city never slept. Kind of like *brides-to-be.*

I pressed Kat's number on my speed dial and the phone rang. One ring. Two. Three.

I cut it off.

My heart was racing. It was all too much. I was feeling the aftereffects of the pitcher of drinks we'd consumed. I didn't need to wake Katrina.

I pulled my robe around me, feeling the dull headache of my mojito hangover, staring out at the blinking lights of Manhattan.

And then my cell phone sprang to life in my hand and I gasped. I quickly checked the number. It was Kat.

"Hi, I didn't mean to wake you."

But before I could apologize further, she cut me off.

"So you did look at it," she said sleepily.

"Yes."

"I'm sorry."

"Sorry for what? What does it . . . ?"

"The fingerprints?"

"Yeah?"

"They have nothing to do with Colin."

I didn't get it. She was exonerating him? I was ecstatic and confused.

"But this is great, Kat. You had me totally freaking out."

"That's not all," she said.

I held my breath.

"Those are the partials from the crime scene that couldn't be used. The police could never make a case with them."

What was she talking about?

"I don't know how it was done, but there was another set of prints. They were taken from the hair dryer, the bathroom mirror, and from the suicide note in Farris's bathroom," she explained.

"Other prints?"

"They were deep-sixed in a vault where forensic evidence in this city goes to die. Unless . . ."

"Unless what?" I stammered.

"Unless someone powerful enough wants to hold it in reserve for another day."

"Kat, you're scaring me."

"You'll need to get a sample so we can compare and be sure."

"Be sure of what?" I stammered, knowing full well what she was saying.

"I could be wrong. I hope to God I am, but putting it together with references found elsewhere in the file, those other prints?"

"Don't say it, Katrina . . ."

"I'm pretty sure they're Colin's."

20

I sat on the bed, bleary-eyed, suspended in a state of shock as I watched Matt Lauer interview Colin about the astounding news story he'd broken the previous evening. The phone rang and, after checking to see who it was, I picked up.

"Why didn't you tell me Colin was on the *Today* show?" Abby screamed in my ear. "Madison, this is major!"

"Yeah, I know," I wearily replied, acutely aware that in normal circumstances I would have text-messaged, e-mailed, and phoned every last relative, friend, and acquaintance in the known world.

"Yesterday was nuts, I know," she commiserated. "That little runaway bride thing you did at Bernini's? OK. No need to go into that. But today's a new day and, damn, Maddie, your fiancé has just gone completely global. Can you believe it?"

"I know," I said, tentatively, wishing I could be as psyched as she was. "Colin is really jazzed."

"He has every right to be," she cheered.

"Abs, have you talked to Katrina?"

"No. But I left her a message right after the dress. I told her no matter what, you had decided to let this whole mess go. Because, like you said, he was the *one* and we all knew that and maybe he and Farris had had a thing and maybe not and it didn't matter. Then I worked my way through three manuscripts for an editorial meeting this morning and I was fried and fell asleep. I woke up only to find my best friend's fox of a fiancé on *national television.* Are you excited or what? Yaaaaaaaaaaah!"

The decibel level was comparable to the time the Backstreet Boys blew kisses at Abs and me (and about ten thousand other freaked-out teen girls) from the MTV studio window in Times Square back in the late '90s.

"I think I'm deaf."

"I bet Melanie and Morty Mandelbaum are going crazy right about now," Abby said with a laugh.

"Yeah, they probably would, if I'd phoned them."

"What do you mean, *if* you phoned them?!"

I filled her in about the envelope and Katrina and why I now needed to get Colin's fingerprints and how I was a total mess. I hadn't the faintest idea about lifting prints other than having watched TV and movie investigators dusting a surface with some kind of powder.

I didn't have any idea what to do, only that, according to Katrina, I needed to do it. Maybe they wouldn't match. A girl could dream, couldn't she? Abby stayed on the phone with me as I went to the bathroom.

"What do you think? Baby powder?" I said, going through Colin's medicine cabinet.

"Gee, Madison. I don't know about this . . ."

"We've got some kind of foot talc. A bottle of bath buds. No, probably get too soapy."

I went for the foot powder and looked around.

"This may be the weirdest thing I've ever done in my life, Abby."

"OK, you're not trained or anything. How could Katrina have even asked this of you? Just wait, I'm coming over."

"Abby . . ."

But she was already gone.

I shook my head. I went into the kitchen and looked around. There were a few glasses, the light switch, and then I spied Colin's favorite coffee mug he'd no doubt used that morning before rushing off to share his newfound celebrity with the world. I stared at it and then the powder. I decided to phone Katrina.

"Madison, for God's sake," she responded when I told her what I was doing. "Bring it down here. I'll get someone to run a print on it."

"I can't do that, Kat," I protested. "You're talking the DA's office. I won't be responsible for putting Colin under suspicion four days before our wedding."

"Are you saying you're still going through with it?" she asked in disbelief.

I stopped cold.

She'd asked the question yesterday but now, with the fingerprints and all, it had me spooked. If the prints matched, what would I do? Were there any circumstances in which I could turn in the man I loved? Would I marry a murderer?

The whole rattling scenario was so beyond my capacity for reason that my head began to hurt.

I turned back to the television to hear Colin answering questions about the City Hall scandal he had uncovered. He sounded so calm, so smart and professional. Matt Lauer was fawning all over him. He was the good guy, unwavering truth seeker, the dedicated journalist who had boldly uncovered a crime and serious breach of trust at the highest level of government in America's largest city.

My heart didn't know what to do with the battle going on inside between the pride I felt swelling within me and the forces of fear beating it back down.

Wait, *what was it Matt was asking him*?

"Just an aside here, Colin, but our producers tell me we've had dozens of inquiries about your *marital status* during the course of this interview," Lauer said with a grin.

Colin was taken aback, and then he broke into an embarrassed little smile.

"Correct me if I'm wrong," Matt probed, "but word is that you are actually getting married this week. Is that right?"

"Katrina," I spat into the phone. "Matt Lauer just asked Colin about our wedding."

"I'm watching. Oh, God . . ."

The call waiting buzzed. I switched over.

"Mom?"

"Madison, are you watching this? My God, the ladies at Bergdorf's are going to absolutely kill themselves. Your fiancé's a genius. Why didn't you call? Sshh, listen."

"Yeah, that's true," he answered, breaking into an ingratiating little grin.

Was he blushing? I could melt.

"I'm getting married in four days to an amazing woman who is, for the record, the total package. Everything a man could want."

"Wow," Matt exclaimed, impressed. "Bet you just scored major points with the in-laws."

"Major," my mother whispered into my ear.

"Well," the *Today* show host declared to the camera. "There you have it, ladies. Colin Darcy, who broke the City Hall scandal and apparently more than a few hearts this morning, is already taken. Good luck to you, Colin. I have a feeling we're going to see more of you around the network. Let's head back to Ann Curry for more of this morning's news."

"Oh my God. He's amazing. Why didn't I see that? Wait, your dad wants to say something."

"No, Mom," I protested. "I've really got to . . ."

"Blue Eyes. You've got a star on your hands. You must be over the moon. I'm so happy for you, honey. Tell Colin well done!"

"I will, Dad," I said, shaking. "Gotta run. Talk to you later."

I stared at where Colin had just been on the screen, his words still vibrating within me.

He had just expressed his love for me before the whole world! How was it possible that this man could have ever done anything sinister or criminal? My heart was incapable of imagining such a thing.

I looked down at the powder and the mug and heard the buzz from the phone telling me Katrina was still waiting, urging me to bring her a sample of his prints. But my mother, the buzzkiller, had finally come around to Colin, I protested silently. Her timing was completely ironic, but still . . .

I felt full and empty and excited and scared all at once.

Was it possible to have everything and nothing at the same time?

My cell was nagging in my ear, demanding a response.

And despite my feelings, I heard my brain once more insist that ignorance was not an answer. That would be like having the wonders of the world laid out before me while I remained in a prison of *what if.* The doubts would even poison the love I had for Colin. I wouldn't live like that.

And with that thought, I knew what I had to do. Not in spite of my love but *because* of it. I clicked on the phone.

"Sorry about that. OK, Katrina," I said, bracing myself. "What do I have to do?"

21

Tuesday, 8:25 a.m.

NYPD Forensics Lab, Lower Manhattan

4 days, 11 hours, 35 minutes to the wedding

Katrina was waiting for Abby and me as the cab pulled up to the address located somewhere just below TriBeCa. Getting out, I cradled my bag with its traitorous contents of Colin's favorite mug against my chest as Abby and I gazed up at the ten-story fortress of gray stone. There was a depressing vibe about the place, as if we were about to enter the world of *The Matrix*.

Katrina hugged both of us, then pulled back and gazed at me. There was warmth in her eyes, but also the cold grit of determination that had been there for as long as I'd known her.

"You ready?" she asked.

"No," I said, smiling uneasily.

"Come on," Katrina coaxed. "Finnbar is an old friend."

"Finnbar?"

A moment later, we were inside the strange citadel and passing through a guard station.

"They'll know we don't belong here," I whispered to Katrina as we emptied our belongings through the metal detector. "They're going to be suspicious."

"I've got it handled," she insisted confidently.

"Hey, Rick," she called out, greeting the young, halfway hunky guard as we cleared security.

"Ah." He grinned. "Look what the *cat* dragged in."

"You see, ladies. This is what passes for 'wit' amongst our city's finest."

As she signed us in, I glanced worriedly over at Abby.

"So Katrina, to what do we owe the pleasure?" he quipped.

"My friend Madison here, and her assistant, Abby, are working on an art montage featuring forensic evidence."

What?

I saw the guard looking us over. Was that suspicion in his eyes or was he checking out the merchandise?

"You don't say?" He grinned.

His eyes found Abby's breasts and stayed there.

OK. Horndog.

"Yeah," Katrina spun. "Fingerprints, bullet fragments. Wild. You know, all those *CSI* shows, the public loves that stuff."

"Is that right?" he muttered, his gaze not budging from Abby's chest.

"Hey, blue boy," Kat fired. "Eyes straight ahead."

"You're my hero, you know that?" Abby told her.

"Men are like dogs," Katrina observed as we walked away. "They pee on your carpet. You gotta rub their nose in it. Only way they learn."

"I thought you were done with men?"

"I'm holding out for that one good puppy," Katrina cracked as we entered the elevator.

She pressed the button for the top floor and looked at me.

"Hold on, Maddie. We're going to get some answers."

The elevator spasmed, causing me to gasp. And then, with a loud whine, it surged upward.

22

After reaching the tenth floor, Katrina led us down a long dark corridor to a door marked FORENSICS LAB: PRINT, BLOOD ANALYSIS/DIGITAL IMAGING. I half expected something out of Frankenstein. I was surprised to walk into a facility brimming with gleaming workstations, where people were busy with long-necked silver photographic machines and infrared devices that looked alien and that, Kat informed us, were state of the art. She navigated the maze of equipment, leading us to a worktable at the far side of the lab.

"Finnbar," she said to the white-coated man peering into a monster of a microscope. "These are the friends I told you about."

The man glanced up. He was, as Katrina had explained on the way up, a fifty-five-year-old Irish American with a bushy crop of salt-and-pepper hair and weathered features. His smile was warm and gentle and nothing like what I had feared.

"Welcome to Oz," he quipped with a big grin.

"Finnbar and I go way back," Katrina explained.

"Her dad and I have been friends since I moved to this country as a kid. We were real tear-ups. Caused some serious trouble back in P.S. 89." He laughed. "Of course, he ended up going off and making millions on the market while I settled on a world of bullet fragments and blood samples."

His eyes found mine.

"You must be Madison?"

"Yes," I said, surprised.

"And you're Abby." He smiled. "Kat talks about both of you all the time."

The cold reality of the room and the reason we had for being there rattled my brain.

"I understand you have something for me?" the man asked.

I swallowed and looked at Katrina, my eyes searching hers.

"Whatever we find, Finnbar will keep it in the vault," she assured me. "I'd trust him with my life."

The man glanced over at Katrina and he seemed genuinely moved by her words.

"Your friend's a kick-ass ADA," he told Abby and me, turning to her. "I am as proud of her as I would be if I had a daughter."

I saw an uncharacteristic emotion flicker on Katrina's face, and I knew it was the kind of acknowledgment that she'd love to hear from her own father.

I reached into my bag and anxiously pulled out the mug. Finnbar reached for it, removed the plastic, and placed it on a small silver tray.

"Morning, Finnbar."

We all looked to our right as a striking dark-haired fortyish woman dressed in a navy blue power suit passed by.

"When you get a minute, I need you to look at something that came in last night," she said with authority.

"No problem," Finnbar replied with a quick wave.

As he began pulling on a pair of latex gloves, I glanced back protectively to make sure the woman had gone.

She was still there, observing. Catching me eyeing her, she nodded, flashed a little smile and, thankfully, moved on.

"Kate Trask," Finnbar commented dryly. "Brilliant mind. Lousy administrator."

"And she's a woman," Kat teased, "and a decade younger than you?"

"Katrina Fitzsimmons," Finnbar shot back, pretending to be hurt. "I am not sexist and you know it." He paused. "I just think a woman has to know her place."

He laughed at himself.

"The three of us can take you, easy," Kat ribbed.

"Will you let me do my business?" he said with mock solemnity.

I glanced at Katrina. I knew she was trying to keep this thing light, but she didn't fool me. I saw the layer of worry beneath her grin.

"What is *this*?" Finnbar asked, pointing to a touch of white dust on the lip of the cup.

"Um," I admitted, fidgeting. "Foot powder?"

The man lifted his eyebrows and looked back at Katrina, who shrugged.

Turning back, he next sprayed some kind of mist from a little orange can onto the cup and held it up beneath an infrared light, rotating it with a thin instrument, studying its surface.

Kat, Abby, and I pushed in closer to get a better look. As if by magic we watched as clear fingerprints emerged on the side of the coffee mug where a blink ago nothing had been visible.

"Excellent," Finnbar said softly.

Reaching for a square white patch, he gently pressed it onto a spot on the cup and then gently removed it and placed it on a clear mat under a nearby camera. He repeated the ritual several times at various spots along the mug and its handle. Then, as we all looked on anxiously, he maneuvered his chair over to the camera. He shot a series of photos of the cup and the white patches that were apparently instantly scanned into his large-screened computer.

"Katrina?" he asked.

Abs and I looked over, uncertain of what was happening.

Kat had reached into her leather case and was drawing out a brown evidence envelope. She opened it, taking out the set of prints she had told me about in the early hours of that morning; the ones apparently taken from the hair dryer, the bathroom mirror, and from the suicide note in Farris's bathroom.

I swallowed hard and squeezed Abby's hand.

She pulled closer as Finnbar took the prints and ran a scan over them, entering them into his computer from which it was now clear he would compare those he'd just lifted from Colin's mug.

"And now," he exhaled, eyes on his screen. "The moment of truth."

He hit a key and a banner reading Print Analysis appeared at the top of the screen.

There was a beat of silence, a nanosecond in which my life and dreams seemed to pass through me. I'd stopped breathing as I stared over Finnbar's shoulder, Kat and Abby pulling in protectively around me.

And then the screen flashed its answer with breathtaking certainty.

23

Match Confirmed, the screen read.

That was *it*? No room for doubt? This was how a dream died, with the simple stroke of a computer key?

I let out a small gasp and my legs buckled. Abby and Kat reached out to steady me. Finnbar O'Shea looked at me, his gaze sad and solemn.

I stared back in disbelief. And as the confirmation in his eyes tore through me, I backed away from him and my friends. Shaking my head, refusing to accept it, I turned and bolted from the room.

Katrina and Abby intercepted me in the corridor as I lost it, my angst-filled screams reverberating along the corridor.

"We're going to get you through this, Madison," Kat asserted, pulling me aside from the prying eyes of passing lab workers.

"No, no, no, no, no!" I lashed out as Abby joined her and, together, they aggressively guided me into a nearby ladies' room.

"This doesn't prove he did it," Kat declared.

"What?" I shouted back, pulling away. "You're the one who got me down here so we could prove it one way or another," I reminded her accusingly. "Well, there it is, Katrina. You saw the screen. The prints match."

"OK, OK," Kat said, and I could see her mind grasping for something, anything to placate me with.

"What do I do?" I said, looking at both of them wildly as I paced the marble floor outside the stalls, mind racing. "His dad's arriving. This will probably kill him. And my mother. Just this morning she finally got over herself and told me how great Colin was. Of course, he had to become the toast of the network and appear on the *Today* show to get her to come around, but she did. And now, look who's telling me to take it easy," I objected. "You've been practically pushing me to find him guilty and call off this wedding."

Katrina stared back, face flushed.

"Don't attack Katrina," Abby stepped in. "She's done nothing but try to help you."

"I won't turn him in. No way. I can't do it."

"Of course not. No one's asking you to do that, Maddie," Abby pleaded.

"My whole life has blown up." I lashed out, confronting Kat. "I don't think I can take any more of your help."

"All right." Katrina nodded, looking as if she might crack. But then she fired back. "I know I've pushed but it's because I'm scared for you, all right?"

I stopped and glared at her.

"I know what bad marriages look like. I've been an eyewitness to one my entire life, and I don't want one of the people I love more than anyone in the world to go through anything approaching the disaster my parents have inflicted on themselves *and* me." Her face was red, her voice shaking. "I've got your back, Madison. The way you've always had mine. And if it pisses you off to find answers you don't like, then go ahead, call me whatever you like. Just remember, I'm on *your* side."

Hot tears of shame coursed down my wet cheeks.

"Now there might be a small opening here."

"What?" Abby inquired with surprise.

"Stay with me here," Kat said, thinking aloud. "As far as forensics are concerned, the print match *only* means that Colin was there in the Farris apartment at some point in and around her death. If this were a trial, it would be circumstantial but not definitive. You would still need to prove motive."

"Katrina . . ."

"Madison. Listen to me," she urged, her eyes flashing. "I grant you,

Colin may have lied. And, I admit, this print match doesn't look good. But it doesn't mean an end to the case."

"There's a case?" Abby asked.

"Stop feeding me a line," I snapped. "I've got to face this. God, I can't breathe. What I am going to . . ."

I began to hyperventilate.

"Abby and I have a plan!" Katrina suddenly blurted out.

"We do?" a panicked Abby let slip.

"Yes," Katrina insisted, eyes still on me. "We do."

"Well, what is it?" I demanded.

Kat hesitated, eyes searching.

"I'm working on it," she barked.

As I stared at my friends I felt the weight of hopelessness seize me. None of us had an answer. The prints matched. Colin was guilty. I felt nausea take hold of me.

"I'm going to be sick." I gulped and made for the nearest stall, collapsing to my knees and tossing my guts out.

I had nothing inside me. I was empty, and still the heaves continued. I became aware of Abby's hand on my back, stroking me softly.

Strange the things that enter your head at a moment like that.

I thought of how my mother could never do that when I barfed as a kid. The sound alone made her sick. Sympathetic nausea, she insisted. At the first convulsing upchuck, she'd flee the room, leaving me, all of six, to fend for myself. But Abby and Kat had never been like that. Neither was . . .

"Oh my God," I said, jerking my head out of the toilet.

I whipped around.

"What?" a startled Abby asked, taking toilet paper and wiping off my lips.

"The time of death. They must have a coroner's report or something?"

"What are you saying?" Abby stammered.

Kat was already consulting the file she was carrying.

"They put time of death between six and eight on the evening of July fourth."

I shot up, energy jolting through me.

"Madison, what's going on?"

"Colin *couldn't* have done this," I insisted.

"What are you talking about?" Katrina responded, confused.

"It's impossible," I said, growing increasingly excited. "He was with me."

"Whoa, girlfriend," Katrina exclaimed. "How can you be so sure?"

"We were in Brooklyn at this new bistro!" I shouted, getting up out of the stall, suddenly energized. "The plan was to eat and then head over to the bridge to watch the fireworks. But I got sick. Bad seafood," I yelled, pacing like a crazy person.

"Maddie, what are you . . ."

"I mean I blew my guts out in the ladies' room of a bistro in Brooklyn, and Colin was there," I exulted. "He was right there and I was so shocked because, you know, barfing is not an intimate experience and normally you can't have anyone around, except, well, you guys, 'cause we basically have waxed ourselves and wiped each other's asses since like forever, but I remember being really embarrassed but totally impressed that Colin stuck with me through a thing as horrible as that."

Abby screamed and I grabbed her and we bounced like we were back in grade school before collapsing in each other's arms, completely pumped.

"Madison . . ."

I looked over at Katrina, who still had this sour expression on her face I didn't get.

"Katrina, he didn't kill her." I laughed. "Are you hearing me? He didn't do it."

"I know I said it doesn't prove that he committed a crime, but Madison," Katrina cautioned like the ADA she was, "his prints were still in her apartment on the day she died. Doesn't that concern you even a little bit? Don't you want to know why?"

"Yes, I do," I answered with a grin. "And you know what, I'm going to ask him. And he'll have an explanation and I am going to have my answer and get on with my wedding week that I've been waiting to enjoy."

Kat stared at me, still troubled.

"I appreciate everything you've done for me," I said, hugging her and practically lifting her off the floor. "Really, I do. And I'm so sorry that I accused you of trying to ruin my wedding. I know you're my sister and that you always have my back. But hey, if I can let go for the moment, so can you. Put your energy on some real criminals. Go try a case or something."

We gazed at each other. And though it was slow to come, Katrina finally let go and allowed herself a tiny smile.

"Better. And you"—I turned to Abby—"you go find the next bestseller. You're already late for work."

"You got it." Abby laughed. "And don't forget, Thursday night the ladies are going to partaaaaay."

"Whooo-whooo!" we three screamed.

We were so jazzed at my having remembered where and when Colin had been on the fourth that I dared Abby to flash the guard. Outside, I hugged both of them and sent them on their way. Next, I quickly put in a call to Colin and was thrilled when he answered.

"You, mister, were fantastic this morning. I am blown away."

"Thanks, Maddie," he said. "I'm on my way to do a follow-up at City Hall, and they've got me doing a two-minute on the network tonight."

"Are you serious?" I screamed.

"Madison, this is turning out to be the best week of my life. How about you?"

I didn't even want to go into that one.

"Colin, we need to talk about something tonight, OK?"

"I know," he teased. "Your vows. I haven't forgotten. Gotta run. Don't forget we're meeting at my dad's hotel and taking the car to your folks. And whatever you do, don't mention the dinner when you see my mother."

"Your . . ."

"Wish me luck."

"Good luck," I said, but he was already gone.

With all I'd been through, I'd completely forgotten about the tête-à-tête with my future mother-in-law, the grand and glorious Diana Darcy.

I glanced back up at the gray building.

I'd run out of the lab so fast I hadn't even thanked Finnbar O'Shea. The truth was, it was hard to feel gratitude for the person who'd just confirmed your fiancé's handprints had been found in a dead woman's apartment.

Katrina was right.

I would have to find out why Colin had been at Rebecca's house. It wouldn't be an easy conversation, but I was so relieved, right then, I didn't care.

Even the thought of tea with Diana Darcy couldn't ruin my mood.

24

Tuesday—2:30 p.m.

The Palm Court of the Plaza Hotel

4 days, 5 hours, 30 minutes to the wedding

Diana Darcy was the kind of woman you couldn't imagine had ever gone unnoticed.

She could draw men in while making women envious of her secrets. And, like Naomi Campbell, she could drop you with a cell phone.

Thrice divorced, Colin's mother had long prided herself on her fierce independence. She claimed a special sisterhood with iconic, one-of-a-kind women. Not long after Colin had taken me to the Fifth Avenue to-die-for penthouse miniestate she'd called home ever since splitting from husband number three, an oil man and apparent Viagra addict, Diana had insisted I join her for a screening of *The African Queen.*

Mesmerized, she watched Hepburn boldly handle Bogart, leaning over to me on her gold-braided sofa and observing, "Now, *that's* what women could be like if they developed some balls."

I wanted to suggest that her desire to acquire balls might have been part of the reason her three marriages broke up but decided against it.

We haven't spent all that much time together for many and assorted reasons, mainly boiling down to the fact she seriously *freaks me out.* But the get-together today was not optional. She had insisted on this future mother-in-law/daughter-in-law sit-down before the wedding and so here we were, at the Plaza, surrounded by silver trays and fine china, sipping tea like perfect ladies.

I gazed over at her ever-present smile. (Was that her default setting 24/7, the mask she showed the world?)

"I enjoy the Peninsula," Diana observed airily, taking in the graceful, formally dressed musician now playing harp. "And they do something rather nice at the Pierre. But still"—she winked—"the Plaza is special."

She gestured around her.

"So civilized, don't you think?"

"Mm-hmm," I agreed and sipped my Earl Grey, just wanting to survive this without a faux pas.

"I suppose it's the years in England. No matter what was happening in our busybee lives, we always paused for a proper tea. *High* tea, of course."

She giggled and made this high-pitched sound that was quickly sucked back down her throat as if she couldn't spare it.

"Now, Colin loves a good tea," she said, her eyes suggesting that I make a note of it.

"Yes, yes, I know," I quickly replied between bites of the cucumber tea sandwiches I was downing.

"My goodness, dear," the grand Diana remarked as I devoured my third salmon puff. "You'll want to be able to fit into that wedding dress."

"I didn't really eat today," I offered with an embarrassed smile, deciding to resist the teensy egg salad sandwich I was eyeing.

"Yes, well, you must take care of yourself now. It is the only way you can be there for Colin."

What was she talking about? Colin was in better shape than any of us.

"Now, dear," the woman said as she faux giggled, "as it so happens, taking care of my son is the very topic I wanted to discuss with you. Girl to girl." She grinned, lifting her eyebrows which, given her love for Botox, was a remarkable feat.

"Holding on to a husband in today's world requires some unusual skills, Madison, dear," she said.

I nearly coughed up a salmon puff.

"One must be prepared."

Back up. Stop. Hold the cheese, Louise. Was Diana Darcy *actually* about to offer me advice on what had to undoubtedly be the last subject in which she might have possessed any practical knowledge or useful insight whatsoever, that of *how to keep a man*?!

I knew about chutzpah. My mother possessed it in family-size servings. But what I was facing here across a tray of scones and clotted cream was CHUTZPAH on a scale previously unknown to man.

"Firstly, darling," she observed, putting down her tea and leaning in, "you must at all times make a man feel in charge. Now, he's my son, of course, and he naturally possesses my genetic confidence, so that's already half the battle."

Battle?

"But, Madison," Diana added, narrowing her eyes, "you don't have to give up your own ideas. Simply put them out there and credit *him.*"

How's that?

"It worked masterfully with Gregory, my first husband. I'd suggest magnificent vacation plans and he would automatically toss them aside. So I simply learned to package them differently."

She gave a sly smile and cleared her throat.

" 'I didn't really want to do Santorini in the spring, darling,' " she complained, as if I were someone else, " 'but your brother and his wife cannot stop raving about their trip and I know how you love Greek food so' "—she exhaled—" 'what can I say, *you* win.' "

She winked, clearly pleased with herself.

"Needless to say, we were taking in the Aegean by April."

"That's amazing," I said, intent on nabbing another scone and loading up on cream and jam.

"On another, more delicate subject . . ."

I looked at her, midbite.

"We're both women. We know how men can be."

Looking around, she drew closer.

"I don't want to get overly personal, dear, but you must 'please' them, if you know what I mean."

No, no, no, my brain pleaded.

"I've always found that to keep a man coming back, one must *cultivate* her courtesan qualities, getting in touch with one's inner whore."

I swallowed half a scone whole and coughed.

"Careful dear. That's another thing. Keep your body toned. They are going to look elsewhere. Of course, they are, they're men. Animals, really. But you must make sure they cannot get it better anywhere else."

Can I go now?

"Madison, I'm going to give you one word of advice. This word has helped me in all of my relationships. If done well, it will help you smooth over any disagreement and will keep my son as loyal to you as the day you met."

She leaned in, lowering her voice as if we were coconspirators.

"Fellatio."

"Diana . . ." I sputtered.

"Darling, I know most brides don't have this kind of honest conversation with their future mothers-in-law, but I want our relationship to be different."

"Uh-huh," I gasped. "Because I'm perfectly fine with the normal way this usually goes."

"Nonsense," she replied with a wave of her hand. "We are women of the twenty-first century. Sex is a means to an end, dear. We both know that. I want Colin to be happy. I want the same for you. To be happy together requires effort. It's not going to be handed to you. Definitely not. There is a blueprint."

"Really?" I said, halfheartedly.

"Oh, yes. You must be adventurous. Keep him surprised. And, by all means, develop *dexterity.*"

"I see."

"You have no idea," she nodded. "Would you believe I once massaged Colin's father to orgasm while Mimi was in her death throes in an inspired production of *La Bohème?*"

I nearly spat out my tea.

"Twice I copulated Hugh orally while crossing the Atlantic," she recalled as if it were an afterthought. "Naturally, we were in first class."

Dear God, let the earth open and swallow me whole.

"Oh, yes, Madison. Being 'deliciously naughty' is not optional if a woman is to succeed in today's convoluted world of relationships. It's a necessity. Develop these skills early and Colin will be a contented man."

Unbelievable, I said to myself, incredulous. *She is pimping for her son!*

The waiter arrived and checked our hot water.

"I think you can take this away," Diana said, gesturing to the tray where several choice sweets remained. "A little too tempting for some of us." She softly jabbed in my direction with a squeal of laughter.

"Diana, if your skills are so considerable, how is it that all your marriages have ended in divorce?"

My heart was pounding like a street drummer, but I was secretly pleased I'd put an end to this unbelievable farce.

Diana Darcy didn't flinch. Taking a sip of her tea, she slowly returned the cup to her saucer and fixed me with the steeled tenacity of a Hepburn.

"I should think that would be obvious, Madison, dear," she said with a sly wink.

"My men simply didn't know how to keep a *woman.* "

25

I couldn't get out of the Plaza fast enough. As I headed down Fifth, I wasn't sure which experience that day held the greatest "ick" factor—the visit to the creepy forensics lab in the morning or the Playboy Channel tour of marital sex provided me by my future mother-in-law.

I had to meet Abs at Tiffany's to pick out gifts for the bridal party. En route, I left a message for Colin telling him that given the last two hours I'd just spent with his mother he owed me big time and I planned on collecting. I reminded him that we were meeting his father at the Peninsula at five thirty, where a car would be waiting to take us all out to Long Island for *Dinner with the Mandelbaums,* adding that I looked forward to getting back to the city afterward and having a little talk.

"Sorry I'm late," I said to Abby, breathless as I barreled through the door. "It was hard to walk out on Diana. She had such *useful* advice for me."

"Like what?" Abby inquired, already eyeing the magical world of luxury before us.

"Oh, little things," I said lightly. "Like how to be her son's whore, her talent for fellatio. Little things like that."

"What?!" Abby exclaimed, her mouth falling open.

"May I help you, ladies?"

We looked over to find a hottie standing behind the counter. He had creamy-rich butterscotch skin and his smile revealed more white teeth than a toothpaste commercial.

"We're looking for bridesmaid gifts," Abby said, brightly.

"Oh." He grinned. "Just a moment." He called out, "Weddings!"

"OK," Abby suggested, looking around. "This isn't meant to be a storewide activity."

"I apologize," the man said with another grin. "There's someone here who lives for this. She'd kill me."

"Yes, yes," said an excited voice to our left.

Abby and I looked over to find a bouncing fortysomething woman, her hair pulled tightly back into a ponytail.

"A wedding." She clapped her hands. "How wonderful."

"Um, we're looking for bridesmaid gifts?" Abby offered, seemingly unsure whether to talk to the eager woman or feed her a bone.

"And are you the bride?"

"I am," I acknowledged.

"Wow." She grinned, inspecting me. "Lucky woman."

Abby couldn't resist.

"Her fiancé was on the *Today* show this morning. He's a reporter."

"Oh. My. God. No way." The woman nearly freaked. "The one with the City Hall scandal?"

Abby nodded, smiling over at me.

"I caught that. Let me tell you, he is Clooney HOT. You are one fortunate lady."

The blonde was gazing at me with that look of envy that's like chocolate to a woman's ego. I could feel myself ballooning with pride. I turned to Abby.

"She can help us."

"Something not too expensive," Abby pleaded hopefully.

"OK." The woman nodded, barely able to look away from me. "But, just so you know," she half-joked. "You're in *Tiffany's.*"

Yes, we knew. She motioned for us to follow her to a long glass case in the back of the store. It was filled with stunning bracelets studded with tiny diamonds that had to cost the GDP of a small country. Abby freaked.

The woman reached below the glass case and retrieved a modest rectangular box. She laid it out on the counter and opened it. There, nestled in velvet, was a small, exquisite sterling silver necklace with a tiny "b" letter attached.

"These are alphabet necklaces designed by Elsa Peretti. You add a lowercase letter for your recipient's name so it has a personal touch. Simple, lovely. They are extremely popular as bridesmaid gifts and"—she leaned in, whispering—"they're pretty much the least expensive item in the store."

Abby and I looked at each other.

"We'll take them," we said.

"Gold or . . ."

"Silver," we chimed in unison.

"Perfect. Just write down the letters you'll need," she said, offering a pen and a small pad of paper. "I'll assemble them and have them wrapped for you in fifteen minutes."

Abs wrote down the letters for the bridal party.

I relaxed. After the day I'd had, finally something had been easy.

With a few minutes to kill, we crossed Fifty-seventh. We were window browsing at Louis Vuitton, not looking to buy, but there it was—a perfect honeymoon ensemble reaching out and talking to me.

"I have *got* to try that on."

Abby glanced over at the mannequin wearing the beautiful soft green and gold outfit I was eyeing.

"Go for it," she urged with a laugh.

The two of us popped into the store, found my size, and raced off to the changing room.

"I'm out here if you need me," Abby called out, shutting the curtain.

I quickly undressed and put on the outfit. It was so soft; it felt like slipping into cream. I checked my look in the mirror. Oh, yeah. I grinned. Colin would love it. Perfect for that little villa in Tuscany we were headed to after the wedding.

I heard a rustling behind me.

"Abs?" I said, not turning around.

There was no answer.

I turned to open the curtain and stepped on something. Glancing down, I found a paper folded in half. I laughed, bending to retrieve it.

"Abs," I called out, shaking my head with a smile.

I looked back at my ass in the mirror. *OK, not bad,* I told myself. I glanced down and unfolded the paper. It was written in large, red-blocked letters.

POLICE TIMELINE MISTAKEN.

HE DID IT.

YOU WANT PROOF?

CALL ME.

A FRIEND

I reread the chilling note several times.

"Madison, what's up?" came Abby's voice. "The gifts are ready. How are we coming?"

She opened the curtain and glanced at me curiously.

I looked at her as if I'd seen a ghost. She came in, taking the note from my hands.

"No," was all she could say.

26

"I am going to fry his ass," Katrina raged as we reached her on speaker-phone outside the store.

"It's him," I said, shaken. "The caller, the man in the yellow taxi. He knew we were here."

I gazed into Abby's eyes, frightened. "Someone's watching me. Us."

Abby held on to me, both of us freaked as we stared down at the red-marked message. We moved around the corner and into an alcove.

"What do I do?" I blurted.

"Shouldn't we call the police?" Abby said worriedly. "I mean I edit books. Madison, you work at an art gallery. Kat, you should know who to talk to."

"Whoever this is seems to know everything we do," Katrina insisted. "I go public and I drag down Colin and Madison, Abby, days before the wedding, which, if possible, we're trying to save here." She paused. "I say we make this guy show his hand. Let's see the proof. Then we'll decide."

"He tells me to call him and he doesn't even leave a damn number," I stammered, angry and frightened.

"Maybe he did," Kat offered, mysteriously.

"What do you mean?"

"A FRIEND," she repeated the word as if puzzling it out. "Check your number pad. A.F.R.I.E.N.D. That's two-three-seven-four-three-six-three. I'd bet 212 area code since he didn't stipulate."

"You serious?" Abby shouted into the phone.

"I don't think she has a choice here," Katrina replied evenly. "We have to find out what he knows or says he knows. It's the only way to clear Colin's name, Madison, and the threat this guy has over both of you."

I glanced nervously at my watch.

"I'm supposed to meet Colin and his father at the hotel in twenty minutes," I snapped, frustrated.

"Phone him, Madison," Kat insisted. "This jerkoff's going to show his hand somewhere, and we're going to bust his ass when he does."

I hesitated, panicking.

"But what if he really *does* have proof?" I found myself asking. "Why hasn't *he* already gone to the police?"

"I don't know," Katrina said. "Something doesn't add up. Look, I'm in a meeting. The attorney general's staff is down from Albany and we're all on a leash. Text me back, no matter what."

I hung up and looked at Abby. The fear I was feeling was right there in her eyes.

And then, with my heart in my ears, I took hold of my cell and phoned A FRIEND.

27

"Hello?" I said, surprised as someone on the other end actually picked up.

"I knew you were clever enough to figure out the number."

"Listen to me . . ."

"Clever girls deserve better than Colin Darcy."

"You son of a . . ."

He went right on, cutting me off.

"You think Colin is innocent because of the time of death on the report. But someone altered the report ever so slightly."

And now I realized that I was talking to a recorded message. And worse, whoever it was seemed to be aware of conversations held only that morning in, of all places, a forensics lab's ladies' room.

"What is he saying?" Abby asked nervously.

"It's a tape," I whispered desperately. "Ssh. I'm trying to get it all . . ."

"Rebecca Farris died, not between six and eight p.m. but *a.m.*" the caller explained in a steady drone. "A simple alteration. You weren't *with* Colin that morning, were you?"

I swallowed hard and forced my brain to try to remember, but I was too busy trying to figure out who would have changed the report and why.

"The proof of Colin's guilt, by the way, is something you will particularly appreciate—a work of art hidden in a queen's painting. Good luck."

The phone went dead.

What was that? A *queen's painting*?!

I quickly told Abby everything I'd heard.

"It's like suddenly living inside the Da Vinci Code," Abby squirmed, shaking her head with disbelief.

How had this caller known what the girls and I had been saying that morning? It made no more sense than the reference to some queen's artwork. The queen reference triggered me and I flashed on Colin's dad, who liked to boast of his distant cousinhood to England's monarch and who was, at that moment, standing in the lobby of the Peninsula Hotel, waiting for me with my fiancé, his son.

I clenched my fists.

Either, as this sicko would have it, Colin was guilty and I was about to marry a cold-blooded murderer, or else this madman was bent on taking my fiancé down and wrecking both our wedding and our dreams.

I grabbed Abby.

"Contact Katrina," I instructed, adrenaline rushing to my head. "Tell her everything. We have to figure this all out. But right now, I've got to go have a family dinner toasting me and a man who may not be who I think he is, with a mom who feels I've finally done something right."

A ball of fear forming in my chest, I hugged her and bolted out of the alcove and down Fifth.

28

The Peninsula was luckily only two blocks away at Fifty-fifth and Fifth, but those were two New York City blocks. With my heart pounding and my brain on overload, I ran to meet my future father-in-law.

My heart stubbornly refused to accept what the caller was saying. There was no proof against Colin. There couldn't be. But the *what if* my head couldn't let go of was chilling. Because if the *what if* became the *then what,* I had my answer.

I could make out the back of Sir Hugh's head from half a block away. He was standing by the car we'd arranged, conversing with the driver. But there was no sign of Colin.

"Ah, at long last, the lady of the hour arrives," he greeted me as I arrived, winded.

Pushing the hair out of my eyes, I gave him a rather clumsy hug as I gasped to catch my breath.

"My goodness, dear," he said, with that ever so brief hiccup of sound that passed for British laughter.

"Sorry to make you wait, I had this thing," I rattled, looking around. "I have no idea where Colin is."

"Oh, he left a message. Said he'd been trying to reach you. Had a very important last-minute interview," he said. "Strictly hush-hush. Told me he'd find a way out to your family's home and that we should go on without him."

I was disappointed and, at the same time, relieved. On the one hand, I was nervous to see him. Colin could always read me like a book, and I knew he'd know right away that something was seriously wrong. At the same time, after today's tea, I wasn't sure I needed any more one-on-one time with another of Colin's parents.

Sir Hugh motioned the driver away and elegantly opened the door for me.

"My dear," he smiled broadly. "Your chariot awaits."

I knew where Colin got his gallantry. I loved those little British flourishes, though I could hardly enjoy them given the day I had had.

The car started up, pulled away from the curb, and joined the snake of city traffic.

"I hope you'll forgive me, Madison," Sir Hugh said, turning to me, pushing a rumpled, silvery thatch of hair off his forehead as he held out his BlackBerry. "I see I have a call to a fellow barrister that must be returned. I'll be but a minute."

"No problem," I replied.

I was relieved to be spared the need to make conversation. As he punched in the number I found myself staring at him and wondering what Colin would be like when he reached that age. Would he have all his hair as his father did? My tummy lurched. Would we be together?

Without wanting to, I recalled the unsolicited advice Hugh's ex-wife had given me that afternoon on how to keep a man. Suddenly, the uncomfortable image of her groping Sir Hugh in a dark opera box flooded my head, and I burst out laughing.

Sir Hugh looked up and over at me.

"Sorry," I said, instantly turning my laughter into coughs. "Just a little tickle in my throat."

He nodded, returning to his call.

How to explain Sir Hugh Aubrey Darcy?

The man appeared to have walked out of an English novel, stiff upper lip and all, and yet was given to flashes of flamboyance like a better-coiffed Donald Trump with an accent. He was British to the bone. Wherever he went he seemed to carry his country with him; wherever he placed his foot, *there* was England.

"The Crown would frown on such extravagant waste," he'd remarked after witnessing the monster-sized sandwiches at the Carnegie Deli. "Good lord, one could feed the colonies for a week with that bit of excess."

Colin had gently reminded his father that, of course, there were no more colonies.

"Yes, well," Sir Hugh had declared, as if it were a source of deep regret, "pity. When we were running the world, we'd have never let this financial business get so out of hand, I can assure you. Preposterous."

And he had a definite opinion on New York taxi drivers after trying to engage a Pakistani immigrant at the wheel on the relative merits of a new novel by Pakistani-born, London-based novelist Nadeem Aslam.

"If the driver cannot discuss the latest literature, the state of politics, or the economic trends of the day, I ask you, of what bloody use is he?"

And yet, for all his preening and pompousness, I had the feeling he was a softie at heart, a pushover for a pretty face and some attention. Neither of which I could offer at that moment.

His call ended, Sir Hugh turned to me.

"Now, my dear, I'm all yours," he announced. "My son tells me things have become rather *exciting* around here. I want to hear every detail."

He gazed at me expectantly.

I gave my best thousand-volt Julia Roberts smile and produced a sound I recognized as the high-pitched squeal of Diana Darcy.

29

Tuesday night, 6:38 p.m.
West Hempstead, Long Island
4 days, 1 hour, 22 minutes to vows

Morty Mandelbaum was in his element.

He loved meals with *extensions,* meaning the importance of the get-together was such that he was required to slide the extra wooden panels into the family dining table to expand to the occasion. He had no doubt reviewed the selections of historical trivia with which he would entertain his special guest, remarks we had no doubt heard a thousand times over but which we would do our best to humor as it gave him so much pleasure. In another life Dad would have been a history professor or that guy who writes the books about 1776 and our founding fathers.

Becoming a CPA had been his mother's, my late Grammie Mandelbaum's, idea. For her, becoming an accountant was like a rite of passage for a Jewish boy, like circumcision and picking up bialys every Sunday morning for the woman who bore you.

Since his mother's death he'd grown even closer to my bubbe who, well into her eighties, made Rachael Ray look like a slacker. By the time I arrived with Sir Hugh it was obvious Bubbe had worked her particular magic in the kitchen. She loved having the assistance of Sally, a beautiful, fifty-nine-year-old woman from Barbados who was the latest in a long line of revolving-door housekeepers employed by my parents. But, other than the rolls and bakery-bought dessert, the cooking was all Bubbe, who'd prepared her chicken liver appetizers and famous brisket, whose recipe was a closely guarded secret along with that of her exact age.

I had long marveled how this supernatural ability with food had somehow managed to bypass Bubbe's daughter. But as my mother liked to tease while serving the one meal she knew how to put together, *scrambled eggs à la Melanie* (scrambled eggs with a lethal dash of Tabasco), "it's like my innate sense of style, Madison, honey," she'd say, glancing at the outfit I would have chosen for that day. "Talent often skips a generation."

"Sir Hugh," my father ventured eagerly, "did you know that in 1775 the people of this area on Long Island actually signed their own declaration of independence, a full year before that of the thirteen colonies?"

"You don't say," Sir Hugh responded with disinterest, turning to Bubbe. "Madame, these canapés are sublime."

My father was clearly disappointed, but Bubbe couldn't be more proud.

"During the Revolution"—Dad tried again—"the patriots of Cow Neck, now Port Washington, actually invaded South Hempstead, which was still occupied by your people and their Tory sympathizers."

"Morty," my mother cautioned.

"Yes, well," my dad added, quickly wrapping up with a nervous smile. "The rest, as they say, is history."

"Quite," Sir Hugh acknowledged in a way that said he didn't like being reminded that his great empire had been at the short end of that stick.

"Can we freshen your drink, Sir Hugh?" my mother asked brightly, her eyes sending another wordless signal to my father that he should take care of that.

"I heard from Pearl and Jack," Bubbe bubbled. "They'll be at the wedding."

"Pearl and Jack?" asked Sir Hugh as he wolfed down another dollop of chopped liver on a cracker.

"Rose's friends from California," Dad explained. "She's eighty-five, he's, what, ninety-three, Rose? *Amazing* dancers. Taught Madison to tango when she was four."

I kept looking around at the door, wondering when Colin would arrive and how I would react when he did. This was supposed to be a celebratory dinner. But after the note in the dressing room, the taped message, and the talk of proof against him, I couldn't feel less like the bride I wanted to be.

I took in my parents, each trying to impress Sir Hugh, who was scarfing down appetizers chased by tumblers of bourbon, which led me to believe he rarely enjoyed home cooking or simply had nothing of his own to say.

Only Bubbe exchanged glances with me, as if she suspected something was off. She could always tell. I did my best to avoid her eyes as I forced a smile and tried a little of her salmon.

"Your son has made quite a splash in this town," my father said, reading the signal from my mother. "You must be a proud man, Sir Hugh."

"Ah, yes, the mayor's financial scandal." Sir Hugh grinned, buttering a roll. "He has a keen nose for dishonor in high places. I suppose we'd have to credit his mother for that." He laughed and refilled his own glass.

"You should have seen the women at Bergdorf's," said my mother as she jumped in. "Couldn't get over the fact that *my* daughter was marrying this dashing investigative reporter. Of course I told them that I'd been certain all along that he was destined for great things."

I'm pretty sure my mouth dropped open.

"Madison deserves the best," my bubbe insisted.

"If I might," my dad said, lifting a glass. "Sir Hugh, I know how proud you are of your son but let me say how very proud Melanie and I are of our daughter. Colin is an impressive young man, but, for my money, he's the one getting the prize."

"Daddy," I said softly, looking at the pride in his beaming face.

"Morty, that was lovely," my mother said, flashing a slightly embarrassed look at Sir Hugh. "Let's just say they are both getting what they deserve."

"Here, here," Sir Hugh declared warmly and, raising his glass, joined everyone in a drink.

Getting what we *deserve*? After the day I'd had, I was beginning to wonder if I had *any* good karma left.

"Sorry I'm late," said Colin as he came through the door. "Today has been one long and crazy ride."

A cheer went up in the room.

I rushed to Colin and clasped my arms around him forcefully, as if by holding on, I could shield us both from the doubts jangling in my head.

"Hey there." He grinned, hugging me back.

"Let me look at you," Sir Hugh said, rising.

The two shook hands and exchanged a quick hug. Sir Hugh turned and lifted his glass to his son.

"To you, Colin. Every inch an Englishman."

My father stepped forward, clearly emotional.

"To Madison and Colin," my father added. "The perfect couple."

"Come sit," ordered Bubbe as she jumped into serving mode, heading for the kitchen to let our housekeeper, Sally, know it was finally time for dinner.

I gazed up at Colin as we walked to the table. The *perfect couple*. It's what everyone had called us since the moment we'd met.

"Damn!"

We all looked over to find Sir Hugh pushing back from the table where he'd just sat down, a full glass of burgundy wine having just found its way into his lap.

"My God!" my mother cried out.

"Just a little, it's all right." Sir Hugh tried downplaying it. "Just my tailored casuals."

"A little salt," Bubbe called out.

My mother rushed over, grabbing the saltshaker and energetically sprinkling its contents onto Sir Hugh's pants.

Colin found a napkin and held it out to his father as Bubbe made her way around the table to see how she might help.

"I'm terribly sorry, Sir Hugh," my father apologized amid the three-ring circus of my parents and Bubbe hovering over the Englishman.

"Here, for goodness' sake," insisted my mother as she began energetically dabbing her napkin in Sir Hugh's wine-drenched lap.

"There, there, madam," he said with a little laugh. "That's not at all necessary . . ."

"Melanie," my father implored.

"Good heavens!" wailed my mother, her hand moving over his crotch stain.

At the height of this fiasco, the front door blew open. We all looked up as Abby and Katrina burst in just as Sir Hugh, fending off all the attention, fell back and tumbled to the floor.

"Wow," Kat said, checking it out. "You guys know how to party."

Colin and I shot forward and helped his father up as my embarrassed parents issued a multitude of apologies.

"I'm fine, really," the man declared, holding his arms at the ready to keep off any further assistance as he turned to my friends.

"To what do we owe the honor of your spirited appearance?" he inquired.

"We're surprising our best friend," Katrina explained, pulling on me.

"Ladies?" my father called out. "If you didn't notice, we're having a really important family dinner here."

Kat and Abby blinked at the wreck our dining room had become.

"Looks like a lot of fun," Kat said with a shake of her head. "But our girl gets married only once."

"You hope," Sir Hugh quipped.

"You want to tempt the evil eye? Pu, pu," my bubbe admonished, spitting on two fingers.

"We don't believe in that. The evil eye?" my mother rushed in, turning to Sir Hugh to clear the matter up. *"Old* Jewish superstitions," she offered with an embarrassed shrug. "Not anything we have anything to do with."

"I see," Sir Hugh replied, no doubt confused that it mattered that much.

"Colin, we love you," Abby called out.

"Have you completely lost it?" I hissed, turning to Abby as she forced me toward the door. "What are you doing?"

"You need to come with us. Just do it, Madison," she insisted.

I turned back and shrugged sheepishly at a stunned Colin and the rest of the family.

"A bride must listen to her maids of honor! Sorry to miss dessert," I yelled out, apologizing.

"Maddie?" Colin called out.

"Madison!" my mother roared.

"What is it?" I demanded as Abby and Katrina dragged me out to Kat's secondhand BMW convertible.

"The proof the caller told you about, the one in the queen's painting?"

"Yeah?" I stammered.

"We're pretty sure we know where it is."

And as Colin ran after us down the driveway, calling after me, his face flushed and unsettled, Kat slammed on the gas pedal and took us roaring into the Long Island night.

"You're taking me to Queens?!" I yelled above the wind.

"The 'queen's painting,' " Abby explained, calling back. "Rebecca Farris wanted to become a professional artist. She lived there. It's the only thing that makes sense."

"We're going to a dead woman's apartment?" I stammered, horrified.

"There's not a dead woman living there now," Katrina commented, in a tone meant to put me at ease.

"Oh, spectacular," I spat. "You think whoever is living there now is going to just let us in to look for some painting we only *suspect* exists and have some wild guess it might be in there?"

"Not necessarily," Kat acknowledged as we hurtled through traffic. "We're definitely going to need some luck."

I didn't respond to that ridiculous statement. *Luck* and I parted company with that first anonymous e-mail to the gallery. And all I could think of right then wasn't the painting or the proof the caller claimed it contained or the total mess I'd left behind at my home—it was the look of shock and hurt on Colin's face as we'd driven away.

That look haunted me now as we sped down the road, a desperate bride and two reckless maids of honor, racing the clock on one outrageous quest.

Katrina eased the car down the street in the Lindenwood section of Howard Beach filled with small, modest-looking apartment buildings. Pulling to the curb, she came to a stop in front of a two-story building where, according to the address in the police report, Rebecca Farris had lived and died. We gazed up at the white, slightly chipped and weathered exterior of the apartment building.

"You sure this is it?" Abby asked.

"Yup," Kat replied, shutting the car off.

My heart was beating in my ears as Katrina put the top up and we all got out and stood on the uneven sidewalk, waiting for someone to make the next move.

"John Gotti used to live around here," Katrina noted.

"Good to know," I nodded, unsteadily.

"Apartment 2A," Abby said, checking the Post-it on which she'd scribbled the address.

"We're not dealing with a brain, this caller of yours," Katrina stated as we headed for the stairs on the left side of the building. "I'm thinking he wants to make it easy. And I can't figure out why."

A minute later, we'd climbed the railed stairway to the second floor. We came to 2A and stopped, looking at one another nervously.

"OK," Kat announced. "If I think we can get away with it, I'll flash my ADA badge and we'll have a look around."

"And if it doesn't look like we can get away with it?" Abby worried aloud.

"We'll immediately go to Plan B."

She lifted her hand to knock on the door.

"What is Plan B?" I asked, barely taking a breath.

"I haven't figured that out, but it'll come to me."

She knocked on the brown door with three frosted windows at its center.

I'd have been willing to bet money that if the beating of our collective hearts could have been hooked up to a sound system, the decibel level would have blown Queens into Brooklyn.

"Who is it?" came a rather strong female voice.

"ADA Fitzsimmons. Ma'am, could we speak to you a moment, please?"

"Who?"

"Ma'am, if you could just open the door. This is official business."

There was the sound of a chain being slipped and a deadbolt sliding. The door swung open. Standing there with an expression that said, *You better have a damn good reason for bothering me at this hour,* was a sturdy African American woman, a baby in her arms, and an even larger male figure behind her, his police officer's shirt unbuttoned to his T-shirt.

"*What* official business?" the woman demanded with a scowl.

Abby and I turned to Katrina, who looked panic-stricken. And that's how we knew we were headed for . . .

"*Plan B,*" Katrina said with a broad smile. "It's a recovery company for families of individuals who have passed on. It's our belief that the last tenant here was an aspiring artist and may have left behind a precious painting that her mother has contracted with us to locate."

"You're talking about that suicide girl . . ."

"Harold," objected the woman. "Not in front of the baby."

"We really hate showing up this late at night . . ."

"Damn right, it's late," the big man complained. "Roll call's at five a.m."

"And we don't want to interfere with your duty or your private time,"

Abby added. "But this information has just come to the young woman's family and they are desperate to have something she might have created before"—she stared at the baby in the mother's arms—"she was gone."

The man scratched his head while his wife continued to study each of us.

"There some kind of reward for this item?" he asked.

"What's the matter with you, Harold?" his wife said, glaring around at him. "We're talking about a dead woman's family."

"Thank you, ma'am," Abby said, warming to her role. "The mother is not well. They live in Chicago. She was hoping to see her daughter's last painting before the dementia kicked in completely."

"Oh, my," the woman said as both Kat and I glanced over at Abby, startled and impressed.

"My husband's people come from Chicago," the woman said.

And to our utter disbelief, she pushed her husband aside and, cradling her baby, gestured to the three of us.

We were in.

32

We stood inside the door, looking at the modest yellow living room with its overstuffed sofa and matching chairs fit for sumo wrestlers. I had no idea where we would begin.

"How do you people go about this?" the woman asked, glancing at us curiously.

I realized this must look suspicious. We were carrying no equipment, not even a clipboard.

"Well, first"—Katrina jumped in—"there's the obvious, but we have to ask. Were you the first to move in here after . . . ?"

"Yes," the woman interjected. "They offered a reduction in the rent because of the unfortunate incident," she reported, turning to eye her husband. "These things get around the station pretty fast and *someone* took it without even checking with his spouse."

"Don't look at me like that, Cheryl. We saved some serious money," Harold asserted, defending himself.

"And that's important, given the economy." I dove in for the first time. "Our question is, did you find a painting of any kind when you moved in?"

"No," Harold answered. "And my guess would be that the blue team would have removed any of that anyway."

"As we thought," Katrina replied, nodding. "Then, it's probably somewhere they wouldn't have thought to look."

"You mean, hidden?" Cheryl asked, giving the baby a pacifier as the little girl rode her mother's hip.

"Exactly. Could we just have a quick look around?" Abby asked sweetly. "We'll try not to touch anything."

"Well," the woman said, fidgeting. "I didn't expect guests, the place is a complete mess and all."

"Not to worry," Katrina responded.

"OK, well," the cop said as he stepped back. "Go ahead. There's this room, a kitchen, and two bedrooms down the hall. Let's get a move on 'cause *Ace of Cakes* is coming on. We never miss it."

"We toy with the idea of opening a bakery someday," Cheryl offered, shooting a smile now at her husband.

"And we're going to, baby, don't you worry," he insisted, giving her a peck on the cheek.

"All right, then." Kat jumped in, wanting to move on before things progressed any further and we were hurried out the door. "Abby, why don't you look here and in the kitchen. Madison, you and I'll each take a bedroom," she instructed. "Folks, we'll be quick and let you get back to your evening."

"Yeah, I'd appreciate that. Cops have a hard day, not like those fruit loops who prosecute what we hand them."

Abby and I held our breath and eyed Katrina. She was biting her bottom lip in that scary, serious way that meant she might blow. Thankfully, she squeezed back and forced a smile.

"OK, then," she declared. "Let's see if we can grant a mother's wish."

Abby immediately went into the kitchen as Katrina and I headed into the bedrooms.

I scanned the space, filled with a queen bed, clothing, and some stacked plastic containers. Entering the large built-in closet, I got down on my stomach, running my fingers along the carpet like I'd seen in the movies.

The truth was, I hadn't the slightest idea what it was I was looking for.

A painting that the caller had insisted was proof of Colin's guilt. The idea horrified me. It couldn't possibly exist. But on the outside chance that it did, then I had to find it.

I continued my search, probing along the base of the closet, beneath and around the shoe rack and assorted boxes. There was nothing. Getting back to my feet, I found a baseball bat standing in the corner of the closet and, lifting it, began poking the ceiling overhead for hidden pockets.

"Anything?" Kat whispered, jolting me by her sudden appearance.

"Nada," I said, lowering my bat. "Katrina, this was probably a setup," I told her, keeping my voice low. "Someone's making me jump through hoops, and you know what, I don't need this and neither do you."

I marched past her, and she reached out to stop me.

"But you know you're not sure of him anymore, Maddie."

"How can you say that?" I protested.

"Because, babe," she said. "You're *here.*"

33

According to forensics, Colin had been in this apartment, maybe in this very room. I looked over at the bed. Had he slept with her? Were they lovers? I felt dizzy.

"Guys, in here," Abby called out.

We hurried down the hall to the one room we hadn't checked yet. I paused at the door. This was the bathroom. Rebecca Farris had died here. Taking a breath, I stepped in after Katrina. The bathtub was on my left. I flashed on the photo I'd seen of her lifeless hand hanging over the lip of the tub. It felt as if we were trespassing on a dead girl's space.

"Up here."

Abby's hushed voice cut through my reservations as I looked over to see her teetering on the edge of the toilet. Out of the corner of my eye I could make out the couple whose apartment we'd entered under false pretenses standing curiously at the door. As Katrina stepped forward to steady her, Abs reached up and pushed against the wallpapered panel above the modest water heater wedged into the corner. Astonishingly, a little door popped open.

"What the . . . ?" The man's surprised voice spoke from the doorway.

I held my breath as Abby poked her hand inside the hidden storage. Carefully she withdrew a long, thin rectangular case and gave it to Kat. Katrina handed it back. I opened it, discovering several tubes of paint and a variety of artist's brushes. I passed them back to the man.

"There's something else in here," Abby reported breathlessly.

And reaching as far as she could stretch, she grabbed hold of whatever it was, inching it forward until she had freed it. Awkwardly, she drew a large flat object wrapped in a pillowcase out of the opening, handing it down to Katrina and climbing back down.

"Is that it? You found it?" asked the excited woman behind us as the baby began to cry.

"Give us a moment, ma'am. Sorry," Katrina said, reaching back and closing the door. "We'll be right out."

I held my breath as Abby removed the pillowcase and let out a small gasp.

It was a painting of a man, naked to his waist. Young, handsome, confident, vibrant.

It was Colin.

I reached out to the counter to steady myself.

"There's something on the back," Katrina said, turning it over so Abby and I could see. There was a typed note taped to the back of the canvas.

"If you find this," it read, *"then I'm no longer here. He's the reason why."*

My heart lurched as I stared up at the stunned faces of my friends. And then everything went black.

34

After reviving me with cold water and some *overly* ambitious Kat slaps, we stumbled out with the items we'd found, thanked the startled couple profusely, and made our getaway. We raced back to Abby's place in Chelsea and there spent the night listening to Katrina's debating courses of action, Abby's attempts to soothe me, and the sound of my tears.

Somewhere in there I had Kat check the voice mail I didn't want to face. There was a concerned call from my dad letting me know Colin and his father seemed somewhat rattled but that he had done his best to smooth things over and assuring me they'd all be on time at the Conservatory Garden the next morning.

I'd forgotten about *the dedication.* Sir Hugh Darcy had arranged for a private donation to the Conservancy of Central Park in honor of Colin's and my wedding. It was to take the form of a sculpture to be placed appropriately for him in the English garden at the Conservatory and would bear the famous sonnet by Elizabeth Barret Browning—"How Do I Love Thee." I remembered being overwhelmed when I'd first heard the idea. How many brides and grooms got a sculpture in Central Park? But right then, with all I'd been through, the thought of it made me nauseated.

Kat listened to the next message and spared me the lengthy lecture left by my mother. Then there were several from Colin, who expressed confusion at my having run out on our special night with his father and in the middle of what was the greatest day of his career to date. It meant everything to share it with me. In spite of it all, Katrina repeated as she listened, he wanted me to know he loved me.

His message made my heart feel like it was getting sucked down a sewer. I was afraid to see him, to talk to him, and yet, it was all I could think of.

"Maybe they had a fight, and it was an accident. He was too afraid to tell the police," Abby suggested.

"Wow. Listen to you," I said, drained of tears. "Making excuses for him." I shook my head slowly. "I don't think I can anymore."

"Then you need to go to him. Tell him that. Present him with the evidence, Madison. Make him confess the truth."

"And then what, Dr. Phil?" Katrina spat. "Turn him over to the people I work for? Have the bride send her groom to jail?"

"What do you think she should do?" Abby stammered.

"I'm the last one you want to ask," Kat shot back. "I want to string him up by his balls."

Abby considered it.

"Yeah, I could see that."

I was still stuck on Colin's message. How he wanted to share everything, including his career. That it mattered. Reminding me that he loved me. His words cut deep, but for a lifelong romantic they died hard.

"I need to see his face," I announced.

"You aren't saying you're actually going through with the dedication, are you?" Kat asked incredulously.

"Have to," I said, getting up and turning to them as the plan formed in my head.

"Rebecca Farris was killed by electrocution. It was an incredibly painful and ugly way to die. If Colin had something to do with it, then I have to know. And it can't be just all about *knowing* in my head. I've got to *know* in my heart. You know?"

They glanced at each other.

"Yeah," Abby responded hesitantly. "I guess . . ."

"Bad idea," Kat fired back. "You're a *love whore,* Madison. You can't resist. You'll definitely fold. You could barely say *no* to zit-face Joey Kagen in the ninth grade!"

"I won't fold. After the dedication ceremony, I'll confront him with the painting and the note. And then, I'll really know."

I looked at Abby on the sofa wringing her hands, Kat pacing behind.

"Can you do this with me?"

Abby turned back to Katrina, who had stopped and appeared as if she might just explode.

"This is a freaking bad idea," she said, shaking her head.

"How about this?" I said, my eyes lasered in on hers. "You see me fold, you have my permission to haul out the painting and confront him for both of us."

That got her attention.

"Well, all right." She nodded approvingly, considering that option. "Kick some ass. I like that."

"Then what?" Abby jumped in.

"What do you mean?" I asked her.

"You know, after you've confronted Colin with the painting or Katrina here has strung him up by his balls, what then?"

I stared at her. I realized I had no idea.

If he didn't have an explanation, if he couldn't make me believe him, I was lost.

I shrugged and gazed at her with a sad smile.

"I don't know. Where do you go to bury your dreams?"

35

Wednesday morning, 10:00 a.m.
Central Park, Conservatory Garden
3 days, 10 hours to the wedding

The headache that had started in the base of my brain the night before had grown exponentially by the time our cab pulled up to the Vanderbilt Gate the next morning.

The three of us hadn't really said much since leaving Abby's apartment. What was there to say? I was going over it and over it in my mind as the painting rested on my lap. After the dedication and photos, I would show him it. What would he do? Would he offer up excuses? Would he break down and confess a horrible crime? Or might he have an explanation that by some New York miracle could allow me to believe in him as I always had, right up until the calls, the diary, the handprints, and now, most of all, the note and painting?

How could our love have been an illusion? I knew what I'd felt. Was my heart a liar, too? Or did it just want to believe so badly that someone who'd seemed so perfect could actually and honestly love *me*?

We walked through the gate at 105th and Fifth.

Months ago when I'd met my dad for a daddy-daughter lunch at the appropriately named Marche Madison, a private little celebration after Colin and I had become engaged, we'd walked over and he'd gone on about this gate. It had originally stood in front of the chateau of Cornelius Vanderbilt at Fifty-eighth Street and Fifth Avenue. The mansion had shared a plaza there with the actual Plaza Hotel. Today, on the site of that mansion stood my mother's workplace and glory—Bergdorf Goodman.

Katrina, Abby, and I paused at the steps to the central section of the Conservatory Garden, looking out at the symmetrical lawn with its single fountain jet at the rear.

"I just need a moment," I said.

"Madison," Kat said softly, clinging to the cloth-covered painting with her right hand. "We don't have to . . ."

"I'm fine. Fine," I said, trying to convince myself. *Come on, Madison Mandelbaum,* I told myself, shaking my arms and trying to get rid of the butterflies having their way with my stomach. I closed my eyes and took a breath. Opening them, I nodded my head.

"Let's do it."

We walked down past the tiny crabapple trees, the rich lawn of the Italian garden before us. To the right was the French garden arranged in concentric circles around bronze figures called the *Three Dancing Maidens.* Katrina, Abby, and I paused to gaze at it. I was sure we were all thinking the same thing. The three of us used to come here whenever we visited the park as young girls. We decided back then that these three figures were us and we named them accordingly. We danced wildly around the circle back then, making a promise to always remain *best friends.* And there was one more vow we made—to dance at one another's weddings.

We moved on. To the left was the English garden composed of wide concentric bands of shrubs, magnolias, and lilacs punctuated by a water-lily pool and a sculpture based on *The Secret Garden. Yes, there were secrets,* I whispered to myself. But not for long.

"Madison!"

I looked up and found my mother marching toward me, her voice reverberating through the garden.

"Thank God you're here," she said. "After last night's little fiasco, I didn't know if perhaps you three had made other plans?"

"Melanie, you look fantastic!" cried Abby.

She knew my mother. You used flattery on her as an attitude adjustment.

"Really?" said my mother, melting slightly. "It works, I think."

"Blue Eyes."

My father made his way over to us.

"Quite a day, huh?" he murmured in awe, gazing at me.

"Careful, Morty," my mother commented as he started to tear up. My dad hugged me.

"Have you seen Colin?" I asked, my voice faltering.

"He was the first one here," my mother asserted, her tone a swipe at our ever so slight tardiness with an unfamiliar note of pride I found jarring.

Suddenly she was *his* champion, an unbelievable turn of events that might have only been more shocking had she actually become mine.

As we entered the English garden, Diana Darcy wrapped me in a ferocious hug.

"The woman thinks she's the center of attention," my mother cracked in a whisper just behind me. "Look at that extravagant getup." She sprang to life. "Diana, darling," she called out, moving around me. "You look truly divine."

I pulled back and saw Diana for the first time. She was dressed in a jumpsuit of shimmering gold, her hair done up in a jeweled tiara like a Russian empress.

"Thank you, Melanie. And you," she said through her teeth.

Before my mother could say something he'd be sorry for, my father stepped in.

"Hello, Diana. Exciting day. I hear the *Times* will be taking a photo."

"Madison, my dear," said Sir Hugh, coming over. "Come Saturday, you are going to be the most beautiful bride anyone has ever laid eyes on."

"I seem to remember you saying that to me once, Hugh," Diana taunted through her smile.

"Yes," he replied, eyes glimmering mischievously as his gaze remained on me. "But this time I *mean* it."

An official moved purposefully toward us.

"I believe we're all here. May we proceed to the dedication, Sir Hugh? Just over here," she said, ushering everyone over to a corner of the garden.

I spied Colin by the water fountain and froze. He was looking at me in his signature way that I adored. He did this little gesture of placing a hand over his heart that got to me. Seeing him do it now, despite my misgivings and everything I was prepared to say to him that morning, I couldn't help it—my heart leaped. And no matter how strongly my head commanded it otherwise, the fragile but resilient little organ inside my chest wasn't listening.

"Easy, girl," Katrina breathed in my ear.

"*Look* at him," I softly pleaded, staring at his stunningly handsome face and the open vulnerability in the way he was gazing back at me.

And then, like two magnets, we began moving toward each other.

"Maddie, we're here," Abs called out.

I waved but never turned back.

We stopped in front of each other, and Colin seemed to devour me with his eyes. He took my hand and placed it on his heart.

"Madison, you are so beautiful."

Something way down deep inside of me gasped.

Not because he hadn't spoken those words before. He had, and like an addict my soul responded as it always had—*gimmegimmegimme*. But at this moment, with his character and our love dangerously in the balance, I believed him.

He leaned in and kissed me.

Oh, boy, my brain uttered. *Good luck with all that* and immediately abandoned me to my emotions.

I turned and saw my girlfriends gazing back at me, Kat chewing on her lip, Abs holding her breath, eyes narrowed with worry.

"Can we have the young couple over here for the dedication, please?" cried the woman from the Conservancy.

Colin placed his hand on the small of my back. I closed my eyes and felt myself weakening. And then we were walking together toward the bronze sculpture that Sir Hugh had commissioned.

Delicate, young lovers held hands, their faces shining with expectation. Below their perch was a tablet; on it Browning's poem was etched for all to read. The ceremony began with a few opening words from Sir Hugh, after which the official thanked him for his gift that would be enjoyed by all who came searching for beauty and to celebrate love.

And then, Colin stepped forward. He turned to me and, in that British-inflected voice, read aloud the immortal words of the poem.

> How do I love thee? Let me count the ways.
> I love thee to the depth and breadth and height
> My soul can reach, when feeling out of sight
> For the ends of Being and ideal Grace.
> I love thee to the level of every day's
> Most quiet need, by sun and candle-light
> I love thee freely, as men strive for Right.
> I love thee purely, as they turn from Praise.
> I love thee with the passion put to use
> In my old griefs, and with my childhood's faith.
> I love thee with a love I seemed to lose
> With my lost saints. I love thee with the breath,
> Smiles, tears, of all my life!—and, if God choose,
> I shall but love thee better after death.

I looked over at my best friends. Katrina was staring back at me, the covered painting at her side.

I gazed at Abby. She seemed suspended, unable to move, as if she couldn't bear to cross the space from this moment to the next. I knew the feeling.

I looked back at Colin, the passionate words of the poem still reverberating between us, but also the excruciating doubt.

"I'll say *what* I want, *where* I want. It's my business!"

I whipped around. There, by the fountain, facing off like two bitches in heat—my mother and Diana.

"When you bring it into the middle of my daughter's wedding, then you make it my business too!" my mom fired back.

"Just take care of your husband," Diana snarked.

"See, that's it exactly," Sir Hugh declared, crossing to his ex. "You think the whole world's your business."

"This isn't a courtroom, Hugh. And I'm not your wife anymore, so, as we say on this side of the pond—*butt out,*" Diana spat.

"Gladly, *lovey,*" Sir Hugh declared, red-faced. "But the rest of us would be ever so grateful if you'd refrain from sharing the largesse of your stupifyingly inappropriate behavior."

"Mom. Dad, could we talk over here?" Colin asked.

"Inappropriate, *me?!*" sniped Diana. "Her husband has been eyeing me since I arrived and *I'm* inappropriate?!"

"What?" My father sputtered with surprise. "I most certainly . . ."

"Of course he's been staring," Sir Hugh noted with a sly grin. "You've had your breasts raised to your chin and everything else with it. Right, Morty?"

"I have *not* been staring!" my father snapped, his face beet red.

"Morty, your blood pressure," insisted my mother, obviously delighted at the dissing Diana was getting from her ex.

"Hugh Darcy. You will pay for this!" shouted a mortified Diana.

"I believe I already have," Sir Hugh parried.

I couldn't believe the scene. The world was falling apart in one preposterous catfight. And like that, something clicked inside of me. It was now or never. I marched over to Kat, grabbed hold of the painting, and taking Colin's arm, I led him over to the fountain where no one else could hear us.

"We have to stop them before they kill each other," he insisted.

"Let them," I said.

"What?"

"Colin, I'm scared to say what I have to say, so I'm just going to say it. You lied to me."

"What?"

"Rebecca Farris."

His smile disappeared.

"The police have your handprints from her bathroom. The forensics lab confirmed it."

He was astounded.

"Forensics? Madison, what are you talking about?"

I removed the cloth from the painting and held it up.

"This is what I'm talking about."

Colin stared at it as if he'd just been slammed in the solar plexus.

"There's a note on the back of this painting . . ."

"Madison . . ."

"Here, read it," I said, turning the canvas over. *"If you find this then I'm no longer here, and he's the reason why."*

Colin's mouth fell open as my heart died inside of me. I watched as he stared in horror at the words on the paper. My God, it was true, my brain blared. He *was* guilty. Look at him.

"Madison, listen to me. Where did you find this?" he suddenly demanded.

"In your girlfriend's apartment," I said bitterly.

"She wasn't . . ."

"How did it happen, Colin?" I demanded. "Wasn't I good enough?"

"You? Madison, this isn't what you think it is."

"I thought I knew you. Everything about you seemed so real," I said, backing up, my voice breaking.

"Madison," Colin pleaded. "You have no idea what you've uncovered here."

"I have a pretty good idea," I countered.

"No, you don't," he insisted, eyes flashing. "This message isn't *about* me, Madison. It was meant *for* me. You have to believe that."

I gazed up at him.

"I don't know what to believe, Colin," I said, drained of emotion. "I just know I can't go where my heart won't."

And then, taking back the painting, I turned and walked away.

"Madison!" he shouted, but I didn't turn back.

When I'd reached Abby and Katrina, I paused and gazed deep into their eyes, sad but determined. It seemed everyone was shouting my name.

Without a word, the three of us linked arms and strode from the Conservatory Garden, up the stairs, and out of the park.

36

I asked the cab to drop me at my apartment back down in the Village. Along the way I filled the girls in on Colin's guilt-ridden response and his desperate attempt to explain that the words of the note meant something I didn't understand.

"It's like this assault and battery perp," Katrina cracked. "Eyewitnesses saw him go into the bodega, beat a worker unconscious, and rifle the cash. Perp comes back swearing he's a Good Samaritan who was only defending himself and had taken the money for safekeeping until the worker came to."

"Unbelievable," Abby exclaimed.

"Yeah," Kat nodded. "And the craziest thing? Man passed a lie detector."

Abby and I stared at her.

"People can make themselves believe anything," she said.

I felt like I couldn't get air. As we headed down Ninth my breathing grew shallow, like someone was sitting on my chest. I shouted out for the cabdriver to pull over.

"What is it? What are you doing?" Abby asked with alarm as we skidded to the curb.

I climbed over her, threw open the door, and tumbled into the street.

"Jesus, Madison," Katrina cried, jumping out the other side as Abby bolted out after me.

"No, no," I called out, hands gesturing them back, feeling the blood rushing to my head.

"I can't breathe . . ."

"Maddie . . ."

"I can't breathe . . ."

"Let us help you," Abby cried out.

And there on the corner of Forty-third and Ninth, my fairy tale shattered, I let loose with a scream that would stop traffic—and did. Cars screeched to a halt.

"Hey, lady, you all right?" called one driver as pedestrians walked on by, giving me odd looks and shaking their heads.

Abby and Katrina led me back into the taxi, and we rode the rest of the way in silence.

Over on Jane Street just off Washington, I said good-bye to the girls.

"Let me come up," Kat insisted, poking her head out the back window. "I'll be quiet, promise."

"Katrina," I said with a quick smile. "That would be impossible." I looked off up the street then back at them. "You guys are the best. I'd never have gotten through this without you. But I need some alone time. OK?"

"Call me?" Abby begged, not wanting to let go.

I nodded and waved as the cab pulled away.

Turning back, I took a deep sad and sobering breath and headed up to my apartment, alone.

37

According to Bubbe, a *kochleffl* was someone who stirred the pot, an agitator, a troublemaker. The freak who'd called and e-mailed about Colin had played that part royally. But as I slipped the key into my apartment door, it caught me off guard to realize that it wasn't raging vengeance I was feeling toward this person.

Would part of me have preferred to walk down the aisle in blissful ignorance? But with the utter heartbreak now enveloping me like a body glove, I was also struck by the question at the heart of all: You could love someone with all your heart, but what was that worth if the person you loved *wasn't* actually the person you had fallen in love with?

It would be like loving a forgery, wouldn't it? You might admire the technique, the uncanny resemblance to the real thing, but once you knew it for what it was, how could you take it into your heart?

I opened the door of my apartment and nearly jumped out of my skin.

My father stood there in the squat living room, his face drawn and creased with concern, waiting.

"Sorry, hon," he said. "I figured you might come here and let myself in. You look terrible. Blue Eyes, what's wrong?"

"I just have to go to the bathroom," I said, pushing past him and slamming the door. Folding my arms around myself, I broke down and cried.

"Madison?" my dad said from outside the door.

"Be a sec," I said, choking on my tears. I stared at my swollen face in the mirror. Who was that looking back at me?

I turned and pulled my bathrobe from off the hook on the back of the door.

And then, blowing out a breath that seemed filled with dead dreams and cast-off floral arrangements, I went out to face my dad.

38

"Your mother couldn't even speak after you walked out."

"Wow," I said as I slumped grimly onto the sofa. "That's gotta be a first."

My father pulled over a stool from the kitchen and sat down opposite me.

"Colin left without a word. Sir Hugh went on about all that was wrong with America. His ex-wife countered with all that was wrong with him. Your bubbe seemed to be chewing out everyone. It was like a *Simpsons* episode," he observed.

He and I used to watch the show together on the nights my mother was off on one of her Bergdorf buying trips.

"How long have you and Colin been in a fight?" he asked.

I sat silently for a moment, everything racing through my head.

"How well did you know Mom before the two of you were married?" I said finally.

"Oh," he smiled, remembering. "I thought I knew everything there was to know."

"And?"

"I knew bupkes."

"What do you mean?"

"Is that what this is about? How well you know Colin?"

I didn't respond.

"Blue Eyes," he said, shaking his head, "what you know now only skims the surface. You have a lifetime to find out who the other person is. That's part of the fun. And the nightmare."

I looked at him. He wasn't kidding.

"Your mother is a very complicated person."

"But if you'd known her back then, really known her for who she was, who she'd be, I bet you'd have never married her."

My father looked at me, surprised.

"I'll take that bet," he half smiled. "Listen, the only one who maybe has a knowledge of how you're going to turn out is God and he's not talking, at least not to me personally. If he had, maybe I wouldn't have invested so heavily on tech stocks back in the '90s, but that's neither here nor there."

I looked away.

"Madison, I'm not who I was back then, and neither is your mother. We fell in love. We took a chance. We've been married over thirty years. That's not chump change."

"But you've been miserable, Dad," I said, turning on him with a force that seemed to surprise him. "I've seen you."

"I've had tough times, I've had good times. And I'd do it all over again."

"There you go," I quipped bitterly. "That's where I get the fatal dose of romanticism."

"And what's wrong with being a romantic?" he countered. "Yes, I put up with your mother's business trips and whacked-out schedule. The way she has an opinion about everything and everyone. Her lack of talent in the kitchen, her need to feel important, *be* important."

"Why?"

He smiled, shaking his head.

"*Because* of all of that."

"Oh," I said, dismissing him. "So what you're telling me is, you're nuts."

"Definitely. You take a chance on love in this cuckoo world; you got to be at least half certifiable. What's the alternative?"

"You don't make the mistake in the first place," I stammered.

"Mistake?" my dad said, staring back at me. "You think my life with your mother has been a mistake?"

"I think maybe you could have done better, yes," I shot back.

"You judge your mother but there are things you don't know."

"I know enough to see how she treated you, and us."

"Your mother has suffered, OK? Let's give her a break."

I smarted.

"Melanie Mandelbaum suffer? What, they were out of the perfect black shoe at Bergdorf's and she had to settle for beige?"

"Is that all you think of her? That all that matters is the superficial and surface?" My father let out a long sigh. "When your mother was seven, some kids were playing in the kitchen and a vat of boiling oil tipped over. She was in the hospital for a month recovering from the burns."

What? My mother had always said the discoloration on her chest was from a skin condition.

"Kids can be cruel. They teased your mother from then on. As a teen, she had to deal with the looks she got from the other girls when they would change at school. She had to listen to boys getting dared to go out with the freak."

"I didn't . . ."

"She wants to be pretty, the center of things, take back what was taken from her. Why shouldn't she?"

"Why did she never tell me about this?"

"It's still painful for her to talk about. And you? From the moment you were born, you have always been so beautiful and absolutely perfect. I couldn't stop looking into your amazing blue eyes. Not sure where they came from 'cause no one else in the family had eyes like yours." He laughed. "To me, you were a miracle. And your mom wanted fiercely to protect you. She went out of her way to warn you against anything that would make you feel as bad as she once had."

His face displayed the toll that had been taken.

"But it came from a place of love."

I didn't say a word; my head was on overload.

"It was your mom who put food on the table when I had my heart attack back when you were ten, did you know that?" His face flushed, recalling it. "For all her noise, she's always made sure I'm on my meds, getting exercise. Nagged the hell out of me to be sure I'd be around to see . . ." He stopped, his voice catching.

"Dad?"

"Your wedding."

I got up and went to him, hugging him from behind like I did when I was a little kid and would ride on his shoulders.

"Dad, with Colin and me? There's just some complications right now . . ."

My father nodded and we remained like that, my arms around him, my tears falling at the sadness of it all.

It felt comforting, his being here in the middle of my nightmare. I remembered the time he'd been summoned to school after I had stolen the answers to a test in the fifth grade, which I'd done because, one, they were lying there on the desk completely begging to be taken and, two, I was tired of always getting a lower grade than Tiffany Galloway, who was impossibly brighter and blonder than anyone had a right to be. He'd been embarrassed, I'm sure. Humiliated, angry, disappointed, wigged out, but he loved me and he stayed with me during the inquisition conducted by my commando-inspired principal who thought making kids sweat was a sacred duty. My dad was still there an hour later when I'd had to stand up in front of the class scarlet-faced and publicly admit what I had done.

And now, when he spoke, he said the same words he'd shared with me then when I'd asked him why he'd stayed at the school with me.

"You don't run when things get uncomfortable or hard, Maddie. That's what it means to love somebody."

I hugged him tighter. Could Colin ever be there for me like this?

"You know my only regret about your getting married?" he said softly. "You won't be a Mandelbaum."

"Of course I will," I insisted.

"Well, yes, naturally, you'll always be because you're my daughter, it's just, I know you've decided to take the Darcy name and I don't blame you . . ."

"Dad?"

"No, it's silly, I know," he acknowledged. "Your grandparents only had one son. My sisters couldn't wait to drop the name. So I'm the last of the *Mandelbaums.*" He shrugged sheepishly. "Male ego. It's a terrible thing."

He smiled sadly. "Hey, someone has to be. No big deal. Now," he said, straightening up. "Madison *Darcy,*" he uttered as if putting it up on the screen for consideration. "A little too Jewish maybe, but it'll do," he teased, and gave me a hug.

And then, arms around me, my father began to laugh.

"What?" I said, as we pulled apart.

"I don't know why but I just got a memory flash. You were five or six, maybe."

"Yeah?"

"Your mother and I, we'd come in to peek on you."

"OK."

His shoulders began to do a funny quake at the memory.

"You are sound asleep when all of a sudden out of your tiny body comes this gigantuan fart."

"What?!"

"Woke yourself up and you began to bawl something wicked."

"Get out," I blurted, giggling slightly, mortified.

"Biggest damn thing I ever heard. Your mother and I were on the floor. I swear, we didn't stop laughing for weeks."

Suddenly he unleashed this great tumble of laughter, tears coming to his eyes, and despite the giant sadness filling me, I felt a dam breaking. It was contagious. I couldn't help myself and, just as we had when I was little, the two of us dissolved into fits of uncontrollable hysteria. It was a big, uncontrollable, cleansing kind of laughter and for that one moment, I was trouble-free.

And when the laughter had begun to subside, as reality slowly crept back in, my dad wiped away his laugh tears and turned to me.

"He's a good man, Madison. He'll stick."

Immediately, the pain reignited in my heart.

I gazed into his eyes. They were pleading with me to fix it, to smooth things over, to bring back the smile he always searched for in my face.

I wanted to tell him that, just like when he'd married my mom, he really didn't know bupkes. But what I said was, "I just need some rest."

"Yes," he agreed, getting up to leave. "You get some rest. Maybe a hot bath. You'll be yourself again."

He came over, pinched my cheek as he had when I was little, looking me deep in the eyes.

"Whatever's going on with you and Colin, it's nothing the love you have for each other can't fix. I'd put money on it."

I did my best to force a smile.

"I can't wait to escort you down that aisle," he said. "But, Blue Eyes, you will always be my little girl. You'll do what you need to do."

He kissed me on the forehead and brightened visibly.

When we got to the elevator, he was in a better mood. As we waited, he turned and gazed out the window onto Jane Street. I knew what he was thinking. The exact same sentiment he had every time he visited me in this apartment he'd helped subsidize in the West Village.

"Can you believe that Aaron Burr lived in this neighborhood when he dueled Alexander Hamilton?"

(The fact that Jackson Pollock and Robert Rauschenberg had also lived on these streets and that Jasper Johns still owned a garage on my corner didn't impress Morty Mandelbaum. No. Dead men and history. And a nice pastrami.)

He stepped into the elevator, blew me a kiss, the doors closed, and I was, once again, alone.

I stood there a moment, his words winding through me.

Whatever it is between you and Colin, it's nothing the love you have for each other can't fix. I'd put money on it.

Like a crude comedian, my head spat—*You'd lose.*

My heart, for once, was silent.

I returned to the apartment to find a message from Colin.

"Madison, who else knows about the painting and the note?" he asked, sounding agitated. "You could be in danger."

Was that a warning or a threat? Whichever, it scared me, pushing me further into my fears.

"Listen," he went on. "After you left, it took a while to calm down my parents, which, as a feat, has to rank up there with Lance Armstrong's seven titles in the Tour de France, and I got this call from City Hall. The mayor wants to do an interview with me, one on one. Tell his side. Blew my mind, Maddie. Seriously. This is huge."

Of course, I knew that.

"I'm supposed to be there in one hour, but I'll stall them if we can talk. Madison, we can clear this up."

It was difficult even hearing his voice.

"Look, I'm on my way over to your place right now. Please be there. We need to talk."

I panicked. Coming here? *Now?*

There was no way I could deal with that. I couldn't trust myself with him. How could I believe anything he said? I needed to get out of there and fast. Throwing on some sweats, I grabbed my purse and hurried out to lose myself in the labyrinth of the Village.

I raced down Washington Street, needing to put some distance between the apartment and me.

Was I actually rushing from the possibility of seeing Colin? I'd become someone else. Not in my wildest, sci-fi dreams would I have ever imagined running away from him. Our love was real, but so was this mad shakedown of circumstances I was in. I glanced back to see if I was being followed, not sure if I was more nervous at finding a man in a raincoat and dark-brimmed hat there or Colin.

At Christopher I headed left. On the other side of Hudson, I turned back and gazed at the late morning array of cars, shoppers, and cabs going about their business as if this were just an ordinary day. But there was nothing ordinary about it. Not when a bride was hiding from her groom, a groom who could be hiding a murder.

I sucked in some air and let go. It felt like I was exhaling the dirty world of clandestine trysts and stolen fingerprints. A shiver went through me. How could everything that was so good only a few days ago turn so unbelievably wrong?

I meandered down Barrow, turning left at Bleecker, heading northwest. The iPod in my head was set to shuffle, and memories played out there in no set order.

I recalled Colin and me getting caught in a sudden rainstorm in Central Park. We'd laughed and let it soak us through, and Colin had turned to me and told me he loved me for the very first time. The pain of the memory made me catch my breath.

I saw my father dancing with me to one of his old Madonna fa-
vorites, "Like a Virgin," telling me he was getting in some practice because someday he'd be dancing at my wedding. A wave of sadness took
hold and my throat tightened.

I flashed on the day my mom and I headed for Bergdorf's; she'd
wanted to show me her new office. As we passed by the park we saw a
bride and groom rush out of the Plaza and hop into a hansom cab and
drive away. I was maybe fourteen and wondered aloud about what my
wedding day would be like. *Perfect,* I remember her saying.

I felt my insides twist into a pretzel at the memory. That had been
such a positive response, especially for her, and I think I'd never recalled
the incident until just then. It had always felt like our default setting was
more *American Gladiators* than *Gilmore Girls.*

My dad's revelations about her now flooded through me. I wondered
how it was possible to live with someone your entire life and not know
her whole story. How had I *missed* it?

And then, like a smash cut in a music video, it slammed into
my head.

It was something Colin had said when I'd confronted him with the
note on the back of the painting.

"This is a message," he'd insisted passionately. "Not *about* me, Madison, but *for* me. You have to believe that!"

And whether it was instinct or the glimmering fragment of a hopeless romantic, the question demanded an answer. Was I missing part of
the story *again*?

A car horn blared. I looked up to see I was face-to-face with a NYC
trash truck, its glaring driver waiting for me to move. I bolted forward.

The question energized me as I picked up my pace and turned left at
Eleventh. What if Colin was right? I mean, wrong to have lied about his
relationship with Rebecca Farris but right that she had sent him a message about someone else's involvement in her death? I needed someone to
help me piece this out. I needed Abby and Katrina. And then, passing an

art gallery between Greenwich and Washington, something in the front window caught my eye.

It was a bold red banner announcing an exhibition by Frank Bender, who was heralded as a *forensic artist,* two words I would never have figured went together. An artist was something I was intimately familiar with. "Forensics" was a science about which I'd been forced that week to learn more than I cared to know. Intrigued, I paused and read the man's bio posted next to his photo in the window. It said that as a painter and sculptor, Bender was an expert in reconstructing victims' identities based on the skeletal and dental record. I cringed. In doing so, he'd given countless victims back their identities, leading to the conviction of dozens of murderers. He had joined together with two others to create a crime-solving club in Philadelphia. The Vidocq Society was made up of current and former FBI profilers, homicide investigators, forensic specialists, and others dedicated to solving cold crimes.

I froze. Nothing could be colder than what was happening to me.

A *crime-solving club*? Could someone there possibly help me?

My heart jumped. I became excited. I reached into my pocket and took out my cell. There were a dozen calls from Colin. I knew he must be looking for me, but my idea wouldn't wait. I phoned Katrina and Abby.

They listened patiently and Katrina said it was really a long shot. But I pushed her. Finnbar actually knew someone down there, she recalled. They'd consulted with him on a John Doe case of hers the previous year.

"But this isn't a cold case, Madison. And I doubt we can get in to see anyone."

"Don't tell me what you *can't* do," I snapped back, adrenaline pumping. "Tell me what you *can do.*"

"Whoa," Abby interjected, sounding impressed.

"Yeah, who's this little kick-ass we're talking to and what have you done with our friend Madison?"

An hour later, I had just emerged from a long shower when Katrina called back.

"We owe Finnbar a keg," she said, incredulous at her own news.

"What happened?"

"Finnbar can't figure it out. These people *never* take a meeting, he says. All I know is, first thing in the morning—we're headed to Philadelphia."

There was something I had to do before going to Philly the next morning.

Googling, I found the website I needed and nervously phoned the number on the screen. A woman answered.

"Yes?"

"I'm looking for a job," I said, trying not to sound as anxious as I was. "I hear you employ women with, um, *special talents.*"

There was a pause.

"You have the wrong number," came the curt reply.

"Please," I shouted into the phone before she could hang up.

"How did you get this number?" the woman inquired impatiently. She'd seen through me.

"Don't call here again."

"Wait," I blurted out.

My mind was racing.

"I'm getting married. I have something I think you can help me with."

"I seriously doubt it," came the amused reply.

"A friend of mine told me to call you if I needed to. Maybe you remember her? Rebecca Farris."

There was a pause. I held my breath.

"Meet me at Bubby's, corner of Hudson and Moore. Twenty minutes," she said. "Come alone or I am out of there."

The phone went dead. I blew out the tension in my chest. It felt like I was entering a world of espionage.

How bad could it be, I tried convincing myself, in a place called *Bubby's?*

The girls and I had been to Bubby's for breakfast years back when John Kennedy Jr. was alive, hoping to catch a glimpse of him at one of his favorite hangouts. I arrived on time and suddenly realized I had no idea who I was looking for as I slipped into the homey surroundings of the restaurant, the smell of freshly brewed coffee and just-out-of-the-oven pies in the air.

It was three in the afternoon and the place wasn't overly crowded. I saw an artsy-looking couple in a tense discussion over at one booth and turned away.

"Table for one?" a waitress asked.

"No, actually I'm . . ."

A dark-haired woman in glasses sat back at a corner table at the far end of the restaurant. She nodded to me.

"I think I've found her, thanks," I said and went over.

"You're from Elite Escorts?" I asked.

"I am," she said, pushing her glasses down. "But I'd appreciate it if you didn't do any advertising for us here."

"Oh, of course," I said, embarrassed. "It's just, I realized, I hadn't given you a name or anything."

"You said you were getting married. I just looked for someone who was lost."

"Oh," I said, not quite sure whether she meant to be insulting or funny, but I sat anyway.

"My name's Madison. Thanks for meeting me."

The waitress came over.

"Menus?" she chirped.

"Just tea for me," I said. "Chai if you have it."

I glanced over at the woman in dark glasses.

"I'm having coffee," she said, "and a piece of your strawberry pie."

The waitress left and I turned to her, surprised.

"They make excellent pie here," she explained softly. "You have five minutes."

I panicked at the time reference and then jumped in.

"I am engaged to Colin Darcy, maybe you've seen him on television, he's a reporter?"

"I don't have time for TV," she replied.

"He met Rebecca Farris."

The woman pursed her lips.

"She went by the name Monet. She wanted to be an artist?"

The woman remained silent.

My heart was pounding.

"Was Colin a client of yours?" I blurted.

"I can't divulge that information."

"I know he saw Farris. I'm sure you remember her; she died."

"Yes," the woman said softly. "Suicide."

"I don't think so."

"What are you talking about?"

"There is evidence, suppressed evidence, that indicates she may have been murdered," I explained.

The woman took off her glasses and stared at me intensely. Her eyes were a deep brown. She was somewhere in her late forties and quite attractive.

The waitress arrived with the pie and hot drinks.

"Can I get you anything else?" she asked.

"No, thanks," I said, my eyes still on the stranger across from me as the waitress retreated.

"We're not sure, but we believe it may have been one of your clients."

"We? Are you a cop?"

"No."

"What would a bride be doing investigating a possible homicide?" she asked skeptically.

I swallowed hard.

"I have a wedding set in three days."

"Where?"

"The Waldorf . . ."

"Ooh. Ritzy."

"My mother insisted."

"I see."

She stuck a fork in the pie.

"You don't know my mother. I'm not sure even I know her," I rattled on, "but, the point is, I am trying to clear my fiancé's name—and if you repeat any of this I'll deny it—but was Colin Darcy a client of yours, yes or no?"

I stared at her, breathless and red-faced, aware of the clock overhead ticking by my minutes.

The woman put down her fork. She studied me.

"Man, you are some kind of freaky bride, running out tracking down your man and who he may or may not have had sex with?"

"This isn't about sex," I stammered, checking the second hand on the clock as it kept moving. "Now I've got like two minutes left and I promise I'll walk out of here, but this is about believing in the man I love. Didn't you ever love a man?"

The woman gazed at me, searching my eyes with a fierceness that scared me. Whatever it was she was searching for I guessed I passed because suddenly she was reaching into her bag and drawing out a laptop.

"To answer your question, yes, I loved a man," she snapped, opening up the computer and typing in something. "Tore my heart out a hundred times before I decided I wasn't going to be his rag doll. I figured after that if men were going to screw you no matter what, I at least wanted to get paid for it. That's how Elite Escorts was born."

"Wow," I nodded, impressed at her ability to focus on a business plan in all of that.

"You said Colin Darcy?"

"Yeah," I replied, holding my breath.

She looked from the screen.

"Client 33," she said quietly.

I stared at her, trying to grasp the information I'd sought but never wanted to hear. He had a name. *Client 33.* Like Eliot Spitzer and countless other men who lied to their loved ones and traded money for fantasy they weren't getting at home.

"If it makes it any easier," she said, "he only contracted to see her once."

I nodded as the knowledge that Colin had definitely used the escort service tore its way through me.

"Do you have a record as to when?"

"According to my records, he only saw her once. Last March. But you should know that unlike the other girls who work for me, Monet had a hard time following the rules."

"The rules?"

"She had a tendency to see clients on her own time. I confronted her about it a few weeks before she died. She told me that these johns really cared about her and that she wanted out of the escort business. I reminded her, like I remind all the girls who work for me, that seeing johns on your own time can only lead to trouble. When she was on the clock, I had her back, but if I didn't know what she was up to, I couldn't protect her. And sadly, I was proved right."

"Thank you," I said, and I got up to leave.

"For what it's worth, I don't think your man hurt her."

"And why is that?" I said quietly.

"The note here in his file. Monet says he was the nicest john she'd ever met."

Was I supposed to feel better? *Meet my fiancé. He has a really great reputation with call girls.*

"I never did think Rebecca could have done it to herself," the woman said. "If I can do anything to help you find out who hurt her, you call me. The name's Eve."

She handed me a card. I gazed at it uncomfortably.

"Sweetheart, men and women are different," she offered. "Most who come to us are perfectly good husbands, fathers. They have needs, desires—nobody gets hurt. It doesn't make them bad men."

I studied her, trying to imagine my own father or my boss, Peter, or any of the other men I knew in my life ever picking up the phone and calling her business. I couldn't. How could the man I loved, someone who could have had any woman he wanted, ever have needed to contact a service like this?

"I thought I knew him," I said, smiling sadly.

"So he has a secret." She shrugged. "Who doesn't at one time or another? And we want the people we love to see us the way we prefer to be seen, so we don't tell. It doesn't mean he's a murderer."

She eyed me closely as I shifted on my feet.

"But I'm guessing you already know that," Eve said. "Now you find the guy who hurt Rebecca, you let me know. I'd like to see to it his johnson is out of commission permanently."

I shook my head, unsure what to think.

"And what if it *was* Colin?" I offered, battling with myself.

"Well then," Eve said, looking me over. "I suspect you'll do Lorena Bobbitt proud."

"Be careful what you wish for," I said, putting money down for the bill.

43

Thursday morning, 7:15 a.m.
Amtrak, en route to Philadelphia
2 days, 12 hours, 45 minutes to the wedding

As our train raced through New Jersey, Katrina reviewed for us what she'd learned about the Vidocq Society.

It was an exclusive crime-solving organization that met monthly on the top floor of Philadelphia's historic Public Ledger Building. The group consisted of retired and practicing professionals along with some skilled private citizens who had special talents and a yen for criminal investigations. The men and women used their collective skills to solve "cold cases" for the common good. They worked pro bono, which blew Katrina's mind, and took their name from Eugène François Vidocq, a brilliant eighteenth-century French crook turned detective whose life had inspired Victor Hugo's Valjean and Inspector Javert in *Les Miserables*, as well as characters by Melville, Poe, and Dickens. He was considered by historians and those in law enforcement to be the father of modern criminal investigation.

"I've never heard of him," said Abby, genuinely surprised at the hole in her knowledge of literary trivia.

"Apparently we're meeting with one of the members who sits on the crime panel that decides what cases to review," Kat told us. "He was kind of mysterious when I spoke to him after Finnbar made contact. Said he usually doesn't do this but was making an exception for 'personal reasons.' "

"He doesn't even know me," I said, confused.

"Yeah," Kat nodded. "But he said, and I quote, 'A bride ought to have her wish granted the week of her wedding.' "

"You're kidding," I said, incredulous.

OK, I told God secretly. *Maybe I'll forgive you my barely B-cup breasts.*

My cell phone rang. Abby lunged for it and checked the caller ID.

"We don't need that freak calling you again," she explained protectively, handing it back over after it had passed inspection.

I clicked on.

"Hi, Mom," I said.

"Madison, where are you? Colin's been calling here practically non-stop. Says you weren't at your apartment and he can't reach you. You're not like that runaway bride they had a couple years ago on TV are you?"

"It's complicated. But I assure you, I'm not running away from anything."

"I had this nightmare that you were calling the wedding off. Is the wedding off?"

"Mom," I said instead, changing the subject, "how come we never talked about what happened to you as a kid? The burns, the teasing?"

She didn't speak, which was something.

"Your father had no right to say anything."

"Why? I want to know about you," I insisted.

"Stop trying to change the subject. I'm down here at the Waldorf alone because no one could reach you. We were supposed to be having an early breakfast and going over last-minute details with Emily, remember?"

Emily Cohen-Wasserstein was the wedding coordinator from hell my mother had insisted on. Which meant she had developed buzz, probably due to bizarre brainstorms that would make normal people question her sanity, such as the *edible yarmulke* concept she floated by us, hailing it as a head covering and appetizer in one.

"Sorry."

"What is going on with you? We haven't even touched base on the rehearsal dinner tomorrow night."

Rehearsal dinner?! I'd completely blocked that out.

"Yeah, about that . . ."

"Madison . . ."

"I have to run now, Mom. Tell Bubbe hi. Love you."

I clicked her off.

Abby was staring at me.

"Being out of the loop has got be killing your mother," she said, stating the obvious.

"Yeah," I said, trying to avoid thinking of her stewing back at the Waldorf. "Sorry to take you away from work, again."

"They think I'm editing this chick-lit novel," she explained with an encouraging smile. "Told them I needed a little space."

"How about you, Kat? The DA giving you a hard time?"

"I got it handled," she said, a little too tightly.

"Whoa." Abby jerked up in her seat. "The bachelorette party? At Buddha Bar? That's tonight."

"Abby . . ."

"We cancel there's going to be a lot of questions," she warned.

Kat's cell went off.

"We're on," Kat insisted as she pulled out her BlackBerry. "You," she said, pointing at me, "you need to get *seriously* drunk."

I gazed out the window at a gorgeous forest of birch trees just off the track. She was probably right.

"Shit."

I jerked around to face Katrina.

"What is it?"

She looked up, her eyes narrowed with concern.

"They're asking what I know about a suppressed file." Her face went ashen. "Someone's tipped them off."

"The caller?" I asked, my heart rate taking off.

"Maybe," she said, shaking her head. "Or that hot-to-ingratiate-herself secretary who'd given it to me. Who knows?"

She looked up at me, her eyes showing fear for the first time.

"I don't know how long I can keep them from getting to Colin," she said, shaken.

"My God," Abby uttered.

My head computed the implications of what might happen if they actually arrested Colin.

A sharp pain shot through me like an icy pick to the spine. Suddenly it wasn't just about saving the wedding or even Colin's career.

We could be talking about Colin's *life*.

44

Philadelphia

As if there wasn't enough that had gone wrong, we exited the train station only to discover the city was in the midst of a taxi strike. We stood in panic staring at the line of cabs along the curbs, their drivers marching alongside, their strike placards bobbing in the air.

We couldn't blow our chances with this crime expert because Philly's cabbies were up in arms. I flipped into crisis mode. Looking wildly around, I suddenly dashed out into traffic, flagging down a Domino's Pizza delivery kid and positioning myself in front of his car.

"Come on, lady," the kid shouted. "I gotta delivery to make."

"Madison, you'll get yourself killed," Abby called from the curb.

"How much you making in tips today?" I shouted.

"Thirteen bucks so far," the kid fired back. "What, you gonna rob me?"

I moved over to his door and leaned in. He could have gunned the car past me but his eyes immediately locked on my chest, which, with a little extreme positioning, gave the illusion of cleavage that didn't really exist.

"Fifty bucks if you get us to where we need to be in twenty minutes."

His head shot up.

"Deal. Get in."

I motioned to a wide-eyed Kat and Abby, and we all piled into the tiny green Civic.

"Who *are* you?" Abby asked, shaking her head, impressed.

The kid hit the gas and we ripped out into traffic.

Through the whole ragged ride, Katrina kept checking her watch every ten seconds and, even though the kid did a hell of a job navigating traffic, we were still fifteen minutes late when we skirted Independence Mall and pulled up to the address on Chestnut.

I shouted thanks, dumped the cash on his lap, and we all exploded from the vehicle and made a wild dash across the plaza and into the gray, Georgian-style building.

Inside, we bolted across the ornate rotunda, past a large statue of Benjamin Franklin, managing to just catch the elevator as it was closing with several stuffy types who looked at us as if we'd landed from some alien planet. At the top floor, we scooted out of the elevator and down a short corridor to a large door where we were to meet the gentleman none of us knew anything about.

Kat threw open the door a little too hard and it got away from her, cracking back against the wall with a slam.

"Come in," said a disembodied voice.

We stepped into a walnut-paneled meeting room and turned left, following the sound of the speaker. Sitting alone at the head of a large oak conference table that dominated the room was a dark-haired man with a salt-and-pepper beard. He was dressed in a brown button-down sweater over a crisp white shirt, open at the collar.

He rose to greet us.

"We're so sorry we're late," Katrina gasped.

But he cut her off with a motion of his hand.

"No need," he said as he grinned. "I am a great fan of punctuality, but my secretary back at Keystone Labs reminded me of the cab strike and thought you might have a little trouble. She insisted I give you half an hour's grace period and you made it." He smiled warmly. "Chris Sageway," he said by way of introduction, extending his hand.

Katrina got to him first.

"Thanks for taking the time," she offered. "Katrina Fitzsimmons."

"The ADA. Yes, Finnbar told me about you." He nodded in an elusive manner that begged the question as to what Finnbar had actually conveyed. "You're somewhat of a favorite of his, I take it?"

"He's very special. Hell of a mentor."

"Right," Sageway nodded. "He says you've very good at what you do."

Abby introduced herself, and then it was my turn.

"Madison Mandelbaum," I said.

Sageway took my hand and gazed into my eyes with disconcerting intensity.

"You are the bride," he said, deeply interested.

My face was flushed, and a mix of emotions poured through my system with a rush of adrenaline.

"I hope you can help us," I said, realizing he hadn't let go of my hand.

I couldn't for the life of me figure out why he was being so attentive, but I wasn't about to argue.

"Please," he said to us as he pulled away, gesturing to the chairs on either side of him. "I'm sorry that I can't spare a lot of time, but let's see what we can do."

Kat and Abby sat to his right, and he motioned me to his left.

"You brought the material?" he asked Katrina.

She opened her briefcase and produced a large envelope, placing it on the table in front of her.

Sageway held up a hand, went over to a rather elaborate desk, and opened a drawer, taking out what appeared to be a clear placemat and a pair of latex gloves. Returning to his seat, he spread out the clear mat on the table and emptied the contents of the envelope onto it.

"You know that the Society handles only cold cases, two to three years old and further back," he commented as he carefully focused on the materials in front of him. "It is my understanding that until this week there wasn't even the report of a crime in the death of this young woman. Do I have that right?"

"You do," Kat said.

Our eyes were trained on him as he quickly scanned the diary pages, police report, forensic evidence. Then he turned to the hand-prints from Colin, and I felt a sickening nausea in my stomach that I fought to keep down.

"Do the police know you have taken this?" he calmly asked Katrina.

Katrina bit her lip.

"Dr. Sageway," she began in her most official-sounding voice, "this is a secret investigation launched out of my office. We have reason to believe . . ."

"The answer, I take it, would be no," he responded matter-of-factly, without raising his voice or looking at her.

Katrina paused.

"Yes, sir," she admitted.

"You could be brought up on charges for lifting this evidence and transporting it across state lines. Are you aware of that?" he asked calmly as he took the painting from me and stood, scrutinizing the canvas and frame.

I gazed across the table at Katrina. She glanced up and our eyes connected. She was risking so much for me, and I felt the anguish of having put her in this position.

"I know what I'm doing," she said evenly.

Sageway looked up from the evidence.

"Your friendship must mean a lot to risk so much," he observed warmly.

I looked into Katrina's eyes. She didn't speak but simply nodded. She knew me, knew what I was thinking, she and Abby better than anyone.

"Do you have the other object?" he asked.

Abby and I looked confused as Katrina reached into her bag and pulled forth another envelope. She handed it to him. I was stunned as Sageway removed a hair curling iron from the bag.

"Where did you get that?" I asked, shocked.

"It was deep-sixed alongside the other evidence," Katrina explained. "I didn't want to examine it. I was afraid after we'd found Colin's prints from Farris's apartment. But Finnbar told me this might be a long-shot chance to exonerate him."

I stared at her.

"Or convict him," I said, frightened.

Sageway examined the curling iron, peering at it from every angle before placing it on the mat.

"We have a method of finding latent fingerprints that might normally go undetected."

"But this was presumably in water," Abby noted. "Wouldn't that ruin the possibility of any prints that might be there?"

"Not necessarily," Sageway said. "It's not the best, granted. But using what we call an SKP, or scanning Kelvin probe, we can see things on metal objects invisible to the naked eye. We're able to scan even curved objects like this. If there are latent prints that have survived, and if they are not the deceased's, we may have something to use. I will have to be quite circumspect about all this, of course."

"Dr. Sageway," I said, emotions pumping through me like music in a workout class. "I am supposed to be married to this guy who up until this week . . ." I broke off. "I've been getting mysterious phone calls and uncovering evidence suggesting I might not have known him as well as I thought I did." My eyes searched his. "I'm lost here. If there's any way . . ."

"You love him," Sageway said softly. "I can see that. I've also seen how love can blind someone from the truth, even crimes," he added, turning his piercing steel-gray eyes on me. "I've had many cases where a young woman never saw the darkness in her mate. Some end up as unwitting accomplices, some meet a far worse fate."

I gazed at him, my heart fighting his implication.

"I have a daughter," he said quietly. "Emma Rose." He smiled sadly. "She was married last year."

"Congratulations," Abby chimed in, trying to brighten the mood.

"Her mother and I didn't think much of her choice. He was a cliché, the struggling artist. Had no prospects, nothing to recommend him. We, of course, wanted her to marry this young lawyer who was after her." He shrugged. "But she told us Jared loved her and she him and that was all the recommendation we should have needed."

He grew silent and we all sat there, uncomfortable and bound by his sadness.

"I think she was probably right," he said, his face evincing the pain that seemed to run deep as a river inside of him. "And rather than have the wedding of *our* dreams, they left here and eloped."

He grew silent. I looked at Kat and Abby then back at him.

"We received a card at Christmas. They're out west somewhere, we think. But she's not talking to us. I don't know if she will or"—he paused—"or, if they have a child, whether I'll ever get to meet him or her."

He appeared to withdraw into himself.

"I'm sorry," I said.

He took a deep sad breath and let it go.

"Just have to stay tuned, I guess. Hope for a little forgiveness."

He turned to me.

"So. If you believe in this guy and if we can find anything useful, I don't know." He smiled a little, putting out his hand on the table as if he might take mine but thought better of it. "Maybe I can help another bride."

I reached out and placed my hand on his.

"Thank you," I said, moved.

"Now," he said, pulling himself together and shifting gears. "This meeting never took place," he explained, eyeing all of us in turn. "The Vidocq Society is a pristine organization that serves the public good. What I do now I do for personal reasons that have nothing whatsoever to do with the Society. This is a social visit. I believe one of you is involved in publishing?"

"Yes," Abby responded, somewhat surprised.

"Then you are interviewing me for a prospective book. It happens all the time. Are we clear?"

The three of us looked at one another, then back at Sageway.

"Of course," we all agreed.

"I'll take this," he said, indicating the curling iron, "and the handwriting to the lab and work on this tonight. I'll phone you if we turn up anything. Meanwhile, you need to look at motive, alibis, who might have had cause to want the woman dead. Have you done that?"

We looked at one another.

"The evidence didn't lead us anyplace else," Katrina said, troubled.

"It doesn't sometimes. It can seem a dead end, and then you come across something small," Sageway said, gathering up the evidence and placing it in the envelope. "Some phone call, an e-mail, jewelry, some tiny clue that helps make a connection no one ever saw. We are all mini-Vidocqs. We all have our specialties where, when you come across evidence, you know it in a way others might not. You can't be afraid to follow where it might lead," he said as he rose.

"I'll have all of this sent back to Finnbar," he told Katrina. "We should leave separately. I have a back entrance to my car. You'll forgive me for not escorting you out."

Abby and Katrina thanked him, and then I stepped forward. I reached up and gave him a hug. Sageway seemed to freeze a second before allowing himself to accept it.

"Thanks for that," he said softly, and then headed for the back door.

"Oh, by the way," he said, turning back. "The Society's motto is *Veritas Veritatum*—The Truth of Truths. Let's hope it's what we find."

He waved and strode out through a door by the stone fireplace behind us.

"I feel like we're in a Harry Potter story and we just said good-bye to Dumbledore," Abby remarked.

Katrina and I stared at her.

"Well, he was a lot younger and definitely hotter, of course," Abby qualified.

I went over to Katrina.

"You are amazing," I said, hugging her, then reaching out to Abby. "You both are."

The three of us stood there a moment in the wood-paneled inner sanctum.

"Something small," Katrina said.

"A phone call or jewelry, some tiny clue," Abby added.

"You can't be afraid to follow the evidence," I said, repeating Sage-way's words.

His words stayed with me all the way down to the street, where we found a shuttle to the Thirtieth Street Station for the train ride back to Manhattan.

Somewhere along the way, it triggered a memory.

Colin had been afraid to follow up on an investigation that involved Rebecca Farris. Who else had been afraid to let him?

Veritas Veritatum.

I had an idea, but it would have to wait. Of all things, I was headed for my bachelorette party!

45

Thursday night, 8:30 p.m.
Meatpacking District, NYC
1 day, 23.5 hours to the wedding

At one time all you would find in this area just north of the West Village were actual slabs of meat hanging from giant hooks like I'd once seen Sylvester Stallone punching in a *Rocky* rerun. Now it was one of the places to see and be seen, especially at night. How I would get through this I had no idea.

"Alcohol," Kat answered the question in my head. "In massive doses."

We hit the Buddha Bar with its hot DJ-propelled music vibrating the high-ceiling, multiplatformed space, head masks hanging on the walls, its giant red-lit Buddha dominating the dining room. Julie Raskin, with whom I'd roomed at Wellesley, instantly handed me a coconut mojito.

"Hey, Maddie," she said, planting a kiss on my cheek. "You look fantastic."

Four days of no sleep, nausea, vomiting in a government building, old clothes, infrequent showers, nonstop crying, and complete emotional meltdown—I was quite certain *fantastic* was the last thing I looked.

"AHH," screamed my cousin Deanie, in from Connecticut, racing for me from the bar. *"There* is the luckiest woman in the world. Madison, I am watching your fiancé all over the tube. He is hot as jalapeño."

She handed me something called a Hello Kitty, some kind of cocktail laced with butterscotch. I sucked it down.

"You are going to get so bombed," she teased.

"Amazing Maddie," Bonnie Judaken said, throwing her arms around me and planting a kiss on both cheeks.

"This is a major deal, Madison Mandelbaum," shouted Loren Bosse above the chaos. "The first of our group getting married. Damn," she said, growing emotional. "I told myself no crying."

Loren and Bonnie had been interns with me at MoMA. They'd become the kind of friends you could count on for movies or a late-night coffee and were always plugged into the latest exhibitions and artists.

"Hey, hey everybody," Abby announced, gathering everyone into a circle as we were each handed a spectacular-looking drink. "Raise your glasses, ladies."

She motioned to the DJ, who magically cut the music. Abby grabbed my hand and marched me into the dining room and in front of the giant Buddha. Everyone eating and drinking in the place was looking at us.

"Ladies and gentlemen," she shouted "This is my best friend, Madison. And this is the new signature drink created in her honor—*The Maddie!*"

"Yay, Maddie," the crowd cried out as if they'd rehearsed.

God, let me live through this. A signature drink? My head was spinning from the alcohol and the thoughts of Sageway and the text message Katrina had received on the train down to Philly.

"She is an astounding woman, a remarkable friend, and, knock on wood, is going to be a drop-dead gorgeous bride come Saturday night."

The place roared like a rock concert.

"Abby," I said, protesting.

How could she be doing this, saying these things, given everything that was going on?

"Come on, get 'em up," Katrina called out. "You men as well," she cracked, and the place went nuts.

She turned to me.

"To our friend, our precious Maddie," Katrina called out, lifting her glass.

"Only joy," she toasted.

I looked at her on one side of me and Abby on the other. They were all I could see. This was their way of telling me to hold to my dream and no matter what happened they were with me.

I hugged them and lifted my glass along with the dozens of strangers all around us.

"Veritas Veritatum!" Katrina roared.

And to the hand-clapping and table banging and shouts urging me on, I threw my head back as Kat and Abby poured and, in quick succession, chugged down a mojito, a shot of tequila, and one more Maddie.

Amid the craziness and fog of alcohol, the ladies led me toward our table. All of a sudden, I was aware we had stopped. I looked at the girls around me. They were all staring straight ahead. I glanced up and into Colin's eyes.

"Looks like a hot party," he said, grinning uncomfortably. "Would you ladies mind if I had a quick word with my bride?"

"Hey. You're the freakin' groom," Julie shouted, sounding only slightly drunk. "Go for it!"

I glanced over at Katrina and Abby, who each had placed an arm around me.

"I know how important she is to you," Colin said to them close enough so the others couldn't hear. "She's pretty important to me, too. Please."

I looked at both of them and, shaky as I was, nodded.

"I'll be OK," I told them.

Reluctantly they drew back as Colin led me through the growing crowd and out the door.

46

We stood opposite each other on the sidewalk, a dozen feet away from the restaurant entrance. I tried concentrating on his face through my alcohol buzz. I was pretty sure he looked like he needed sleep.

"You run away. Don't return my calls. All but accuse me of murder," Colin said, pacing in front of me. "Madison, what the hell is going on?"

"Could you maybe stop moving so much? I'm getting a little seasick here," I said, watching him zigzag back and forth.

"I'm trying to figure what I ever did to make you treat me this way?" he said, still on the move.

"You lied, for one," I tossed out there, my words slightly slurred.

"I may have shaded the truth. Omitted something. Everyone does it."

"Not with the woman you're going to marry."

"Especially with that woman."

Gratefully he stood still.

"Madison, I am madly, deeply, insanely in love with you," he said with great passion. "I want us to build a life, have a family. But we have to be on the same side."

I gazed up at him. He looked terrible.

"Let's start with being honest, OK?" I blurted, the tequila and mojito rum working my tongue pretty good. "Where'd you go to college?"

"What?"

"Before Columbia. Where were you?"

"You know that already," he insisted, shaking his head. "Ox . . ."

"Uh, uh, uh. Bzzzzzzzzzzzz!" I shouted. "I checked. You were never at Oxford."

He stared at me.

"What?" He half laughed. "You actually checked up on me?"

"Yeah. You do it for a living. Got a problem with that?" I shot back.

"I love you," he said, his head shaking as if he couldn't wrap his head around what was happening.

"It's not enough," I responded, waving my hand in the air wildly. "Love can be easy, I'm thinking," I stammered, trying not to sway too much. "*Truth* is hard."

He searched my face as if trying to locate something he recognized.

"I want the woman I fell in love with," he shouted.

"She doesn't exist," I answered, fighting through the tipsy fog. "I've changed. I need more than a sprinkle of honesty in my love potion," I insisted. "You got any of that?"

"I was protecting you."

"From what?" I countered.

"Things that make the world dirty, all right?!"

"You never went to Oxford."

"Madison . . ."

"Who are you, Colin, really?" I demanded.

"I'm the man you said yes to when I asked you to marry me," he exploded, eyes flashing. "Yes, I might have shaded the truth. There are things I'm not proud of, but down deep you know who I am. I love you. I'd give up all the hype and attention I'm getting this week for you to believe me."

"I'm fighting for you, Colin, don't you see that?"

"No," he said, shaking his head vigorously, making it appear to my alcohol-induced eyes as if there were three of him. "All I know is that I love you, Madison Mandelbaum. And that's the truth. Believe that."

"Hey, you all right?"

I glanced back to find this Incredible Hulk of a bouncer outside the Buddha Bar entrance.

"Yeah," I thundered, bloodstream pumping tequila, Maddies, rum.

"Look. Maybe I should call you a cab?" implored Colin, looking ragged and worried.

I glanced up at him.

"I don't need a man to do that," I insisted through my haze. "And I don't need to go home."

I weaved toward the door.

Colin started after me but the behemoth bouncer stepped between us.

I looked at Colin once more, then turned for the door and the promise of liquid oblivion.

47

Friday, 7:30 a.m.

Battling a major hangover, I stood by the curb in Chelsea next to Katrina's car, already on my third cup of java.

"We could just hook you up and pump it in intravenously," Kat suggested.

"Sorry I can't go with you, Maddie," Abby said as she handed me a bagel for the road. "They're going to kill me at work."

"I know," I assured her, holding my head a second.

"DA's going to have my head as it is," Katrina added, looking hesitant about what I was doing. "I have to show. Are you sure you need to do this?"

"I can handle it," I insisted, trying to convince them and myself at the same time.

"I know you can," Abby said unconvincingly.

"Give them hell, kiddo," Katrina called out. "I'll phone when I hear anything from Sageway."

"Look at you, you're Nancy Drew," Abby quipped, trying unsuccessfully to hide her worry as she reached in.

I gave her a quick hug.

"See you," I said, slipping into the vehicle, turning the key, and easing away.

"Madison!"

I hit the brakes.

"Rehearsal dinner. Tonight. What do we *do?*"

I hadn't the slightest idea how to answer. There was way too much on my mind, and the caffeine hadn't kicked in yet.

I shook my head, hit the gas, and sped off.

I could see them in the rearview mirror, still watching me as I headed west toward the river. They were the best, beyond the beyond. But they couldn't do what I had to do. I couldn't let them take the risk. My fiancé was a wreck. My family thought I'd lost my mind. And maybe I had. But all I could think of was that I needed to do what Colin hadn't, to see if there was any *there* there.

I owed Colin that much . . . and maybe myself as well.

Hungover and growing jittery from the caffeine now flowing through my veins, I headed north on I-87, determined to find the *truth of truths*.

Two hours later my head was just clearing as I stepped into Jamison Walker's office in the state capitol. My insides felt like Jell-O.

"I need to see the attorney general," I announced, slightly off-balance.

"Do you have an appointment?" the tony receptionist asked brusquely, eyeing me dismissively, certain in her knowledge that I didn't.

"No," I answered. "But he'll see me," I assured her, taking a bracing breath. "Tell him I'm here about Rebecca Farris."

Friday, 9:30 a.m.
Albany, The Office of the Attorney General
1 day, 10 hours, and 30 minutes to the wedding

At forty-nine, tall, preternaturally white-haired, lean and handsome, Jamison Walker looked like Hollywood's idea of a political leading man.

I had seen him on television and Colin had once remarked "Walker is as good as a pol gets." Like Bill Clinton at his peak, Walker's charisma, his playful banter with the press, and his sincerity when bringing down those who had broken the law made him a natural. But until he appeared in the doorway of his office, his grim expression morphing instantaneously into a compelling grin, I never knew the jolting power of his presence.

"Mr. Walker, I tried to tell her . . ."

"It's all right," Walker assured his flustered receptionist. "I've got it handled. Ms.?"

"Mandelbaum. Madison Mandelbaum," I said, the hint of a quiver in my voice that I hoped he hadn't detected.

"No need to be nervous, Ms. Mandelbaum," Walker coaxed with polished warmth.

He'd caught the quiver. *Damn it, Madison.*

"Won't you come in?"

He motioned me into his office.

"Hold my calls," Walker directed his receptionist.

I glanced over my shoulder back at the woman. She was eyeing me with barely concealed contempt. You'd think I was stealing her boyfriend.

Walker ushered me into his dark-wood-paneled inner sanctum. (What was it with men and their *inner sanctums*?) There were photos of him with the president of the United States, the governor of New York, and other dignitaries prominently displayed, no doubt, to better intimidate.

Walker gestured toward two broad-backed stuffed leather chairs in front of his wide mahogany desk, behind which, in each corner, the flags of the nation and of the State of New York stood as silent witnesses.

"Now, Ms. Mandelbaum," the attorney general said, propping himself on the edge of his desk, towering over me. "What can I do for you?"

Sinking into my seat, I was forced to look up at him. Walker smiled that thousand-watt smile, and I knew instantly he had used it to charm a million others. Still, I was surprised that, even with my mission, it had kick.

This was how he disarmed the public, I told myself. *Don't fall for it. Do what you have to do.*

"You knew Rebecca Farris?" I asked.

Walker thought for a moment, looking genuinely puzzled.

"Forgive me," he said, furrowing his brow. "Rebecca who?"

"Rebecca Farris. She died last year?"

Walker scratched the back of his head.

"No, I don't recall that name," he said, still smiling. "I thought my receptionist had said you were here about Rebecca *Harris.* She's a distant relative. I'm sorry you wasted your time."

His phone buzzed and he picked up.

I sat there, annoyed and confused. This was not going as planned.

My mouth was dry and I looked around for a glass of water. As I did, my eyes fell on the photograph of his family, angled just enough on his desk for anyone seated here to view.

They were a good-looking family, altogether: a frat boy of a son, about twenty. He looked familiar in a way that all young college kids do. Next to him sat a strikingly beautiful daughter, just slightly older. Between them sat an attractive, fortysomething wife, a brunette with large expressive Angelina Jolie eyes and a prominent gold necklace with a striking pendant at her throat. I was drawn to the unusual ornament. I had seen it once before but somehow couldn't place it.

"Ms. Mandelbaum?"

I glanced up. Walker stood at his desk, clearly waiting for me to leave.

I panicked. I hadn't come this far to let him slip away. It was my only chance of saving everything.

"Mr. Walker," I said, my heart pounding in my chest. "You have a beautiful family," I noted, my eyes on the photograph.

"Thank you for saying so. Now, if you don't mind, I have pressing business . . ."

"I'm due to get married tomorrow night," I blurted.

"Well, isn't that lovely. Congratulations."

"So you'll forgive me," I said quietly. "I don't have the time for you to play games with me."

Walker was taken aback.

"Excuse me?" he said, his voice rising indignantly.

"You heard me," I said, eyes flashing at him, strength coming from who knew where. "You're lying about not knowing Rebecca Farris, and we both know it."

Walker turned beet red.

"What gives you the right to come into the office of the attorney general and waste my time? . . ."

Triggered, I got to my feet.

"You took the meeting," I insisted, beating back my fear in his house of power.

"I was merely trying to help . . ."

"Don't feed me lines, sir," I declared, asserting myself as if I were channeling, well, my mother.

"I have reason to believe you were seeing Rebecca Farris," I went on. "She was a private escort. How's your memory now? She provided evidence that you were threatening her before she died under mysterious circumstances."

The pretense was gone. He went ballistic.

"You are way out of line here," Walker erupted, his voice thundering. "You do not want to challenge the highest judicial officer of the state."

I did not look away.

"And you don't want to mess with a bride one day before her wedding," I shot back, my voice steady. "I need answers."

"Madison, is it?" Walker said, eyes glowering. "You seem like a nice young lady. Maybe this is wedding jitters, I don't know. I'm going to ask you to step out of my office now with my warmest wishes for you and your fiancé, what's his name?"

"Colin Darcy."

Immediately, I caught the look of recognition on Walker's face as he stared at me. He looked dumbstruck. And then, changing gears, he smiled, a little too broadly.

"Ah, the reporter," he acknowledged.

I could see his mind working behind that grin.

"I have a dear friend who heads up one of the news divisions where your fiancé works," Walker offered pointedly. "I would hate to see Mr. Darcy lose his job over his young bride's *indiscretion.*"

He took a few steps closer, his gaze boring into me with high-wattage intensity.

"Are we clear, Ms. Mandelbaum?" Walker said, the threat cold and evident.

I stared back into his menacing glare. Amazingly, I felt no fear. Colin had been right. There *was* something to this story.

The door opened, and one of his aides walked in.

"Excuse me, Mr. Attorney General," the officious young man said. "It's nearly time for your press conference."

"That's fine," Walker said, his eyes still locked on mine. "Ms. Mandelbaum is through here. Would you see her out?"

I held his gaze, refusing to back down.

"Ma'am?"

I turned to the aide. He gestured for me to follow him out. With one last unflinching glance at Walker, I turned, reluctantly, and followed.

As we came to the door, I paused. I took in the painting hanging in the recessed panel in the wall. It was a portrait of Walker. He was seated, his fingers interlaced in his lap, his gaze steady, confident, if not a little whimsical, a twinkle in his eye. It immediately brought to mind the work of Britain's Lucian Freud. It had a noticeable *impasto* whereby the artist applied paint thickly enough so that the brush or painting-knife strokes were visible. It gave the work texture, making the paint seem as if it were coming *out* of the canvas. There was talent here, but also a rudimentary quality that suggested the artist was perhaps still new at this approach.

"Ms. Mandelbaum?"

I ignored the aide, my eyes instinctively searching the lower-right corner of the portrait. At first I didn't find the name. I stepped forward. And then I saw it, tucked in at the edge of a dark rug, barely perceivable, initials hidden in a curved brushstroke that stood out from the canvas.

RF.

I stared at the two letters. Like Sageway had suggested, we are all mini-Vidocqs. We all have our specialties where, coming across evidence, you know it in a way others might not.

I was unable to move, staring at the painting and its implications.

And then, Walker's assistant placed his hand on my arm and literally pulled me through the door.

Tiny explosions were going off in my head as I hit the street outside the capitol building. I searched my memory of the painting we'd found of Colin that had been hidden in Farris's old apartment. Though shocked to come across it, I had recognized it was an accomplished work, detailed, even bold. There was a playful touch of Gauguin-like surrealism about it I'd found surprising.

My breath quickened.

All of my advanced studies in art, my skills with recognizing style and technique, approach and methodology, now told me one thing loud and clear—the portrait of Colin and the one of Walker had been created by two *very* different artists.

50

It was less than an hour later, as I drove down I-87 back to Manhattan, that I got the call from Katrina.

"Sageway found two prints on the iron. Neither came from Farris. He can't be sure but there is a strong chance the iron didn't even belong to her. Someone else put it in that tub."

"How could he know that?"

"Farris was a blonde. He found an undetected microspecimen of hair trapped in the handle of the iron. It was from another head. He ran a DNA on it and cross-matched with the DNA listed on the Farris report I'd supplied him. They didn't match."

"Whoa," I reacted, swerving from a truck trying to pass. "Then again, there's the possibility a visiting girlfriend could have used it. Not some murderer bent on frying her."

"You're good. You ever want to leave the art world we may have a place for you downtown. How did it go in Albany?"

"You're talking to New York's new public enemy number one."

"Wow."

She grew silent.

"Kat, what is it?"

"Meltzer called me in about the file. Asked for a full briefing and accused me of keeping vital information from him."

"God, Katrina."

"I think someone's breathing down his neck. He seemed to know more than he let on."

"Katrina, I'm so sorry I got you into this."

"I'm a big girl, Madison."

"What about the other one?"

"The other what?" Katrina said.

"You said Sageway found two prints on the iron."

There was a beat. I knew what was coming.

"Right," Katrina said reluctantly. "It belonged to your guy."

My fingers tensed around the wheel.

"Of course it did," I muttered, hoping for other news.

"Madison?"

"Gotta go."

"Kat . . ."

"Abby and me, we've got your back."

"I know."

"But if I were you," she added, "I'd start watching it, too."

51

Friday, 1:23 p.m.
NBC's New York affiliate, 30 Rockefeller Center
1 day, 6 hours, 37 minutes to the wedding

As I made my way across Rockefeller Plaza, I thought back to that first time I'd come to WNBC with Colin. We'd only been dating two weeks and he'd taken me for a tour of the studios used by the New York news team. The station was cool and all that, but mostly I liked the fact that Colin was trying to impress me. Me? Madison Mandelbaum. It blew my mind.

As I entered the station, Colin's co-workers buried me under an avalanche of *mazeltovs* and *you go, girls* and off-key renditions of "Here Comes the Bride" that I did my best to smile and acknowledge.

"Colin's not here," Rick Pembleton, one of the news producers, told me. "I hope he's taking a nap. Not to get personal, but I don't think he's been sleeping. It's been a big week. And of course, the two of you are getting married so, hey, I can understand."

"Yeah, yeah," I said, looking around, distracted.

"Something really strange though," he said, pulling me aside. "He turned down a chance to appear on *Dateline*. I just couldn't . . ."

"Whoa, whoa, what?" I said, not sure I'd hear right. "Say that again."

"Crazy right? I realize the wedding's tomorrow and all, but he could have taped this afternoon or even in the morning? It's not like him to pass up a shot like that."

"He turned down *Dateline*?" I repeated.

"Didn't he tell you?"

"No," I said as it computed. "No, he didn't."

"Well, when you see him, see if you can talk some sense into him. He wouldn't listen to me."

"Right." I nodded. "Thanks."

I turned around and nearly bumped into the very man I'd come to see, a well-dressed woman at his side.

"Mr. Hopkins," I said, startled. "I was actually coming to see you. I wanted to . . ."

"Ah Madison, isn't it? This is my wife, Mary Beth. Dear, this is Colin Darcy's bride-to-be."

"How wonderful," the woman said, her face lighting up. "Nothing beats wedding week. Most exciting time of my life," she gushed.

"Yeah," Hopkins commented with a wink. "And the rest has been downhill."

"Now you," she teased back. "Don't pay attention to him, hon."

"No," I said, looking over at Hopkins. "Actually, sir, I had a few questions."

"We're just on our way out. Look, if you leave word with my secretary. Or pass whatever you need on to Colin. Your boy's probably written his ticket to nationals after this week. Definitely going to require a salary bump. Ouch."

"Mr. Hopkins . . ."

But he was already on the move, noticing someone down the corridor.

"Jack, did you get those new visuals?"

"Mr. Hopkins?" I called after him.

"Story of my life," his wife said, shaking her head with a little smile. "We got married right out of college. Thirty-four years I've been sharing him with his mistress."

I looked at her curiously.

"His work, dear," she laughed softly.

"Thirty-four years, wow." I nodded and, just to be polite, asked, "What's your secret?"

"I went in with my eyes wide open." She grinned. "That and a news-free night once a week," she insisted. "I'll give it to Bob," she said as she looked down the hall after him. "A slip now and then but, for the most part, he's honored that request." She smiled, adding with an arched eyebrow, "Of course, the house in the Hamptons doesn't hurt, either."

I nodded. Her manner was impressive. I could only imagine the sacrifices, the roller coaster she'd ridden to get to here. Looking at her now, I noticed the necklace she was wearing. It was gold with an unusual pendant. The same ornament I had seen earlier that day in the photograph in Walker's office. It was, of all things, a piglet. And now, seeing it again, I remembered where I had first seen it—around the neck of Rebecca Farris.

"Mrs. Hopkins," I began.

"Mrs. Hopkins is my mother-in-law." She grinned. "Mary Beth, please."

"Mary Beth? Do you mind?" I asked, as I moved closer to examine it. "That's such an unusual necklace. The pendant, where did you get it?"

"Ah." She smiled, patting the piglet. "The Porcellians."

"*Poor* what?" I inquired, having never heard the word.

"Porcellians."

"I've never heard the word before."

"Bob's final house at Harvard. Very *chichi.*"

"Final house?" I repeated, another term with which I wasn't familiar.

"Final houses. Kind of like secret fraternities."

"Like Skull and Bones at Yale?" I asked.

"A bit like that," she said. "High-powered boys' clubs, really. Big men on campus, the elite, they like to think. Once you're in, you're in for life. They say if you haven't made your first million by the time you're forty, your Porcellian brothers hand it to you."

"Nice club," I said.

"Only members get to purchase these precious little piglets. They even stamp the backs so you know they're authentic. The men think they've handed you a diamond. Oh, they take a lot of pride being Porcellians all right." She laughed. "These guys stick together longer than a lot of marriages, I'll tell you that."

"Mary Beth!"

We looked up.

Hopkins was motioning for his wife to follow.

"He actually reminds me of a little pig once in a while." She grinned slyly. "Husbands get like that. But you feed them, wash them, give them a tickle once every so often, they do all right." She smiled. "Looking forward to the wedding, dear. Best of luck."

And she was off.

I stood there in the corridor, repeating the name in my head.

The Porcellians.

Hopkins must have been protecting his fellow porker when Colin had wanted to launch an investigation of the attorney general ten months earlier. He'd even threatened to end his career. Colin had recently gone back to that file and someone had found out.

Was it just the sex scandal Walker feared, I asked myself leaving the studios, or had this little piggy committed murder?

52

"Why pigs?" Abby asked when I'd reached her at work.

"Something to do with a prank played back in the 1790s when they started the club," I explained as I read her information I was now Googling on my BlackBerry. " 'In keeping with the classics they chose the name *Porcellian* from the Latin *porcus*. Their motto is *Dum vivimus vivamus*—while we live, let's *live*.' "

"You can't argue with that," Abby remarked.

I heard another voice.

"Tell them I'll phone back," she told her assistant.

" 'Some members sport golden pigs on watch chains, neckties, or jewelry. They have a clubhouse above a clothier on Massachusetts Avenue opposite a gate to Harvard Yard that sports a boar's head, called the McKean or Porcellian Gate.' "

"You get your own gate at a place like Harvard, you have to have some serious pull."

"What do you think?"

"Look, maybe you're right, Maddie," she said. "Walker and Hopkins are brothers in this secret, exclusive whatchamacallit. But what does it prove?"

"Walker had guilt written all over him when I confronted him in his office. And he had her painting hanging there."

"They were initials," Abby argued. "Madison, you can't be sure it was her work."

"You remember what Sageway said. It's the *small things*. I know it in my gut, Abby."

I stopped in the middle of the sidewalk, searching on my BlackBerry for the e-mail and attached photo of Colin and Farris I'd received a few days earlier.

"I've got it here, I know it," I said, ducking into the foyer of a building to better see.

"Maddie?"

There it was. I clicked on the photo attachment and tightened on the pendant. A small piglet came into focus.

Yes!

"This is it!" I shouted. "This connects Walker."

"But Maddie," she said, sounding worried. "This evidence is no more definitive than that against Colin. You are accusing the attorney general of the State of New York of homicide, and that case had better be airtight. Even if you could tie him to the necklace, there are the diary entries, fingerprints, painting, the note from Farris—they all point to Colin."

I stared at the necklace in the photo as my brain kicked into overdrive.

"Didn't it say in her diary that he liked seeing his gift around her neck?"

"Yeah, I think so," Abby said, sounding puzzled. "But she was writing about your guy."

"How do we know that?" I pressed my point as I said, "Maybe she was writing about someone else, and she wanted Colin to expose him."

And then, like an unexpected wedding gift, a crazy idea emerged.

"Gotta run," I said excitedly.

"Where?"

"To see if my head's as smart as my heart," I responded. "See you at the hotel."

"You're going ahead with the rehearsal dinner?" she was shrieking as I hung up and flagged a cab.

I seriously needed a miracle.

And if there was any luck reserved for a bride the day before her wedding, I was about to get one.

53

"E ve," I told the voice answering machine as the cab carried me up-town. "It's me, Madison Mandelbaum. You said to call if there was any-thing I needed to help find out who may have hurt Rebecca Farris."

"You got it," she said, picking up. "Shoot."

"You told me that Monet had a problem with seeing her clients on her own time. Aside from Colin Darcy, did she ever tell you anything about a deepening relationship with one of her regulars? Someone who wanted her to leave Elite Escorts?"

"I was only concerned with Rebecca's visits that were on my time. And if any of her clients were trying to cut me out of the deal, I certainly didn't know about it."

"Got it. But maybe if you just think back . . ."

"Only exception she ever made was for your man," she replied. "I told you."

"Eve, please?"

My cab rounded Columbus Circle as I waited anxiously. And then, she came back on.

"Sorry," she said. "I don't have anything in my records."

My heart did a nosedive. I muttered the f-word, the s-word, and a flurry of combinations.

"Maybe it's not in your written records, but maybe there was one particular client who was a bit too rough? And it kept Monet from working?"

Eve was silent. Had I pushed too hard?

"There are some clients who like to play a bit aggressive." She paused. "There was one. I can't betray his confidence. He could destroy you, me, your fiancé, and your wedding."

My heart sank. "Can't you give me anything on him?"

"You said you had her diary? Maybe she called him by her pet name for him. What was it she called him?" she asked herself, clearly scanning her brain. "It was a kind of animal, I think."

"You mean a pet?"

"Give me a minute," she murmured.

God. A little help, please?

"Not a cat. No. No. A dog?"

My heart sank.

"No! It was a pig," she declared triumphantly.

A jolt ran through me.

"Pig?" I said with hushed excitement.

"Yeah," she replied, a rush in her voice. "Because he was bringing home the bacon."

All right. It wasn't perfect. It might not hold up in court. But it was something. Some*one*. *Not* Colin.

Rebecca Farris had been talking about someone else in her diary, someone who'd given her a Porcellian necklace, someone who had hurt her. It confirmed the story Colin had told me when I'd first asked about Farris earlier that week. I was ecstatic.

And then my heart sank.

I suddenly remembered the diary referring to the man having met someone new, someone who'd majored in art at Columbia, a woman who now managed an art gallery, someone Farris said she hated and wished were dead. It seemed certain the reference was to me.

I felt like I was in free fall all over again. One step forward. Two light-years back.

And then, as we approached the park, I grasped at the only possible explanation.

I took out my cell and phoned Katrina.

"I have a huge favor," I said. "It could mean trouble."

"Maddie," she said. "You helped get me through my parents' divorce, my mom's breast cancer. I'm a hard-ass and you're my sister. What do you need?"

I told her and had barely gotten off that call when another came in.

I knew at once who it was. This time, I didn't hesitate.

I took the call.

"Wow. What a surprise," I purred, muscles tensing. "I missed you."

"Hello, Madison," said the familiar mystery voice. "You've had a busy day."

I strained around, looking for him.

"Are you following me again?" I asked evenly, straining back to see for myself.

"I think we've started to see eye to eye, you and me. Am I right?"

"You and me?" I asked, barely containing my disgust. "We have absolutely nothing in common."

"Oh, I beg to differ," he replied. "We both agree Colin Darcy is not husband material."

"You sure about that?"

"Quite," he said curtly. "But consider this a friendly warning."

"Oh, goodie," I snapped. " 'Cause you're so good at that."

"Don't go poking your head in places you don't want to be."

"Really?" I said, up on my knees on the backseat, scanning for some sign of him as the driver pulled over by Eightieth and Central Park West.

"You tamper with the file, you'll end up going down with Darcy. Not to mention the price ADA Fitzsimmons might pay."

The cab came to a halt. The driver pointed to the fare.

"Son of a bitch!"

"You don't want to lose your temper, Madison," the caller said in that maddening metallic clip.

The driver froze, glancing back as if he couldn't wait to be rid of me.

I pulled money from my purse, handed it through the window, and bolted from the car.

"Whatever happens to Colin and me, you're going down and I'm going to make it happen."

"I would love to see that," he said with a laugh.

"Be careful what you wish for," I snapped and hung up.

I stood at the entrance to the park, seething with anger. This jerk knew about the file. He seemed to know what I'd asked Kat to do. She was in danger, and it was all because of me. I screamed and threw my BlackBerry to the pavement in frustration. It smacked hard on the surface, cracking the back off and sending the battery skittering across the cement. I was aware of the stares I was getting and angrily went over to retrieve the phone. I picked up the back piece and the battery that had broken free, surprised to find they had survived.

Turning the body of the BlackBerry over, I was about to slide the battery back into place when something peculiar caught my eye. Taped to the casing of the phone, where it would have been hidden had the battery not been dislodged, was a tiny silver chip. I was no *techspert,* but I knew immediately this hadn't come with the equipment. Bugged? It all made sense now.

How had the caller put it in there? Where? When? And why hadn't it occurred to me to look for something like this? I'd read Patterson, Baldacci; I'd seen the *Bourne* films. I felt stupid, violated, angry with myself over the danger I had caused Katrina, Abby, and who knew how many others?

Heart thumping, I ripped the sliver of an object from the phone casing. Throwing it down beneath me, I ground it under my shoe with a vengeance, as if, by destroying it, I might obliterate all that had transpired.

I stared down at the crushed particles glinting silver in the sun.

Snapping my cell back together, I stepped over the smashed chip and headed into the park.

56

It was late afternoon and the gates to the Delacorte Theater were closed, the sign reading REHEARSAL IN PROGRESS. The cast of the Public Theater's Shakespeare in the Park was no doubt preparing for the first summer offering.

Ever since Colin had proposed here, this theater and its surroundings had become a kind of touchstone for us. We'd come in autumn as the colored orange and gold leaves fell around it; in winter, when we'd snuck in and skated across the frozen white wonderland of the stage; in spring, when Colin had boosted me over the wall and climbed over after me where, with the assistance of a nice bottle of pinot noir, we'd reenacted the night of the proposal, just for the two of us.

Following the disturbing news that Colin had turned down a shot to *Dateline,* something unheard of for any up-and-coming reporter with ambition like him, I'd phoned his apartment and his cell repeatedly. I'd even braced myself and checked in with Sir Hugh and Diana, respectively. Neither had seen or heard from him, but both, in their own ways, demanded to know what it was I was doing to their son.

What could I say? That I was racing the clock trying to keep the wedding alive by trying to remove suspicion and disprove the overwhelming evidence that Colin had been involved in a homicide? That their son had somehow hidden the fact from his future bride, back when we'd reviewed all of our partners (does everyone do this?), that he had actually once visited a personal escort service? That he apparently had developed some kind of relationship with the woman even while convincing me that he *was* that into me and that I was *the one*?

Even with all the suspicions that had piled up around him, my love for him was as real as ever. But I couldn't let myself forget that, if I was wrong, if it hadn't been Walker who killed Farris, if, despite what my heart told me, Colin had somehow been involved . . .

I couldn't imagine the unimaginable. And yet, it was what I'd been dealing with the whole week. Still, something had led me here, a need to protect Colin, to tell him to hold on, that there was hope, because I didn't know how to face the alternative and, I was pretty sure, neither did he.

As the gate opened and a burly actor in tights and a rapier emerged, I slid inside the Delacorte. The rehearsal appeared to be breaking up as actors and workers made for the exits. I peered out across the rows of seats, searching. But there was no sign of Colin. Damn. I had been so sure.

Making my way back out, I stood outside the Delacorte, looking up and down the walkway. Nothing. Letting out a deep breath, I shook my head. Obviously I had been wrong. I was just turning back toward the path that would lead me out of the park when a female voice called out.

"Are you Madison?"

I turned back to find a woman about my age, her long black hair pulled back in a scrunchie, addressing me from the box office.

"Yes," I shouted, utterly surprised.

Ducking under the counter, the woman hurried over.

"A man was here earlier. Good-looking guy," she said, a little embarrassed. "Said his fiancé, Madison, might be coming by and if I saw a woman fitting your description, could I give her this?"

She held out an envelope. Startled, I took it.

"Thanks," I said.

"You're welcome."

She started off, then whipped back, her face bright with curiosity.

"He said he proposed to you here in the Delacorte. Is that right?"

I nodded.

"Wow," she said, as if blown away. "You're living my dream."

She smiled and headed back.

I looked down at the envelope in my hand. Colin had been here after all, my instinct—*our* instincts—were the same.

A spark of hope ignited in me.

The caller's threats, the disastrous clues, my attempts to discover whether or not he was the man I thought I knew, the exchange outside the Buddha Bar—all of that had driven a wedge between Colin and me. But now, in the park, knowing he'd come here for me as I had for him, I felt a sudden closeness.

Ripping open the envelope, I found what seemed words from a poem.

> *Let me not to the marriage of true minds*
> *Admit impediments. Love is not love*
> *Which alters when it alteration finds,*
> *Or bends with the remover to remove:*
> *O no! It is an ever-fixed mark*
> *That looks on tempests and is never shaken . . .*

Of course he *would* pick Shakespeare. But what did Shakespeare know about his lover's name being tied to a dead prostitute? Or latent handprints on curling irons? So he had to suffer through hostile critics, maybe bubonic plague. Child's play. I was dealing with a groom accused of homicide and the loss of my bridal dreams, not to mention the full-scale fury about to be unleashed by the humiliation of Long Island's most combustible Jewish mother.

I turned the paper over and found there a handwritten message.

> *Madison,*
>
> There is no excuse for a lie, anytime. But that you can even think me capable of a crime, especially this one, has shaken me more than you know. I thought our love was stronger somehow. To say I miss you terribly, the smell of you, the feel of you, would be the greatest understatement of my life.
>
> *Colin*

I stared at the letter, rereading the words. As the meaning detonated in my heart, I felt a force separating me from my body, cutting me in two. My knees buckled. The letter fell from my hand as I sank to the grass.

I stared into my heartache, and the reality whipped me like a bitter winter wind—in chasing the truth, in fighting to uncover it and to rescue *us,* had I lost *him?*

I don't know how long I sat there, staring into space, my tears stinging my cheeks.

Numb, I picked up the letter and got to my feet, no longer thinking of threatening callers, golden piglets, or the mystery of who had really painted the portrait we'd found in Farris's apartment.

"Good luck," I heard the woman in the box office yell after me as I walked away.

I didn't respond.

My brain had shut down.

If I were lucky, my heart would follow.

57

I wandered along avenues replaying scenes from our relationship. Traffic ceased to exist. The white noise of Manhattan was gone. I saw and heard only Colin.

I couldn't tell you if I'd been walking one hour or six. It must have been some inner autopilot guiding me to where I'd planned for months to be this night because sometime around seven that evening, I found myself at the Waldorf-Astoria taking the elevator to the Starlight Roof, where our wedding and the night's rehearsal were to have taken place. The media screen in the elevator informed me it was 7:43 p.m. There was some distant awareness that the rehearsal was to have begun at seven with dinner following in the Marco Polo on the mezzanine at eight thirty.

I had a distinct sinking feeling as the elevator carried me up to face those gathered above. Colin's four groomsmen would be there along with his best man, Big Ben. Sir Hugh was probably half plastered by now and prepared to battle for his son's honor, I had no doubt. And, of course, the inimitable Diana, who, after events in the garden and calls to my mother, I imagined was already plotting on how to destroy my family and me.

I thought of my bridesmaids who would be there. I suddenly felt a responsibility for any damage I would be doing to their dreams for their own weddings someday. I thought of my bubbe and felt a sharp pain in my chest at the hurt this would cause her. I closed my eyes as I ascended, thinking of my dad, who would be crushed, the look in his eyes that would be impossible to avoid.

And then there would be my mother. I gasped for breath. I was certain the combined loss of face and sense of failure she'd now experience (both of which she'd perfected as art forms) would make anything I'd witnessed in the previous twenty-eight years seem like kids' drawings before a Picasso.

The elevator stopped. The silver doors opened. Kat and Abby were standing there. Thank God for small favors. They reached in and grabbed me.

"Where have you been?" Kat asked, her face lit up with concern.

"We've been calling you nonstop," Abby said, hugging me.

"Colin's not here. Have you seen him?" Kat asked, leading me into a corner out of sight of the others.

"No," I answered sadly.

"Maddie, I'm sorry," Abby gasped.

"Yeah," I said. "Me too."

Katrina gazed at me, biting her lip.

"Maybe it's for the . . ."

"Don't say it, Kat," I asked, eyes pleading.

"Right."

It felt like I was walking into a mugging. I could hear the buzz of voices around the corner. There was no way to survive this and no way for me to walk away, either.

I glanced at my friends, took a deep breath, and started down the hall.

58

The first person to reach me was the wedding coordinator, bearing down on me like an uncaged rhino.

"How can a bride be late to a night like this?" she demanded, trying to hide her shock and smile at the same time. She failed on both counts.

"Madison, where have you been?" my mother bellowed.

"More to the point, where on earth is Colin?" Diana demanded.

"Madison, thank God. Are you okay?" my dad shouted.

The room burst into questions, the wave of voices coming at me so fast I thought I would drown in them.

"Please. If you'd just listen to me," I called out, but no one could hear me over the chorus of Emily Cohen-Wasserstein, Sir Hugh's booming barrister voice, the shrill sounds of Diana, and the indomitable white Oprah, my mother.

There was a loud crash.

All eyes turned to where Katrina stood behind me, red-faced, dishes smashed on the marble floor at her feet.

"What's wrong with you people?" Kat said. "The bride shows up and has something she needs to say. You're like animals."

"Preferable to a barbarian," Diana Darcy declared.

"Hear, hear," said Sir Hugh, which had to be the first time he'd publicly agreed with her since they'd both said "I do."

I turned back to the faces before me from my perch three steps up, overlooking the length of the stunning, light-sparkled room. I coughed and fought to clear my dry throat.

"My God, Madison," my mother erupted in frustration. "What have you done?"

"Melanie," my dad threatened.

I nodded, gazing into my mother's eyes.

"That's perfect, actually. That's right, Mom. What have I done?" I said.

I felt my throat close. I wasn't sure I could speak. And then I found my bubbe's face. I had a feeling she somehow knew the news I was bringing as she clasped her hands, reaching them out to me as if to offer whatever strength she had in her aging body to do what I had to do.

"There isn't going to be a wedding."

The room exploded.

And when it died down a little, I continued.

"We should all know the people we're involved with, live with, but we don't always, do we?" I said, gazing down into my mother's eyes. "People keep secrets. And when you find them, it makes you wonder how well you really knew them or even *if* you truly knew them at all."

"What are you insinuating?" Diana tossed off tartly. "Are you saying Colin's harbored some terrible secret?"

I glanced around at Abby and Katrina, then back.

"I'm not insinuating anything," I explained. "Only that trust cuts both ways. And there are things we've each done that have made the other feel less of it."

I stared out at my broken rehearsal party. In the distance I could see the chuppah that had already been erected for tomorrow. I felt faint. My legs gave out. And then I felt arms catching me. I thought they must be Kat's or Abby's. But as I looked up I was shocked to be gazing into Colin's bloodshot eyes. He struggled to get me to my feet as he teetered on his own. It was only then, as the others gasped around me, that I noticed the half-empty bottle of scotch whisky cradled under his arm.

"Greelinks and palpatations everybody," he announced, slurring his words as he circled the bottle over his head, totally wasted.

"Colin," I gasped. "What are you? . . ."

"Hello Mum, Dad, *Maldebaums,* friends," he said, drunkenly gesturing with the bottle as he named each one. "Where's Bubbe?" he called out. "Bubbe?!"

"I'm over here already," she called out, lost in the sea of confusion.

"L'chaim," Colin said, raising the whisky in a toast and taking a long swig.

"Hey, man, maybe you should lay off this stuff?" said his best man, trying to humor him as, at six feet seven, he loped over to confiscate the liquor.

"No, no," Colin warned, keeping the bottle out of reach as he held off his tall friend.

"Colin," Sir Hugh thundered. "Where's your dignity?"

"Dignity?" Colin repeated curiously, checking his pockets. "I'm not sure. If anyone finds it, do let me know."

He laughed riotously and drank again.

"Colin Darcy, stop making a spectacle of yourself," demanded his mother, stepping forward to face him.

"My goodness, Mother," responded Colin with a drunken giggle. "You've spent your entire life teaching me that's exactly what we must do, make spectacles of ourselves. Isn't that right?"

Diana looked genuinely wounded. I stepped in.

"Colin," I said. "You're drunk. This isn't you."

"Ah, the woman of the hour," he proclaimed. "Have you met my bride?" he shouted as he waved his arms wildly. "Isn't she gorgeous?"

"Colin," Kat urged, trying to talk him down.

"And here, ladies and gents, are the two best friends—Princesses Abigail and Katrina. Like Macbeth's witches, you three have completely managed to turn my life upside down."

"Colin, please," I said.

"No." He waved me off.

"I thought I knew you," I said.

"You don't always know everything," cried Emily Cohen-Wasserstein in exasperation. "This is a reason to call off a wedding that has two hundred edible yarmulkes that can't be returned?!"

"OK, *you* we don't need to hear from," my mother declared.

The woman looked stunned.

"Madison received word that cast doubts you were who she thought you were," insisted Katrina.

"Kat."

"She stood by you, Colin." Abs stepped in. "But she can't marry someone she doesn't know."

"What are you talking about?!" Diana shouted.

"The truth," I said.

"And lies, right?" Colin countered.

"And the difference," spat Kat.

"Veyazmeer, enough!"

We all stopped and turned to the middle of the hall.

Bubbe was perched over the scene, standing on a chair in the middle of the room.

"Secrets, lies, truth. What is this, the CIA?"

"No, Bubbe," I insisted. "It's about figuring out what to believe."

"And who?" Colin shot back as he tried to keep himself from falling on his face.

"Talk, talk, talk," Bubbe said, climbing down off her chair. "How does anybody build an honest relationship with such things?"

"What do people do when they don't know what to believe anymore?" I stammered.

"They *love,*" she said, her eyes on me as if there were no others in the room. "They see it all, and they still choose to love. That's how it goes, shayna," she said, coming toward me. "We human beings, we come and go," she explained. "The love, it lives on. We get to hold it for a while, be burned by it, learn from it, experience its pain and its passions. We embrace it, wrestle with it, like Jacob and the angel. And like that all-night wrestling match, if we prevail, even a part of the time, we end up with a blessing."

"Which is?"

She was standing right in front of me now, her face lit up with age and memory.

"That we have lived and loved." She smiled softly. "That we have known what it is to be truly *alive.*"

I gazed into her warm and probing eyes, and I was a kid again.

"Do what you must, sweetheart." she nodded, taking my hand. "But don't walk away from the choice."

She walked over and took Colin's hand so that she stood between us.

"It's the choice that matters," she said, looking first at Colin then back at me. "The meaning is in the *choosing.* You see?"

"What if you get it wrong?" I asked, glancing up at Colin, who seemed to be looking at me through the liquor, wondering the same thing.

"Even if you get it right, you might feel pain. In fact I am sure you will. It's part of the bargain. But," she turned to me, gazing up from her five-foot two-inch height, "the *choice,* the choice is everything. Because it means we go in with eyes and hearts wide open. Trust me, my granddaughter, it's the only way I would have wanted to live my life."

She let go of us and walked the few feet over to where my mother was standing, spellbound as I'd rarely seen her.

"It's the only way to ever find even the possibility of *having it all,*" she said, looking into my mother's eyes. "Otherwise, you're living half a life because you've shut your heart down. And when that happens," she acknowledged, turning back to me, "your head, trust me, Maddie, it doesn't have a compass."

She held me with her eyes a moment.

No one spoke a word.

I looked over at my parents, my father's intense, hopeful gaze, my mother's uncharacteristic silence, as if, for once, she'd come upon a situation she couldn't imprint her will upon or dismiss with blame.

I turned to Abby, her face aflame with concern, wanting to help and not knowing how. And to Katrina, struggling with emotions my bubbe's words had stoked, feelings she normally kept to herself.

Finally, I found Colin. We gazed at each other and I knew, even with the whisky, he was wrestling with the meaning of Bubbe's words. There was so much unaccounted for, my brain insisted. A crime unsolved. Lies unexplained. Future uncertain.

And then and there, as I treaded the murky waters between my mind and my heart, Colin turned from me. Crossing unsteadily to my bubbe, he handed the bottle off to my startled mother and then did the most remarkable thing. Getting down on one knee, he took my grandmother's hand and, with one question, melted my reserve.

"Rose," he said, lifting his eyes to gaze up at her. "Would you be my bubbe?"

Bubbe broke into the smile of a little girl.

"*That* is the most romantic thing I've ever seen," blurted Abs, who'd pulled close to me, overcome by the gesture.

Bubbe was now looking over at me for an answer.

I opened my mouth but heard another voice emerge.

"No!"

We looked back at Katrina, who was staring at her BlackBerry in horror.

"The DA's issued a warrant for Colin's arrest," she reported breathlessly. "Finnbar says the police are in the building now. They're on their way up here!"

The room erupted in chaos.

In a blink I knew what I had to do.

"Tell my father 'sixty-one.' He'll know what to do," I yelled to Abby.

I raced over to Colin, grabbed hold of his hand, and, as the elevator doors burst open, we bolted through the adjacent kitchen, disappearing down a stairway to the only refuge my panicked brain could think of.

59

My dad's boyishly enthusiastic historical lectures had always been something to endure with a little smile and feigning of interest. Until that moment, I hadn't known I'd actually ever learned anything from them.

As I raced down the stairs dragging a sobering-fast Colin behind me, I found myself accessing trivia Dad had conveyed after my mom had insisted on holding the big event at the Waldorf-Astoria. Marilyn Monroe had lived here. Bugsy Siegel. Herbert Hoover. But what got him most excited was the fact that the hotel had its own railroad platform called Track 61 that few people knew about. He'd said it was used to bring President Franklin Roosevelt in privately so people wouldn't see he had polio and couldn't use his legs. "Perception," he'd said, "perception is everything," joking nostalgically that, with YouTube and cell cameras and bloggers, privacy was a thing of the past.

I didn't know how we would find the platform, I only knew the direction—down. We ran raggedly down through a series of seemingly abandoned stairways and across pipe-lined corridors. At one point, Colin struck his head on something jutting down from the ceiling. It clocked him pretty good, opening a cut on his forehead. On the plus side, it seemed to sober him up fast. I realized as we bolted down one long, paint-chipped corridor that Colin hadn't the slightest idea where I was leading him and yet hadn't questioned it. He had simply trusted me.

Finally, we came to a long corridor that ended in a Jurassic Park–sized service elevator.

Frantically we glanced back along the corridor as we pushed the button. It opened and we stepped in, the doors closing behind us. As we descended I flashed on my father's telling me of an elevator big enough to put Roosevelt's car in. Had we found it?

And then the doors opened. Fighting to catch our breath, we stepped out. It was dark and hazy, a few naked bulbs dangling from wires overhead. There were several old railcars sitting at angles before us, and a cold musty smell hung in the air.

We'd found Track 61.

We were safe for the moment.

I turned to Colin.

No wigged-out wedding coordinator. No families or friends.

We were alone.

60

Standing there with Colin, I felt it was odd and strange and familiar all at once, a little like being alone that first time fourteen months ago.

I was glad for the break in the rush of madness swirling all around us. At the same time, the questions and suspicions, not to mention the very real danger of having run from the police, heightened the moment, painting it in fiercely bold colors against the drab canvas of our shadowy surroundings.

"Let's try over there," Colin said, gesturing toward a weathered railway car, its side gaping open. "Better cover."

I nodded, and we hopped down from the platform and walked over the tracks to what appeared to be a once silver railcar wedged between two others.

We peeked in. There were a couple of stools; a striped, dusty mattress; and some beer bottles, empty and lying on their sides.

"The bridal suite, I believe," Colin said, shaking his head.

He held his hand out and I swung up and inside. We took a few steps then, exhausted, slid to the floor to sit opposite each other, backs against the walls of the train car.

"Why are we running?" he asked at last.

I stared at him.

"They were about to arrest you."

"For what?"

"Someone's framing you, Colin, and that someone has connections. They've got evidence, prints, motivation."

"What are you talking about?" he said as if I were talking in a foreign tongue.

"Why did you lie to me about Rebecca Farris? Didn't you think I'd find out you went to her for sex?"

Colin stared at me, conflicting emotions battling on his face.

"It was before you," he said. "Besides, I've never been much of a ladies' man, even if you thought I was."

"What are you talking about?" I said. "You were the talk of the *Today* show."

"Yeah." He smiled sadly. "You think five minutes of fame defines me?" he asked me.

"But women have always fallen at your feet; I've seen it," I insisted.

"They don't want me," he said, gazing deep into my eyes. "They want something *from* me. It's always been like that. Back in England, girls were after me because of my dad's name. There was the money, the prestige. He could get us in anywhere. I never knew whom to trust. I come to America and they love me for the accent or the TV thing or the idea of who they think I am and who they can be with me. No one ever seemed to actually like me for me. Not before you."

"Look, you banged your head pretty good back there," I quipped. "You may be delirious."

"I know it sounds pathetic. I never wanted you to see this part of me."

"Which part?"

"The insecure, *I'm not all that* part. The part that didn't buy my own press."

"You're the most confident person I know."

He looked away a moment, then back at me.

"As a kid, I had trouble reading, and my parents didn't know what to do. During story time, I'd say 'aminal' for 'animal' and 'bizghetti' for 'spaghetti.' I'd mix up P's and Q's and B's. They had their fun with me in school. Couldn't read like my mates. I felt so stupid, Maddie, like someone had put me together differently from everyone else. Finally some doctor told us I was dyslexic and you'd think the world had ended.

"My mother told my father how embarrassed she was, that she didn't know what to do, which, of course, made me feel even guiltier. My father insisted we keep it quiet and get me some help. They were utterly ashamed of me. Do you have any idea what that feels like?" The pain in his eyes broke my heart.

"Finally they sent me to this special school, and I worked hard to overcome it. But being sent away, my parents' attitude, not seeing my friends, I always felt different. I knew then I needed to work hard to get it right, always afraid someone would discover my secret."

"Is that why you told me you'd been to Oxford? Because you wanted to seem like you weren't different?"

"Ah, college? I'd been raised to think Oxbridge, what they call Oxford and Cambridge, was the only route that mattered. My father was determined, despite my disability, that I attend Oxford. He told people I was going: 'Perception is everything.' But I couldn't live his lie. I went to a small college up in Scotland. Worked hard. I wanted to be a journalist." He laughed at himself. "Tell the truth wherever it led. Applied to Columbia Journalism School and, somehow, I got in. Came to the States for a new beginning."

"But the dyslexia? You'd never know."

"I've learned to deal with it. Still, I prefer memorizing my copy and not reading it off a prompter. It's why I'm good in the field. I don't read. I tell the story that's in my head."

I was amazed.

"But why wouldn't you tell me? It's nothing to be ashamed of. In fact, it's inspiring."

He gazed at me.

"Maybe it was the fact that I had lied on my résumé, hoping the Oxford connection might help with job interviews. Then the station hired me and let it be known I was an Oxford man. Maybe I was too much of a coward to correct them. Maybe it was the fact that when I went to your house that first time and your father seemed so impressed, spouting the history of the place and before I could stop you, you'd shared it with your mother who already seemed to suspect me. Guess I didn't want you to look bad in her eyes so"—he shrugged—"I swallowed the lie and figured someday when we were married with kids running around, I'd tell you—when it was too late for you to get rid of me."

He shook his head.

"I hadn't counted on being vetted by my bride."

I looked at him as if I hadn't really known him.

"Why would you go to an escort?"

"I was lonely and it sounded exciting. No ties. No mess. Walk away. Sounded good." He looked down solemnly, then back at me, a strange smile on his face.

"It was the weirdest thing. I get there and all, Rebecca was this knockout, only I couldn't do it. I mean I tried. But the thing just refused to work."

He shook his head as if, even now, he couldn't quite believe it.

"You'd think every guy's dream, right? Beautiful woman, you can have sex with her and walk away, free and clear, only, suddenly, face-to-face with a fantasy, I didn't want to be free and clear. I wanted to be with someone who meant something to me."

I stared hard at him.

"Big Ben teased me about it. Something had to be wrong with me, right? Only I decided I'd felt that way for a reason. And then, a month later, I found that reason," he said, gazing intensely at me.

My mouth was dry.

"What did you do there, with her?"

"We talked."

"You talked?" I said, surprised. "About what?"

"Her dreams. What she wanted to be when she grew up. About my work, our families, her art. After, it seemed we both felt better somehow. Only then she began calling, sending me e-mails, wanting to meet for coffee so she could tell me about some new art piece she was working on.

At first, I went. Only, after the third or fourth time, I began realizing she was becoming attached and I wasn't sure how to get out of it."

"You met her even after we were together?'

"I know how bad it sounds, Maddie. It seemed to mean so much to her, and I was too ashamed to tell you all this, the escort, the meetings I was trying to get out of. I didn't want to upset you when it meant nothing, so"—he shook his head—"I said nothing." He paused. "But I couldn't take the guilt so finally I told her about you and that I didn't feel comfortable seeing her anymore. She got angry and desperate. I didn't know what she was going to do. Don't forget, Diana Darcy's my mother. *Hell hath no fury* and all of that. But then she came to me with the Jamison Walker angle, maybe thinking she could buy my attention with the possibility of a headline. But when Hopkins ran me off the story, I told her I couldn't pursue it and that was that. I never heard from her again."

He bit his lip.

"On July first, I told her that I couldn't talk to her ever again. She died on July fourth. Maybe if I'd kept meeting her, she wouldn't have felt so hopeless."

"She wasn't hopeless," I said. "She was murdered."

He stared at me.

"How can you know that?"

I told him everything.

About the calls, being stalked, the chip in my phone, about Finnbar and forensics and the Vidocq Society, about Walker and golden piglets and secret clubs, about the threats to him and to my best friends if I caused trouble.

Colin listened to all of it, shocked and angry and moved beyond words by what I'd gone through. And when I had drained myself of the story and there was nothing left to tell, he slid across the floor until he was next to me. Filled with emotion, his eyes searched mine. And then, as if they'd been created for this purpose alone, his arms slipped naturally around me, holding me, pulling me to his chest, enveloping me in the only evidence I needed—his love.

We stayed like that for a long time, clinging together as if, after the distance we'd traveled, we couldn't bear to be even an inch apart. And then Colin whispered in my ear.

"Forgive me."

I turned my face to him.

The service elevator sprang to life outside the car. We tensed and held our breath. It was going up. Pressing our heads up by the opening to the door, we waited, hearts pounding.

The sound of the elevator stopped. There was a pause and then it whined again. It was coming back down. I took Colin's hand. I squeezed so hard I was sure I'd cut off his blood supply. And then the elevator stopped at the platform. My mind was racing. How would we evade the police now? We heard the doors of the elevator open.

I looked at Colin. Where could we possibly hide?

And then I heard a loud whisper that made my heart leap.

"Blue Eyes?"

61

Other than the time when Abby and I had accidentally sealed ourselves inside a float of Beauty and the Beast at the Macy's Thanksgiving Day Parade 1991, I had never been so happy to see my father in my life.

I bolted from the railcar and raced over to him, throwing my arms around him in a wild hug.

"Are you all right?"

"We're OK," Colin said as he reached out for my dad's hand.

"Help us, Dad," I blurted.

He gave Colin a warm smile. He looked out at the dimly lit railcars and grinned. It reminded me of how he'd told me he'd reacted as a boy when he'd received his first train set. "Franklin Roosevelt used this platform, can you believe it?" he marveled. "Track Sixty-one. Not so bad listening to your old man once in a while, is it?"

He gave me another hug and then he grew serious.

"We have to wait until the police drop the search. We can't use the elevator," he explained, producing a small flashlight. "Come with me."

I didn't know how in the world he planned to get us out of there, but I didn't doubt for a moment that he would.

Pulling out what looked like a copy of a blueprint marked *New York City's Underground,* he led us down the track a hundred feet or so and then paused. Consulting the map, he turned sharply to his left and proceeded. In another minute we'd arrived at a narrow entryway whose wooden door was marked with a fading but still distinguishable white-stenciled sign identifying it as 50TH ST.

My father handed Colin the flashlight and moved into the tight space that was confined by dark walls studded with some kind of fuse boxes and piping. Dad pushed against the door, but it wouldn't budge.

"Probably hasn't been used in a while," he explained, and tried again. He grunted with exertion.

"Damn this thing."

"Let me . . ."

But before Colin could step forward, I shot into the confined opening and pressed my weight against the door alongside my father. After a few seconds, it began to move and then, with our efforts, it slowly slid open.

"Sons," my dad quipped, obviously proud of our combined effort. "Who needs them?"

We were standing beneath an old-fashioned gas lamp, its golden glow producing giant shadows of the three of us.

I turned back for Colin as he stepped through the doorway.

"Your dad's amazing," he laughed.

"What are you two waiting for, an invitation?"

We both glanced up only to find my father was already at the first landing and hurrying upward.

"Dad, wait up."

"I have to give the signal. The girls should be on the other . . ."

We were only a few steps up the dust- and rust-riddled stairway when we heard the loud crack and the scream and something landing with a thud.

"Dad?!" I cried and scrambled up the stairs, Colin right behind me.

We raced up one flight, calling for him frantically. My heart was in my throat as I whipped around the landing and tore up the next flight.

"Madison, let me go in front of you," Colin called out, but I wasn't stopping. I would have stepped right through the two stairs that were missing and had clearly given away if he hadn't grabbed hold of me.

"Dad?!"

"Morty?" Colin yelled, shining the small light down.

There was a second of silence. Panic raced through me and just as I was about to cry out again, a weak voice called out of the darkness below.

"Blue Eyes . . ."

Colin's light found him where he'd fallen onto crates stacked some twenty feet beneath the stairs.

"Dad, we're coming. We're coming!" I cried.

I don't know how we managed to get to him through the crates with our sole tiny light. He was conscious but in a lot of pain. We were afraid to move him, but there didn't seem to be a choice. We tried phoning out with his cell but couldn't get a signal. He thought he'd broken his leg, and there was blood seeping from his arm. Ripping off his shirt, Colin tore it into strips and did his best to bind my father's arm wound. I next helped him splint my father's injured leg with one of the wooden ribs that Colin salvaged from the broken crate. Adrenaline and immediacy took over. Afraid we could make matters worse, we decided we had to take the risk.

Thoughts of weddings and murders and mysterious callers were nowhere in my head.

This was my dad. Hurt. How serious, I didn't know.

And somewhere in the frenzied, heart-pounding moments it took to carry him down off that mountain of crates and up the stairway and out to Fiftieth where Abby and Kat were nervously waiting, the realization struck me with a vengeance—this was all my fault.

If I'd never investigated Colin, never given in to the doubts, substantiated or not, the wedding would be on track and my father would no doubt be spending a sleepless night, and not lying in pain in the back of Kat's convertible, rushing to a hospital the night before he was to have seen his only daughter married.

62

Saturday, 1:13 a.m.

Lenox Hill Hospital, 210 E. 64th Street

18 hours, 47 minutes to the wedding

We rushed my dad into the emergency bay and, despite the early hour, were immediately met by a frenzy of activity.

"It's like *Grey's Anatomy*," I heard Abs remark, awed as hospital personnel burst onto the scene, taking my father's vital statistics, examining him on the gurney on the run.

I continued to hold his hand all the way in, even as I was aware of Colin's presence right by me, my girlfriends close behind.

We had phoned my mother en route and found her, as I'd suspected, wide awake. Bubbe had been carrying on all night, worried for Colin and me; and my mom, for once, seemed less concerned with the *shanda* of a canceled wedding than the possibility that my father and I could be aiding and abetting a fugitive, never mind that he was my fiancé. I heard the terror in her voice when I told her about Dad; with Bubbe, whom I could hear shouting in the background, Mom was already on the way.

The hospital personnel needed to remove my father's clothing and search for internal bleeding, and we were urged toward the waiting room where they promised to come and give us an update.

"I'm right here, Dad," I said, rushing forward and planting a kiss on his forehead. "Mom is coming."

"I'll be fine," he bravely assured me, though unable to hide the worried look in his banged-up features.

"I'll be right out here," I promised.

Reluctantly, I joined Abs, Kat, and Colin as we headed out to the waiting room just down the corridor. En route we passed a uniformed cop at the nurses' station filling out some papers. I felt a tug on my left hand. I glanced over to find Kat staring intensely at me, her eyes darting from me to Colin.

Oh my God, I realized only then. By being with me here, Colin, too, was in danger.

"You have to go," I said in a whisper as I turned to him.

"No, I'm not leaving you with your dad like this," he insisted.

"Colin, please. Haven't I caused enough problems for the people I love?"

"Madison," he pleaded. "Let me be here with you."

"You won't help getting yourself arrested. There are police everywhere. Look," Kat said, and I was thankful she was taking control, "someone's playing me down at the DA's office. I'm not giving them the satisfaction of getting their hands on you until we can"—she hesitated—"hopefully work this thing out. First things first. Make sure Mr. M is all right, OK?"

She locked eyes on Colin and, thankfully, he gave in.

Colin put his arms around me, holding me with a ferocity that took my breath away.

"He's going to be all right, Madison," he whispered in my ear.

"I know," I said.

He looked into my troubled face.

"It isn't your fault. None of this."

I nodded, touched his lips with my fingers before he turned and hurried away with Katrina.

"Madison, he's right," Abs said, trying to help.

But I knew the truth. All of it was on me. I wanted to scream.

"Are you the daughter?"

I turned back to find a doctor who looked younger than me.

"Yes. How is he?"

"Your father's sustained a broken leg, bruised hip, and lacerations to his arms and face. He's lost blood, but we are cautiously hopeful there is no internal bleeding. We're doing a few more tests just to be sure."

"Can I see him?" I asked urgently.

"Not just yet. We're running an MRI and the attending wants to look at everything, head, internal organs—it's normal procedure. I know it's hard, but hang tight. We'll come get you."

I stepped forward before she could leave.

"There must be something I can do?" I insisted, a frantic cocktail of adrenaline and nervous energy pouring through me.

"She's supposed to be married tomorrow," Abs offered, as if having a dad fall through a stairway beneath Manhattan wasn't reason enough to be going a little nuts.

"Right." The doctor nodded, gazing at me with what seemed a new understanding. "Well," she suggested encouragingly. "I suppose you could donate some blood in case your dad ends up needing some. As his daughter, you could be a match, and blood supplies are kind of low around here."

"Done," I blurted, grabbing hold of her offer as if it were a life raft.

63

Abs accompanied me to the lab.

"Nothing to worry about." She smiled broadly, even though we both remembered how Abby would pass out at the slightest sight of blood.

Silently and with the skill of someone who did this countless times per day, the nurse tied the rubber strap around my upper arm, found a vein, and slipped in the butterfly needle so fast I didn't have time to react. Instantly, the plastic bag alongside my chair was filling up with the rich red liquid.

The whole scene felt surreal. A short time ago I'd been holed up with Colin in an underground railcar, listening to his explanations of how and why he'd lied and hid things from me. I knew I could forgive him for that. But I could never forgive the despicable voice on the phone, the one who had set matters in motion that had turned my fiancé into a fugitive and sent my dad to the hospital. I had a score to settle if there was any justice in the world.

The lab technician removed one bag and attached another.

"Leave a little," urged Abby. "She's supposed to be married today."

I turned to her. Why was she even bringing up what had clearly become an impossibility?

"Don't look at me like that," she answered my gaze. "I believe in happy endings."

"Fairy tales," I said, shaking my head. "If you believe anything, after this week, believe that."

"Yeah?" she said, fixing me with a determined smile. "The week's not over. And I believe in my best friend, and that her dad and Colin are all going to come through this. So how do you like that?"

Somehow in all of this mess, Abby managed to tease a small smile out of me as she planted a firm kiss on my head. I reached up and took her hand as the woman removed the bag and butterfly needle and placed a small bandage on my arm.

"They called down and said you had directed it for a patient," she said, consulting her chart. "Mr. Mandelbaum?"

"My dad." I nodded.

She smiled.

"He helped give you life, dear. Now you help him, you see?" she said. *"That's the miracle."*

I looked at her, surprised.

I'm not sure if it was her kindness or the power of her words that penetrated my angst at that moment. Somehow she struck me as the happiest and sanest person I'd met that whole week. And here she was, toiling in the middle of the night in the bowels of a hospital, collecting blood.

That's the miracle.

I clung to her words all the way back to the waiting room, not knowing I was about to discover that, when it came to miracles—one size did not fit all.

64

My mother had phoned several times while we had been in the lab and I called back en route to the waiting room, giving her what I knew and telling her I was certain they'd be in to see us as soon as she arrived.

Kat was in the waiting room when we arrived.

"Were the doctors in?" I asked anxiously.

"No. I just got here."

"Colin?"

"I took him to Abby's. I just got spooked that someone from the DA's office might be watching my place. He's all right, Maddie. Worried about you."

She came to me.

"You were right about him," she said, softly. "He's a good guy."

It had taken going through hell to get that out of her, but it was something.

"Thanks, Kat."

"That's Katrina logic for you," Abby quipped with a shake of her head. "Man becomes a fugitive, *now* he's good enough for our Madison."

"I'm twisted, what can I say." Kat shrugged.

"Ms. Mandelbaum."

We turned to find the doctor at the door.

"How's my dad?"

"We're just waiting for the results of the MRI, but I can tell you, Dr. Sarkissian—he's the attending—is really a top guy, so your dad's in good hands. He says preliminarily it looks encouraging," she said with a nod.

"That's great," I said.

"Way to go, Morty," yelled Katrina.

The girls each hugged me. Finally, a piece of good news. But I could see the grim look on the doctor's face as she eyed me uncomfortably.

"What is it?" I asked with concern.

"Could we talk for a moment? Alone."

"What?" I responded, my grin fading. "These are my best friends. We're sisters, really. If there's anything . . ."

"Would you mind?" she said to Abs and Kat. "It'll just take a minute."

"Sure," Kat said soberly.

"We'll be right out here, Maddie," added Abs as the two squeezed my arm as they left the room.

I turned to the doctor. She was gripping her chart so tight her knuckles were white.

"OK, what's up? You're freaking me out a little."

"It appears your dad will be needing some blood after all. Just to be safe."

"OK. Fine. I just gave a couple of pints. If you need more?"

She shook her head.

"It's all right, we can get blood for him. We need to prep it anyway. Ms. Mandelbaum . . ."

"It's Madison."

"Madison. I'm Robin. I am probably way out of line talking to you about this. Your friend said earlier that you were getting married and, as it happens, so am I," she said, a tentative smile appearing and vanishing just as fast.

"Congratulations," I uttered, still waiting for the point of all this.

"My mom got the news she has breast cancer right after Tom and I announced our engagement," she shared.

"Oh, I'm so sorry," I said, taken aback by this admission.

"She's fighting it," she smiled bravely. "Allison Cates is a real trouper."

I didn't know how to respond to this.

"One day after her chemo I was in her room brushing her hair out and she told me she knew I must be worried about inheriting her problem. She knew I must be afraid I could pass it on to my own daughters, if we have any. And she was right. Those thoughts did enter my mind."

"Robin . . ."

"That was when she told me I'd been adopted. For some reason she and my dad had chosen to hide that little fact from me but now she thought it was important that I know the truth. She said there were many things she hoped she'd passed down to me, but cancer wouldn't be one of them."

I stared back at her.

"I'm not . . ."

"We can't use your blood for your dad because . . . you're not a match."

"What are you saying?"

"While you were in the lab your mother called in offering blood if your dad needed it. She is O positive just like he is. Your blood came back type B."

I held my breath.

"Lots of fathers and daughters aren't the same blood type. I know I'm not a doctor, but I don't think that this means that I'm *adopted*?"

"Yes, that's true. There are many combinations that could result in a B blood type. An O and a B combination is possible, for example. But two type Os could *never* produce a B."

My mind was exploding.

"So you're saying, either I'm adopted or that one of my parents . . ."

My mother threw open the door at that moment, her eyes darting from the doctor to my stricken face.

"What's happened?!"

65

As soon as the doctor slipped out I flashed a look at Kat and Abby outside the door, and they knew immediately to take care of Bubbe and not to come in.

I turned and confronted my mother with everything I'd just discovered. I was hoping against hope she could provide some logical explanation. Her stunned and guilty expression confirmed my fears. Like someone who had been on the run for years and had, at long last, been cornered, a mask seemed to slip away as she quietly crossed to the tiny sofa opposite me and lowered herself into it, exposed and with no place to hide.

"I had just hit thirty," she began, her voice more subdued than I'd heard it ever before in my life. "We'd been married a year. I'd been strongly encouraged by my parents to jump at Morty. He was a good Jewish man, with a job, a future. I loved him. He was sweet and kind and loved me six ways from Sunday. But I wanted to wait. It was a time of possibility. Women were breaking through. But, in the end, my doubts about myself, my future, they got the best of me and I gave in. Your father was so eager to get pregnant right away and so we tried. And I mean, we tried," she emphasized, her face reflecting the arduous, painful memory. "Weeks turned into months and before you knew it, it had been a year. Meanwhile I was building a career. There were lunches, dinners, people to impress, the next fall line to discover. Morty, he was so romantic, always sending flowers or little notes to Bergdorf's, insisting our luck getting pregnant would change. I was hoping the same but"—she shrugged sadly—"it seemed it wasn't to be."

She glanced over at me with an odd, stricken gaze and then averted her eyes.

"I know it doesn't make sense," she continued, "but these things enter your head and I remember wondering what kind of a woman I was. Unable to conceive? I think it was then I began to withdraw from your father. It was too painful to see and *feel* that disappointment hiding behind the smile."

My mother had never revealed anything about those days other than the most superficial of details. My heart was pounding as her words and confession tumbled out.

"And then, one day, one of the chief sales reps came in from Chicago. Handsome like Redford. Bright blue eyes like Paul Newman. A *goy* god. The girls were falling all over themselves to get his attention, but, for some reason, to their horror and my amazement, he found his way to my counter and began flirting."

She paused, glanced up at me, then away again, a look of shame I didn't recognize on her face.

"The good-looking boys never paid any attention to me in school. I was teased a lot. Made fun of 'cause I wasn't so polished the way I dressed, and I had this burn on my body that some had seen and others heard about. Your bubbe, of course, told me I'd show them one day. I never believed it. Never. Not until that moment when Paul Jansen approached me at the glove counter and looked at me like I was somebody."

I held my breath, waiting, unable to look away.

"What can I say?" She laughed ruefully. "It was flattering. He took me to lunch, dinner. We talked fashion. He told me I would make a wonderful buyer, that I had an instinct for what worked on a woman if I would only allow myself to trust it. I wasn't poor Melanie, covered in ugly burns. I was glamorous, talented, smart. I liked who I was in his eyes," she said, almost pleading with me to understand. "Was it so bad to want to believe I could be that woman?" She seemed to answer her own question, withdrawing into herself with self-recrimination. "And then, one night, after I'd made excuses to your father that I had to go into the city to prepare for a big sale, it happened. We had dinner, lots to drink, went back to his hotel, and I didn't leave until the next morning."

I swallowed hard, thinking of my dad.

"I was thrilled and ashamed and alive leaving him. But I knew deep down, I could never let it go on. He was married and so was I and, despite all this, you must believe me, Madison, I loved your father. I *love* your father," she said, looking at me sadly. "When I was late the next month I went to the doctor. He confirmed the pregnancy. Morty was ecstatic, and I was so guilt-ridden at what I had done I couldn't do anything else but have the baby."

She grew quiet, and I felt my face hot, my blood racing.

"We had you nine months later. I hoped it wasn't that night in the hotel, but I knew it had been. And two years later when we tried for another child and your father's sperm came back sterile . . ."

She broke off, tears filling her eyes. Were they tears of remorse, shame, or sadness she'd never borne another child?

"Our doctor convinced your father that it sometimes happened to men after they'd managed to produce an offspring. It was an aberration, he said, but we should consider ourselves lucky to have received one *gift*. Morty seemed to make his peace with that. But the doctor knew, and so did I." She looked up at me ruefully. " *'Be careful what you wish for,' right?"* She sighed. "I told your bubbe, but I've never told another soul. It was *our* secret," she said, gazing up at me with deep and utter pain. "Until now."

I was unable to speak as her confession detonated in my brain. Her eyes were searching mine, looking for something it seemed only I could offer. I had never served that purpose in her life. At one time I had wanted her to see me as possessing something only I could give her, to feel essential and important to her. Now she was reaching out to me. What was it she wanted? Forgiveness? Understanding? *Love?*

Instead, as I watched her tears fall, something in me altered. I couldn't bring myself to give her what she wanted. Strangely, I felt a certain power making itself known, questions long tormenting me, now answered.

The distance I'd always felt—had I always reminded her of a transgression she could never forget and from which she could never hide?

Her whole modus operandi, the love/hate, giving/withholding way of mothering seemed to come into focus.

My mother reached out a hand for me, more vulnerable than I'd ever seen her. In the midst of this storm, I don't know why, but a heightened sense of myself took over. That, and a fierce protectiveness of what was mine.

"Some secrets deserve their name," I said in a steady voice. "He must never know. It's *our* secret. Are we clear?"

She gazed at me, astounded. It was as if I'd offered her a gift beyond her imagining. But it wasn't for her I was doing this. It was for a man who had poured so much more than blood into me.

"Yes, yes, Maddie," she said, relieved, crying. "Thank you. I'm sorry. I'm so sorry."

And maybe it was for the little girl in her who'd felt she could never be anything, or the young woman who, when she was slightly older than I was, had lost her way and found a daughter she hadn't expected, but there was a sadness I felt for her that compelled me to take her hand.

"Let's go see Dad," I said.

66

My father was sitting up and thrilled to see all of us, even as the doctor gave us the report that, other than the broken leg, a puncture wound they'd closed, some cuts and scrapes, he'd been fortunate.

"Just a lucky guy," my dad said with a grin, wincing from the pain. "Now all I want is to walk my daughter down the aisle. I might need a crutch or two, but I'll be there."

I tried to speak, but my voice caught in my throat. The stunning discovery Doctor Big Mouth had decided to share had shaken me. But I knew I didn't have the luxury to give in to those feelings right then. Colin needed me.

"Take care of him," I whispered to my mother. "I have to go find my groom."

I gazed into her eyes. They reminded me of Colin's.

"Turn on the TV," Katrina yelled, bursting into the room.

Grabbing the remote, Abs clicked on the small flat screen mounted on the wall. The image jumped and came into focus. It was a reporter from Colin's station.

". . . are reporting the apprehension of one of our own journalists who just this week broke a story about the mayor of New York City that gained national headlines. To repeat, after receiving an anonymous tip, authorities have arrested Colin Darcy in an apartment in Chelsea after the DA's office issued a warrant for his arrest for the murder of Rebecca Farris."

"My God," Bubbe cried.

"We've got to go. *Now,*" I shouted, finding Abs and Kat already at the door.

"Don't do anything crazy," my mother worried aloud.

I shot her a look.

"I'm going to do whatever it takes," I said, determined, heart racing.

"Of course she will," my father insisted proudly. "She's a *Mandelbaum.*"

My mother gazed back at me, even more vulnerable than when she'd seen me in the wedding dress, as if some wall she'd spent her life grappling to hold up had, at last, dropped away.

"Yes, she is," she agreed quietly.

I took in the scene of the two of them, side by side, my mother standing by my father as he lay in the bed. She had clung to her secret for a long time, protecting herself. That I understood. But in her own way, she could have been protecting him, maybe me as well.

Was that possible? The whirlwind of anger and shock blowing through my brain somehow found the tiniest fraction of free space to even consider that. She would do, and had done, whatever it took to preserve what she had. I would do the same for Colin. And then, something unexpected clicked in my head and pieces of another puzzle began to move.

"What?" Abs asked, reacting to what had to be the strange look on my face.

I didn't answer.

It was too outrageous, wasn't it?

But as we bolted from the hospital, it occurred to me that, after the week I'd been living, maybe "outrageous" was the only solution that made any sense.

67

After Colin was arrested, it was clear we were being watched. It was 4:40 a.m. when we drove to Katrina's apartment, parked the car, entered the building, and immediately slipped out the back exit. Thankfully, Sasha, bleary-eyed and gulping java, was waiting where she was supposed to be.

"Don't worry. No one knows where we are," she whispered conspiratorially as we crammed into her boyfriend's Mini Cooper and sped off.

Despite the hour, I put in a call to Sir Hugh who, I'd correctly suspected, had gone down to bail out Colin. There he'd been informed that, due to *extenuating circumstances,* his son would remain in lockup over the weekend. He told me Colin had his chin up and was more concerned with my father's condition and my state of mind. I told him my friends and I were working on gathering evidence and not to lose hope.

"My dear," he replied with inexplicable confidence. "I am of the Royal House of Windsor and an Englishman. We stood up to the Germans, I dare say we shall prevail against Manhattan."

I admired his bravado. But, being my father's daughter, I was aware of history as well, though I didn't have the heart to remind him that the British had rather famously *lost* the city back in the days of George Washington.

It was just past five in the morning when we pulled up to the art gallery.

"Are you sure you don't need any more help?" queried Sasha, clearly wanting to be part of whatever clandestine efforts were going on.

"You've really come through for me," I told her, giving a quick hug through the window. "Thanks."

"Call me if you think of something?" she inquired with a worried smile.

I nodded and watched her reluctantly drive off.

Inside the gallery, I led the girls into the office, put on a small light, and immediately went to the drawer of security discs Peter kept locked up. Entering the code, I retrieved the previous week's output and, with Katrina and Abby hovering over my shoulders, began popping them into the computer, racing through the recordings.

"Can't you even tell us what you're looking for?" Abby asked worriedly.

"I'll know it if I see it," I said distracted, removing one disc and turning to the next.

As I worked, I recalled how Brigitte had given Peter a hard time when he'd insisted on this state-of-the-art system. She'd joked about it earlier in the week. If I could possibly be right, who knew what I'd find?

"Maddie, we can help you," Abby urged.

"Will you let the woman work?" scolded Katrina.

With nothing but the sound of my friends literally breathing down my neck, I reviewed three discs from a week earlier and came up empty. Katrina began to pace nervously. By the time I'd slipped in the fourth disc, I was beginning to think I'd been unhinged by my father's accident, not to mention the bombshell revelation that had come with my blood typing. Just maybe I had let my imagination run away with me.

And then something on the screen caught my attention. I stopped the DVD, backed up, and hit Play.

My God—I caught my breath—there it was.

I zoomed in. I was in a discussion with a young man who'd come in claiming his mother had left a package. As I'd suspected, it was when I moved out of the picture to check in the back office that it happened. I'd left my BlackBerry on the desk in the middle of the gallery, and the young man on-screen turned, clicked something in his hand, and then quickly lifted my phone.

Katrina reached past me, tapped a few keys, and tightened the shot on-screen as we all watched the figure deftly slip something out of the BlackBerry, manipulate it, and return the phone back to its place on the desk in a matter of seconds.

"*Damn.*"

Abby's gasping response said it for all of us.

"Who *is* that?" she asked, horrified.

I would have explained, but there was something else I needed to check on. I sprang into action, delegating assignments the way we'd always operated. It had been rare for me to take the lead, but now I didn't hesitate. If the plan forming in my head were to work, I would need the help of an unlikely accomplice.

I phoned Brigitte, waking her. I told her only what I had to about Colin's predicament. I couldn't afford for her to say no to me. Yes, she promised that she would keep Peter away from the gallery and then gave me the piece of information I needed for my plan to work.

"Be careful, Madison," she said before hanging up. "We love you."

I don't know why, but I was struck by her emotion. Growing up, I'd never thought I generated that kind of feeling in anyone other than my two friends, my bubbe, and my dad. Now I realized that I had Colin, Peter, Brigitte, Sasha, even Eve. I had an army backing me.

I glanced up to find Abby and Katrina hard at work, faxing, phoning, researching. I hadn't shared with them the bombshell about my father. I had told my mother it would be *our* secret. The truth was I had shared everything with these two *sisters* all my life. And then I thought of Colin and what he must be going through. I wanted so much to be in his arms; without contemplating it, I knew I would tell him the secret. He was my *partner*, my lover, my best friend. I didn't love the girls less. It was only that Colin would go to places in my heart reserved for him alone.

"You were right—look," Abby said excitedly, showing me images of paintings and expanding them as I bent over to examine the style, technique, the *signatures*.

"And this?" Kat called out.

She brought over a fax of handwriting samples and Sageway's statement suggesting how fingerprints can be lifted from, say, a person's *work desk* and planted on something like a *hair iron*.

"In between yawns he kept mumbling, 'Brilliant,'" Katrina noted. "Still, he worried about the repercussions, suggesting we let the DA build the case."

"Yeah," I said, cutting her off. "We've seen how that's gone down."

I closed my eyes and ran it through my mind one more time.

Painting. Forensics. Access to surveillance. The discovery of Colin's file on Walker. The necklace. Most important—*motive.*

My friends agreed with me that I had as much as I was going to have. Before Colin's fate could be decided by manufactured evidence and malice I didn't understand, I had to act.

I'd always avoided confrontation whenever possible. As a little girl, I would lose my voice if anyone openly opposed me. But this week, between the mysterious caller, Diana, Colin, not to mention my mother, I'd had plenty of practice.

You can do this, I told myself. *You* have *to.*

At exactly 8:00 a.m. I put in the call. Slowly, deliberately, I delivered the message I'd rehearsed with my two friends and then hung up.

Katrina, Abby, and I looked at one another with trepidation. We were wedged between hope and danger and knew it. They each hugged me tightly, reluctant to let go but finally I forced them to. They had tasks to complete, and besides, there was no way the plan could work if they were here. Our suspect would see through that.

No. This I had to do alone.

I could only pray the bait would work.

68

The Closed sign was in the window, the shade pulled down as the minutes ticked down to the time I'd set. So much could go wrong.

What if my suspect didn't show? What if the person had already reported my attempt to the DA? I could be the one arrested for extortion. The system had already been manipulated. What was to stop it from happening again?

But what I was counting on, clinging to with a fierce faith, was the insidious power of *family secrets* that my mother's confession had triggered, that and a remark Colin had made as we'd hidden out the previous night on Track 61.

The clock struck ten.

I panicked. I went to the door and peered out. Normal foot traffic and no sign of the person I was expecting. I raced back to grab my phone on the desk in the middle of the gallery and call Katrina and Abs.

"Kat?"

And then I heard the knock coming from the gallery entrance in front of me.

"Maddie? You there?" a voice was calling in my ear.

But I was now fixated on the shadow framed on the shade in the door window.

"Madison?!" Katrina called frantically on the other end of my BlackBerry.

I drew several rapid breaths. The thought of Colin in a cell, my father injured, my wedding in ruins, steeled me at that moment.

"Gotta go," I told Kat.

Crossing to the door, I cautiously drew back the shade, a burst of adrenaline shooting through me. My God. I had been right.

I stepped back and opened the door.

69

The woman in the stylish, long white coat entered, closed the door behind her, and immediately backed me up against it, running her gloved hands down me like a body check at the airport.

"I don't have a weapon," I insisted.

She took my arm and led me to the back office, expertly locating the security system. In a burst of motion, she pulled the disc from the recording machine and broke it apart in her hands before ripping the entire machine from the casing and discarding it on the floor.

"There," she said, brushing herself off as she escorted me back into the center of the gallery. "Now, Madison. At last we meet."

"We've met before," I said, staring hard at her. "At the Forensics Lab. I later saw a photo of you and the family on your husband's desk. Still, I didn't put it all together. It was only later that I recognized your son in the photograph. I'd seen him a week ago when he'd come in and planted the chip in my BlackBerry."

She gazed at me wordlessly.

"At the lab you use your maiden name, Kate Trask," I said, eyeing her carefully. "But in art circles where, according to your website, you've been showing for years, you use your married name—*Katherine Walker.*"

"I like to keep my professional interests separate," she said admiringly, studying me like some specimen in her lab.

"I don't plan on being here long. Now, Madison, if you're at least as smart as I think you are, you'll hand over the file as promised and I, in turn, will be sure you and your friends are not prosecuted for tampering with evidence in a murder investigation."

I was not giving her the satisfaction of seeing the fear running through me as she ticked off the exact plan the girls and I had in place.

"I have to admit you fooled me with that voice on the phone," I offered. "Then it occurred to me that if you could alter diaries and evidence in the DA's office and manage to surreptitiously plant a forged painting in Farris's old apartment, then manipulating your voice with some device had to have been relatively easy."

"How did such a smart woman become such an unlucky bride?" she purred. "The file. Now," she demanded.

I moved, ever so slowly, over to the center of the gallery as she followed, always keeping her eyes on me.

"Funny," I said. "I was wondering how it was possible for any man to have ever cheated on someone as talented and attractive as you, Katherine?"

"Don't be a little girl," she offered icily. "Men *stray*. It's what they do."

"Yes," I agreed, continuing to move slowly, "which is why I'm guessing that in your eyes your husband's crime wasn't the cheating but that he fell in love."

Katherine Walker's eyes flashed with indignation.

"You're what, all of twenty-eight?" she inquired in a dismissive tone. "You think you know what it is to suffer?"

"I'm a Jewish girl who's been a constant disappointment to the woman who bore her. I'm more than qualified."

"This isn't a game, Madison."

"No, it isn't, Katherine. Because you murdered a young woman whose only crime was to become your husband's obsession. You then doctored her diary and manipulated evidence to implicate an innocent man."

"There is nothing more naive than a bride." She laughed with a shake of her head. "With you it's all so neat. *Love* tied up in a box with a bow, as if everything about it came as a gift with easy instructions."

She gazed up at *The Dance of Life*.

"Like this painting here. Love is a kind of dance. You make accommodations for changes in rhythm, alterations in tempo and mood."

She leaned closer, and I knew she was examining the strokes of the paintbrush, the mixing of colors, the detail.

"Jamison would come home after being with that girl and he was calmer somehow," she said, eyes still on the art. "You find the tempo of a relationship has changed. You make adjustments because you love the man despite his weaknesses," she said, her voice betraying emotion.

"But Colin Darcy? What did *he* ever do to you?"

"The driven Mr. Darcy," she muttered. "He came into Rebecca Farris's life and everything changed. Jamison would go to her, and all the little whore could talk about was her new *white knight*. Unlike other men, she insisted, Darcy listened to her. He'd convinced her she didn't have to wait, that she could have a new life right away. The girl apparently believed it, because she threatened my husband who had stupidly promised to set her up in the art world. She said she'd go public if he didn't follow through. And trust me"—the woman spat bitterly—"Jamison would have done it too. Trade away every contact I had. But I told him I would leak the story of his transgressions myself, that I would bring him down if he tried." Her eyes narrowed. "Comes a point you have to keep a man in line," she said simply. "But the bitch had bite. Farris ran to her white knight with a story that could destroy my husband and our family. And for that, she had to be stopped."

I held my breath, adrenaline pumping through me as I heard her confessing to everything Colin stood accused of.

"It's been nearly a year. Why go after Colin now?"

"Yes." She nodded. "It would seem strange, but, as they say, timing is everything, Madison. We thought we had your man handled. Darcy had been warned off his investigation months back, and we were assured he'd destroyed his notes and would remain harmless. Three weeks ago word came down of the reappearance of a file Darcy had on Jamison. Suddenly we were faced with the very real possibility your groom was bent on causing trouble and making a name for himself at my husband's expense. My family's expense! I couldn't let that happen."

"So you turned the woman Colin loved against him?"

"I had to find someone who could expose the evidence against Darcy," she explained darkly. "Someone not connected to me. So I counted on the one thing a woman always desires—*proof* of her man's love." She shrugged, as if she were commenting on a fatal flaw in all women. "You did not disappoint."

I felt a shiver of horror rush through me. I had allowed her to play me and, in turn, placed Colin, my father, my closest friends in jeopardy. *Your heart tells your head,* Bubbe had counseled, but I had let this woman's lies blur my instincts and reverse the order of that wisdom.

"I'm afraid our little talk is over," Katherine said, reaching into her pocket and pulling out a hand-size silver metallic object she held like a gun.

Unnerved, I stared at the menacing device.

"Six hundred and fifty thousand volts," she said, nodding at the Taser. "A few seconds will incapacitate you. A minute and you won't get up. *Ever.* Now, if I don't get the file you spoke about on the phone in the next sixty seconds, they'll find a note by your body blaming Colin Darcy for destroying the dreams that ended your life. It's that simple. Your choice."

I swallowed, checked the distance to the door, the clock, the out-stretched hand carrying the weapon.

"In the top drawer of that desk," I finally said.

Katherine Walker crossed over and opened the drawer, her eyes still on me. Reaching in, she pulled out the brown legal-size envelope waiting there.

"It's a little late," she said offhandedly, "but someone should have advised you, Madison. Never agree to marry a man thinking he won't fail you. It's the only way to deal with the inevitable disappointment."

"And I realize it might be a little late, but I have a little advice of my own," I said as I watched her tear open the envelope with one hand, the Taser poised in the other. "If ever you get the urge to destroy a man by turning his bride against him?"—I shook my head— *"Be careful what you wish for."*

At that, the door of the gallery flew open and Katrina, Abby, and several of New York's finest burst in.

"Katherine Walker," Kat announced as the men took Walker into custody. "You're under arrest for the murder of Rebecca Farris."

"Officers," the startled woman said, "I don't know what these women have told you, but I am here on official business of the department. I am Chief Forensics Director Kate Trask . . ."

"Save it, lady," Abs said, cutting her off as she held up her laptop that was playing a video of Walker and me. "We downloaded your entire confession off the signal from the gallery. It's streaming on YouTube as we speak."

"That's impossible," Katherine protested. "The security system is disabled."

I walked over to the painting she'd been admiring, the one I'd made a point of leading her to. Reaching up, I felt along the frame and located the microrecording device that Peter had had installed as a fail-safe. It was exactly where Brigitte had told me it would be in our call that morning. I held out the fingernail-size device.

As they read Katherine Walker her rights, Kat explained how they had found Walker's son in a Range Rover across from the gallery and how he was being deposed at that minute.

We looked at one another in disbelief. It was over.

Somehow we had done it, the three of us, together. Recognizing that, we simply fell into one another's arms as I hugged the only sisters I'd ever known.

"I think we better get those edible yarmulkes ready," Katrina said, pulling away with a big grin.

"'Cause tonight we are going to *partay*!!" she and Abby screamed.

We exited the gallery and watched as the police drove Katherine and her son off.

With a heart so full I thought it would burst, I headed out to reclaim my groom and our wedding day.

70

The Waldorf-Astoria
Saturday night, 8 p.m.
Vows at last

Colin was released immediately after the gallery confession. Abs and Kat took me directly there to meet him. I ran down the corridor of the station into his arms, and we held on to each other and let the tears fall. Our bodies seemed to absorb each other's release of emotion—the danger, the hurt, the love that had been challenged. I thought I would never let go.

When we drew back and looked at each other, it was with new eyes. We had both seen secrets revealed that had altered us. But we had also come to know each other on a level beyond any expectations. I knew it would bind us together even closer.

I turned to Kat and Abs. There were no words. We simply gazed into one another's eyes. If you're lucky, you have friends like this who have your back. I shook my head, marveling at what we had. They were truly my ladies of honor.

We offered to postpone the wedding, but Dad was hearing none of it. It would take place that night, he insisted.

Bubbe gave me some special advice before the ceremony that will remain private and that I will always treasure. Then I turned and found my mother waiting.

I wasn't sure how things would play out between us from that day on. There were hurts that maybe only time could heal and unanswered questions that would wait for another day. But the unraveling of her secret had seemingly allowed her to let something go. She told me she loved me, and they seemed more than words.

Hobbling on crutches, my father walked me down the aisle, beaming at the many guests who, only hours earlier, had received startling word that the wedding was once more and irrefutably *on*.

Arriving at the chuppah, my dad leaned in and kissed me.

"I'm proud to be your father," he whispered into my ear.

"I'm proud to be your daughter," I said softly.

Left unsaid was the decision I'd made to *honor* him. He'd find out soon enough.

"Go. Love. Have fun." He smiled through his tears and placed my hand into Colin's.

In a blink, Colin was speaking the vows he'd shared with me earlier in the week at Babbo when he had moved me to tears.

And then, at last, it was my turn.

I had decided not to use what I had written weeks earlier. So much had changed. Gazing into Colin's eyes, I simply spoke what was in my heart.

"When we're little girls, we think of marrying the perfect man. But I've learned that you're not perfect, and I can't tell you how happy that makes me. Because you're more than perfect, you're *you*. Colin Darcy, I vow to love the little boy inside of you, to nurture his dreams alongside those of the little girl in me. And I vow to love the man, to hold precious your tears and your feelings. I promise to be imperfect, to go a little nuts on you now and then, and to always strive to be open, honest, and unyielding in protecting *us*. And I vow to dance on the bed, in the shower, in the street, and to love you with all the madness in my soul."

I took his hand.

"I want it *all*, Colin. And, whatever that is, I want us to find it together."

I beamed at him. "Deal?"

He grinned.

"Deal," he said.

And from just behind us a voice rang out that could only come from my one and only Bubbe.

"Ah-maine!"

71

The next day, the following announcement appeared in the *New York Times.*

Madison Leah Mandelbaum, 28, daughter of Melanie and Morty Mandelbaum of New Hempstead, New York, was married Saturday evening at the Waldorf-Astoria to Colin Wordsworth Darcy, 31, the son of Diana Steinberg Darcy of New York City and Sir Hugh Aubrey Darcy of London.

The reception was highlighted by the announcement of Mr. Darcy's promotion to a national post at NBC.

In a unique twist, the bride toasted her maids of honor after word came down that Ms. Katrina Fitzsimmons was to be named Chief Assistant District Attorney for New York County, the youngest in that office's history. Ms. Abigail Toobin was said to be taking a leave of absence from her editing duties at Random House in order to work on a novel loosely based on the Darcy/Mandelbaum wedding week.

The newlyweds will reside in Manhattan.

The bride will keep her name.

The settings and organizations described in *The Bride Will Keep Her Name* are all based in fact.

The exclusive crime-solving organization known as the Vidocq Society actually exists and meets monthly on the top floor of the historic Public Ledger Building in Philadelphia. Made up of forensic professionals and passionate private citizens, they gather around gourmet meals and seek to solve cold cases, especially murders, when called upon by families or law enforcement. To find out more, check out www.vidocq.org.

The Porcellian Club is a gentlemen's club established in 1791 at Harvard University. In a 1996 article in the *National Review,* Jeffrey Hart, a Dartmouth professor emeritus and former speechwriter for President Ronald Reagan, wrote that the Porcellian organization is "devilishly hard to join. But there is nothing there, hardly a club at all. The quarters consist entirely of a large room over a row of stores in Harvard Square. There is a bar, a billiards table, and a mirror arranged so that members can sit and view Massachusetts Avenue outside without themselves being seen. And that's it. Virtually the sole activity of Porcellian is screening applicants. Porcellian is the pinnacle of the Boston ideal. Less is more. Zero is a triumph." Justice Oliver Wendell Holmes, President Teddy Roosevelt, and Col. Robert Gould Shaw who led the first black regiment in the Civil War are three of its famed members. As the novel points out, poor FDR never made it in. I wish to add that the entire circumstances of the involvement of Porcellian members in the events of my novel are entirely fictional.

Track 61 actually exists beneath the Waldorf-Astoria in Manhattan. Some say it was created expressly for FDR so that the public would not see him having to be brought into the hotel in a wheelchair. It remains unused, a hidden train stop from another era and one of those mysteries that sometimes exist in our neighborhoods and, sometimes, right beneath our feet.

ACKNOWLEDGMENTS

Wow. I feel like the guy giving the toast at the wedding. Where to start?

My unwavering agent, Linda Chester, is a true friend and discerning adviser and continues to guide my career with aplomb. Managing her office, Gary Jaffe is one hell of a mensch and, believe me, it makes a difference.

Shaye Areheart is a wonder woman in publishing. Her embrace of my novels means the world. Kate Kennedy is some kind of wonderful as an editor. Her suggestions raised my manuscript a giant notch and I am most grateful. Thanks as well to the great team at Crown/Shaye Areheart Books—the effervescent Kira Walton in marketing, the amazing Annsley Rosner and Justina Batchelor with publicity; my keen-eyed copyeditor, Laurie McGee; the magnificent production editor, Rachelle Mandik; the talented Lynne Amft and Lauren Dong for the interior design; Laura Duffy for the eye-catching book jacket; and Christine Kopprasch and Anne Berry for magnificent support. Maddie would insist you all be at the wedding!

To the astounding Lynn Goldberg and all at Goldberg McDuffie Communications, especially the powerhouse Grace McQuade for her peerless work in getting the word out. Major bouquets.

I want to send a shout-out to my friends in Ireland where my writing was supported in art residencies amidst the emerald hills: to Sue Booth-Forbes and the Anam Cara Retreat in West Cork and to Pat Donlon and the Tyrone Guthrie Centre in Annaghmakerrig. I'm hoisting an Irish pint in your honor. And gratitude to Jack Berman and Pearl Brown, who graciously provided a writing getaway at their mountain home. They have a seat at the head table anytime.

Friends who have your back mean everything. Lili and Jon Bosse are real-life angels whose friendship is constant and priceless. As dear friends they'd give Kat and Abby a run for their money, as would Loren Judaken, Izzy and Rita Eichenstein, Lee and Fred Silton, David and Jocelyn Lash, Dirk and Linda Wassner, Pat Ogden, and Ken and Karen Scopp.

I am forever grateful for the constant enthusiasm of my family— Linda and Glenn Solomon, Mark and Kyoko Goldstein, Ethel Goldstein and John Eckerson, Mike and Cheryl Goldstein, and my amazingly enthusiastic in-laws—Matt and Marion Solomon—who truly go above and beyond. My children, Yaffa, Batsheva, Elisha; daughter-in-law Stefanie (an early reader who made great suggestions); my stepson, Ari; my little one, Shira; and Andy Chase (ever assisting with the books) each dazzle in their own right and, like the characters in the novel, could collectively rock Manhattan. I'm a lucky guy to have them and, especially, to have had parents like mine. Frank and Roberta Goldstein made all the difference in my life and, like the dreams beating in Maddie's heart, they remain with me always.

At the top of the list there is *my* bride, Bonnie. Best friend, my first and most incisive reader, the inspiration for Madison's indomitable spirit.

Am I lucky, or what?

Jan Goldstein is the author of two national bestsellers, *All That Matters* and *The Prince of Nantucket,* the latter of which was recently optioned for film. His work has been translated into more than a dozen foreign languages. He is the recipient of the Presidential Award for volunteer work in fostering arts in the inner city and was recently chosen as an international artist-in-residence at Ireland's famed Tyrone Guthrie Centre. Jan lives in Los Angeles with his wife, Bonnie, and their family.

For more news on his books, appearances, or to write to Jan, visit his website: www.JanGoldstein.com

Also by Jan Goldstein

**The heartwarming story of a man primed to go far in life,
who first must find his way home**

Teddy is a successful Los Angeles lawyer whose charm and political skills
have made him a leading U.S. Senate candidate. But behind the golden
public persona lie some darker truths: His teenage daughter has barely
spoken to him since his divorce from her mother and he has long been es-
tranged from his own mother. When his sister asks Teddy to come back
to Nantucket before Alzheimer's steals their mother's mind entirely, his
campaign manager sees it as the perfect opportunity for a mother-son
photo op, and Teddy reluctantly agrees to the trip. Once on Nantucket,
Teddy uncovers some stunning family secrets and meets a woman who
challenges everything he thought he understood about relationships—
unexpectedly finding the life he never knew he wanted.

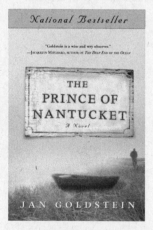

THE PRINCE OF NANTUCKET
$13.95 paperback (Canada: $15.95)
978-0-307-34591-2